THE
DARK
FRONTIER

Wild West Press
Louisville, KY

Thank you for reading! If you like the book, please leave a review on Amazon and Goodreads. Reviews help authors and publishers spread the word!

To keep up with more Wild West Press news, join the Anubis Press Dynasty on Facebook.

WELCOME TO THE DARK FRONTIER

WELCOME TO THE DARK FRONTIER...

Where the ghosts of dead lovers call from the mountain
Where the thick rolling fog erases all that it touches
Where an old devil seeks the powers of a deity
Where a relic releases hungry shadows on the prairie
Where giant monsters harvest souls to feed their young
Where cannibals roam seeking their next meal
Where a mother must shield her baby from evil
Where bikers rule with just a drifter to stop them
Where one family demands the services of new brides
Where supernatural voices seduce all their listeners
Where the afterlife meets the unforgiving desert
Where a gunslinger must serve his Underworld Mistress
Where spirits play games with the souls of the dead
Where a cult of the land's darkest gods rises
Where the abyss whispers to your soul from the dark

Here on the brink of destruction, in the midst of civilization's fall, this western outpost is the last refuge of man, and it breeds evil, darkness, and sadism. The shadow has long since swallowed this final station, turning the west into the Dark Frontier, where you are about to embark upon a journey of desperation, an expedition of dread. Make it across, and you might find a brighter world waiting on the other side – or you might find that the other side has vanished and all that remains are the horrors of this wicked wilderness. Perhaps, you'll find yourself cornered with the darkness closing in all around you, and you're forced to stare into the eyes of evil – eyes that could be your own.

Dare to test your limits with the courage to see yourself. Take a ride where the monsters live, where the soul of man has decayed, where the abominations of infinity hold the heart of the world. Look into the storm that has spread across the horizon, and in it see the mighty wings of judgment and damnation.

Behold the Pale Horse –
Behold the Black Angel –
Behold, the Dark Frontier

CARGO MOUNTAIN
by Charles R. Bernard

L oden has been gone for a month when Heathcoat uncovers her face in their garden. It happens as Heathcoat is harvesting onions, her sweat dappling the sandy ground. She grasps each crisp sheaf of stalk and pulls, freeing the hard little onions one by one. Loden's face lies beneath a particularly robust specimen. When Loden's features are uncovered, half-buried in the dry, pale soil, Loden blinks and then grins. Her mouth is full of earth, her teeth rimmed with it, and her eyes are flat and hard. They shine like two bits of beaten tin.

"The depths are full of dreams," she whispers, and it's unmistakably *her* voice, smoke and whisky and just a hint of barbed wire. Heathcoat lets out a long, shuddering gasp that hitches at the end, almost a sob. "Come dream with me," says Loden. Her tongue rolls once in her mouth like a red fish surfacing in a muddy pond – then Heathcoat blinks, and she is alone again. It's just her and the dead, sandy ground and her little patch of carefully tended crops. They aren't much – onions, melons, a battered stand of leggy corn – but in the midst of this vast, acrid nothing, they're everything.

She hesitates, then digs carefully with her fingertips, but of course there's no Loden there. There's no Loden anywhere, not any more. Heathcoat works the ground

1

until sunset turns the sky the color of a dish of peaches engulfed in flame. Sunsets and sunrises are the only real color to be had this far west, where the dry heat has baked every hue but a dull khaki from the dust, the vegetation, even Heathcoat's clothes. Tall, narrow, and bony, with her shock of bristly alfalfa hair, Heathcoat could be mistaken for a particularly convincing scarecrow.

As the sun sets, the shadow of the mountain swells like smoke. Heathcoat shivers, although heat still rises from the ground and sweat still dots her brow. Her little house – a glorified shack, really – is in need of repair. As the wind picks up from the west (as it does every night) it orchestrates a moaning symphony in the dwelling's many gaps, cracks, and joints. Still, the shack has a sturdy enough door, which Heathcoat bolts shut behind her now, and a good tin roof.

She lights the lantern and sits at the table with a bottle of whisky that tastes like sugar and paint thinner. Loden's chair sits empty, still angled where she stood from it weeks ago. Heathcoat runs her fingers over the table's surface. It's scarred and pitted in many places from Loden's hook, the one that had served as her left hand since an unspecified bit of mayhem in her past that she had hinted at but never directly discussed. She was careless with it, a fact testified to by the table's many marks – careless except when she was with Heathcoat. When they were together, Loden was so gentle that the hook whispered like silk over Heathcoat's skin. Thinking about it, Heathcoat shivers with pleasure, which then collapses into a miserable emptiness that she tries to fill with whisky. She nods off at the table at some point in the long night, with the wind muttering disconsolately in the darkness outside.

It's a little less than an hour's travel from her shack to the crossroads, provided that Heathcoat takes her battered motorcycle. She has made the trip on foot before, when she's run out of gasoline, and has always finished it sweating, cursing, and spitting acrid dust for days. She loves the motorcycle – loves traveling like a low-slung rattletrap comet over the dunes, loves the high whine of the engine and its vibrations that almost shake her apart, even loves the bittersweet ache that lingers in her joints afterward.

The crossroads and its handful of sun-bleached wooden structures stand where two Eastern trade routes from the Free Cities kiss before veering off north and south. No route goes any further west, where the mountain swells out of the sand like a monstrous tumor and the wind tastes like cooked wiring. Where Heathcoat lives.

She pulls the bike up before the least decrepit-looking building – adorned with a sign that reads TRADING POST in neatly burned letters – and pops the kickstand. When she kills the engine, the silence is profound.

The trading post consists of a single room with no windows and a long counter running parallel to the back wall. Inside, the heat is stifling, and the darkness only partially abated by a guttering oil lamp. There are two men behind the counter; a matched set with their soft faces split by identical smiles. They wear long brown cowls cinched at the waist with rope, the hoods pulled back from their bald, shiny pates. They could be twins, and in a sense, they *are* brothers – Brothers of the Knife, members of a monastic order of geldings, their self-mutilation a demonstration of their commitment to the faith, their subtracted genitals, still bleeding, burned as an offering to Ix Buul, the god of pain. It is a small faith, and one hated by even the buttoned-up Puritans of the walled compounds, even though they, too, were forced west for their zealotry.

Sometimes Heathcoat thinks of the desert as the shore of humanity's ocean; a place for trash to wash up.

"Ms. Bobbinet!" chirps one. For the thousandth time, Heathcoat regrets telling one of the Brothers her surname.

"Whisky." Her voice is a husk; her throat feels like a canyon choked with sand. She swings the bike's saddlebag onto the counter with a muted thump. As one Brother turns to rummage through a trunk behind him, Heathcoat lets her eyes wander. For the first time, she notices – with a stab of dread that makes her head hurt – the empty walls, the barrels and boxes with their sealed lids. The Brother turns back to the counter, bottles in hand. "And gasoline?" he asks, and she nods. He turns, tugs on the sleeve of his comrade's cowl, and the other man disappears through the back door without a word.

The Brother reaches below the counter and withdraws a scratched, murky glass, which he holds, waiting. Heathcoat flips over the saddle bag and shakes it gently. The bag disgorges its cargo of onions, a few of which roll lopsidedly; as soon as the produce touches the counter, the Brother sets the glass next to one of the bottles. Heathcoat fills the glass, drinks it down with a shiver of pleasure, and pours another.

"We still haven't seen her," the Brother says. Heathcoat nods, remembers a red tongue rolling in a mouth full of earth.

"We're moving on," he continues, setting an additional two bottles before her. "You understand, Ms. Bobbinet? There's no trade this way, not since the Free Cities burned. And something out there—" the Brother lifts his chin at the blazing expanse outside "—has gone bad. Our animals are dying. Their meat spoils so fast we can't eat it. And it's just the two of us now. Because the others are gone. Something out there seduced them."

The mountain glowers in Heathcoat's mind like a great black toad. She thinks of the west wind at sunset, of a smell like blood and battery acid. "It's getting worse," the Brother says, then, after a moment's hesitation: "More children are missing from the compounds, too."

"Where will you go?" Heathcoat asks.

"South and east."

She nods. Her gut feels as hard and sour as a peach pit, but she drains another glass regardless. South and east – back toward the walled compounds. When the Brothers leave, Heathcoat will be a day's ride from her nearest neighbor. And that's if her fuel holds and the bike doesn't break down. On foot, in the desert…

The Brother who left returns bearing twice Heathcoat's normal order. The fuel sloshes in its plastic tubs as he sets it down. She frowns. "That's too much."

The Brother behind the counter shakes his head and sets another pair of unopened bottles before her. "Thank you for your trade. We wanted to give you more, but we'll need everything else we have."

Perhaps the slug of alcohol has unknotted her a bit already, or perhaps it's her broken, shallow sleep of late. Whatever the cause, Heathcoat is almost overcome by a sudden, fierce wave of affection for the Brothers with their soft faces and gentle, fastidious manners. "Thanks," she manages after clearing her throat.

"May the Ragged One watch over you," he replies.

"No," corrects his comrade. His back is to Heathcoat as he speaks. She can't see his face, but his voice is sad. "Nothing watches over this forsaken place."

Heathcoat dreams of her first kiss. Organdy had been the girl's name, a soft, oft-grinning girl with a sea of jet-black hair and a throaty laugh that made Heathcoat's heart flutter. In the dream, Organdy's lips are sweet and firm, and Heathcoat responds hungrily. A ringing – like great bells, or the song of a metal bowl – splits the air. The scene shimmers, shifts, and Heathcoat is in the courtyard of the walled compound where she grew up. The one she had escaped as a teenager.

"The depths are full of dreams," comes a voice, and when Heathcoat turns, Organdy's eyes glow with a rotten phosphorescence the color of an infected wound. Her features melt around her burning eyes, and suddenly Heathcoat is looking at her mother's face, the mouth pinched by piety, the brow furrowed by judgment.

Heathcoat turns her head, unable to meet her mother's eyes, the depths inside the fierce and glowing colors there. Across the courtyard she sees the two Brothers of the Knife from the trading post. As she watches they undress each other, their movements as tender as any nurse's. Under their cowls, the terrible marks of their Order are revealed; the puckered scars, the red and winding vines of re-stitched tissue where their penises had once bloomed. Once they are naked, each washes the other's scars with water from a broad silver bowl.

CARGO MOUNTAIN

"Full of dreams," the voice repeats, and Heathcoat has no choice. The compulsion to look is both undeniable and unbearable; as she once again turns, Organdy-her-mother – some middling state between the two – scrambles up the wall of the compound like a lizard, her movements too quick, too double-jointed and nimble. When she gets to the top of the wall she faces outward, toward the unseen expanse beyond the wall, and lifts her arms. Her flesh falls away like an old overcoat, revealing a perfect golden skeleton. Its bones are emblazoned with jewels and reflect the sun's fire like a beacon.

Beyond the burning bones, the black mountain rises, rushing to meet the walled compound like the wrath of a primal god, or a great, oncoming wave. Heathcoat wakes, face twisted in a rictus and cheeks wet with tears, with the taste of burnt wires in her mouth. As she claws her way out of the dream, she could swear that the ringing sound comes with her; that its echoes have followed her into the waking world.

Each morning, when she wakes, she genuflects before the porcelain chamber pot and vomits sweet whisky and bitter bile, the wages of her drunken and unsatisfying courtship of sleep. The second day after her trip to the Brothers' trading post, she slouches out of bed at dawn, head splitting, and retches up a long rope of blood and foam. It's bright against the ceramic of the pot; the brightest thing in the shack, which is a study in monochromatic dust and bleached wooden boards. She wipes the blood from her lips and tries to collect her scattered, skittering thoughts. How long has it been since she's eaten? Two days? Longer?

The bottles shine, dull to near-opacity, as she pours their contents into the dirt. The liquor makes a musical, chuckling burble as it flows. As each bottle is emptied, Heathcoat pitches it sidearm into the desert as hard as she can. The movement makes her joints scream and her shoulder give a warning twinge, but it's worth it. The sound of glass shattering brings her the first faint flecks of joy that she has felt in some time. Back inside her shack, she investigates the cupboards; hardtack, jerky, a few ancient cans of beans. Too late now to buy better provisions from the Brothers. Her anger at herself is almost as bitter as the taste of bile that still lingers on her tongue. Hardtack it is, then.

The desert air has kept the bricks of baked flour as hard and as dry as stones. She soaks one in a tin dish of brine until it softens a bit and chews without pleasure, washing it down with a cup of water. At first her stomach cramps in revolt and she has to grapple with her gorge, but after a few minutes the food settles a bit and she feels almost human. Her stomach has awakened and she follows the hardtack with jerky, which she gnaws with gusto.

That day, Heathcoat works the garden hard and relishes it, sweat, aches, and all. The walled compounds are a day's ride, she reasons, but the distance isn't insurmountable. In a few weeks, when she has pulled everything from the earth – when her long efforts have been harvested – she can leave this place to the wind and the punishing sun and the long shadow of the mountain. (And the ghosts, she thinks before she can stop herself.) By nightfall her hunger has returned and she eats an entire can of beans for supper, wolfing the food directly from the can. The sun sets over the hunched black peak in an explosion of brooding color and, for the first time since Loden vanished, Heathcoat feels no dread at the coming of night. Instead, she feels as cool and peaceful as the stars that begin to emerge in twilight's velvety violet. Sleep comes easily.

It's dark when she wakes, dark and oppressively silent. It only takes her a moment to affix the anxiety that accompanies her into wakefulness to its source; she can't hear the wind. Heathcoat can smell it; blood and burnt wiring. She can feel it as well – the pressure sucked and blown upon the shack's many imperfectly joined boards like a pipe organ – but there's no sound. Her anxiety sharpens to panic. Has she gone deaf? Her answer comes as she shifts her weight on the bed and hears a loud, complaining chorus of groans from its battered springs.

Then, almost as if in answer to the bedsprings, a long creak comes from the pitch darkness above Heathcoat, between the shack's rafters and its tin roof.

She stiffens, feeling as though her marrow has frozen inside of her. Long seconds pass in which Heathcoat can feel her heart gallop, and then she hears it again. Loud enough that it seems to make the air shiver: a loud, wooden creak, like the complaint of a rocking chair or the tortured song of an ancient staircase. The darkness in the room begins to withdraw as a cloud that had occluded the moon passes. As the dusty moonlight fills the shack and Heathcoat's eyes adjust, she sees the spidery shadows of limbs in the rafters above her, and although the face is still no more than a black shape, she sees the dull gleam of eyes that shine like diseased fireflies. It's Loden, lost Loden, perched upside-down against the underside of the tin roof. Watching her beloved, as the dead silence hangs and the rushing, phantom wind slips through the shack's perforated walls.

As Heathcoat watches, frozen with horror, Loden tilts her dull, smoldering eyes from side to side, tipping her head at a sickening angle. *Crr-rrr-rrr-rrreak.*

The scattergun rests where it has always rested: leaned against the edge of the nightstand, within easy reach on the off chance that a raiding party were to venture into the desert. It's in Heathcoat's hands before she can think, before she even realizes that she is screaming, and then her scream is drowned out by the thunder of the gun. It sprays a long cloud of fire and lead into the rafters and through the roof; ruined shards of tin, bits of burning powder, and other debris rain down into Heathcoat's face, stinging her eyes and setting the bedclothes to smoldering. And, of course, the rafters are empty; no hobgoblins, no Loden - only a ragged perforation in the tin now, through which she can see the stars. The sound of the wind has returned, as well: she can hear it moan, hungrier than ever and louder even than the ringing in her ears.

Heathcoat trembles like a child as she tears at the loose floorboard, the one near the foot of the bed. She rips one fingernail to bloody tatters as she pries the board loose but hardly notices; beneath, resting in a sheaf of burlap, is a dusty bottle. She uncorks it with numb fingers and gulps whisky. The bottle in hand, Heathcoat sits with her back pressed against the wall and the reloaded scattergun in her lap. She drinks until sleep crashes down like a vast and silent ocean.

The onion top Heathcoat holds is crisp, and white, and very dead. Ignoring her shrieking knees, Heathcoat crouches beside the ruins of her garden and runs her fingers over the sandy soil. The neat, ordered rows of onions have been dug from the earth and the ground is littered with sundered vegetation – and with footprints. Bare footprints that dance and turn pirouettes on the carcass of Heathcoat's garden. If there are prints leading to her ravaged crops Heathcoat can't find them, but the tracks leading away and out, into the desert, are unmistakable. She follows the tracks for a few dozen yards and finds what she expects: they lead in an unwavering line pointing to the black hulk of the mountain.

The little patch of land and its paltry crops that had tethered Heathcoat is destroyed. With it lying in ruins, she feels liberated and weightless, as though her heart were a balloon and its string had just been cut. She doesn't pack much; just water, a few leather-hard scraps of jerky, and the last of the whisky. After deliberating for a moment, she leaves the scattergun propped against the table.

Wind whips through her hair as she rides into the blood-light of the setting sun; bitter wind as hot as breath against her skin. It carries grit that stings her cheeks and forehead. Her motorcycle carries her to the foot of the mountain, about a mile from her destination, before the gas runs out. The engine dies with a stutter and when she rolls to a stop, she pops the kickstand and leaves the bike where it stands. Travel on foot, Heathcoat muses, puts the vast and lethal scale of the desert into its proper context, stripped of the comforting compression of time and distance provided by engines. By the time the sun has receded to an infernal magenta glower she is filmed in sweat and dust and her knees and hips have begun to bite with each step, but she makes it to the edge of the mountain before the light gives out completely.

This is the closest to it that she has ever ventured. Theories about the peak had circulated among the walled compounds that mark the far western reach of human habitation in the desert. They had differed on the details – who had inhabited the mountain, what specific fate had befallen them – but they all agreed on the broad strokes. Someone long-dead had done something there, something powerful and dangerous enough that it had soured the land, scoured it clean of fertility and vitality and left it, picked clean like a bleached skull to rot in the desert forever. Heathcoat thinks of the absent Brothers of the Knife, and of the children of the walled compounds – and of Loden, her terrible eyes and creaking neck – and thinks that she knows something else about the mountain. Something she can't quite grasp yet, but which lurks below the surface of her mind like a hungry eel.

Heathcoat climbs a sandy elevation and finds that that's where the sand gives out: beyond it is a rough, rocky depression, the bottom of which is dotted with ancient and decaying concrete. She follows the depression as it narrows to a dark stone throat carpeted with dust. Heathcoat pulls a small flashlight from her pack and ignites it with a click. The beam pushes back – but by no means dissipates – the blackness at the bottom of the narrow chute as it twists its way to the spot where it meets the mountain's massive cliff face. And there, where the ruins of the road she has been following dead-end, is the terminus of her journey. The terminus, she thinks, of the chain that binds her to the memory of love. She has followed it now to the place where it has shackled her since Loden vanished, although she hadn't known it.

The archway is massive; easily twenty feet tall at its peak, and cast from concrete a yard thick. The years, however many have passed, have nibbled at the edges of the structure and chunks litter the dust where they've fallen away, but it was built to last and it has. Even more impressive than the archway, however, are the doors. They tower above Heathcoat, massive, heavy, covered in rust and corrosion and standing on hinges that have, no doubt, been fossilized solid by time. There's no need to worry about cutting her way through them, though, a task which would have proved impossible, anyway. They stand ajar a few feet – must have stood that way for untold years. The floor of the entrance below the sheltering arch bears a line of bare footprints which lead into a darkness far too deep for Heathcoat's light to penetrate.

The light does, however, pick out the letters stamped into the concrete above it:

CARGO MOUNTAIN COLLIDER COMPLEX
Authorized Personnel Only
Tachyon Badges Required Beyond This Point

The place feels dead, deader than any place Heathcoat has ever been or even dreamt of in her smallest, coldest hours. The entryway yawns like the idiot maw of some unimaginably vast worm; or the mouth of a tomb, adorned by the grave marker left by its vanished sextons. A more recent visitor – mourner or revenant, who can say? – has appended an epitaph in faded black paint: *we are all dreams & the dreamer has gone mad.*

A chill breeze rolls forth from the gap between the doors. It swells and recedes like the breath of a frozen

13

giant. It bears a familiar stench of burning wires, one that Heathcoat knows well from the night wind off of the peak. It's much stronger here, and different; shot through with an organic undertone like a butchery. The reek is so strong, in fact, that she is overpowered for a moment by a dry, jagged coughing fit. By the time she catches her breath, clears her throat, and spits into the dust, she is lightheaded, and the foul taste of the place has made its way into her sinuses and coated her tongue.

That much, Heathcoat muses, she can do something about. Her knees complain as she sinks into a crouch and pulls the whisky bottle from her bag. There are a handful of swallows left and she downs them all, grimacing with pleasure as the liquor burns its way into her guts. The flashlight, propped against her thigh, throws Heathcoat's shadow against the concrete of the archway where it towers over her. When she has drained the last drops from it, she pitches the bottle against the rock cliff wall where it bursts with a sound that is delicate and immediately swallowed by the odd, oppressive silence of the place.

Without so much as a flicker, the light vanishes. Heathcoat curses and slaps the flashlight against her leg, but to no avail: it remains dark. Frustrated and a little drunk, she flings the light in the same direction that she threw the bottle. She is immediately furious with herself and winces when she hears it crunch against the rocks.

"Damn you." Her voice sounds bitter to her in the darkness, more bitter than anything she knew she had within her, and very small. "God damn you." A bit louder, and she can taste the tears and feel the hitch in her breathing. "Oh, god *damn* you, Lo." Tired, miserable, and tipsy, Heathcoat sinks to the dust and lies there, head in her arms. Sleep comes like the onset of a plague; but oblivion carries no darkness deeper than that at the stone threshold of the tunnel entrance at the foot of the mountain.

Heathcoat.

Sleep is a deep pool of tar that doesn't want to relinquish her. Her head throbs; her mouth feels parched and sour and full of the cold wind's burning, greasy taste.

Heathcoat. Get up.

"No," she mumbles, and retches up a rope of something hot. She claws at the caul of snot and sweat left on her face afterward. Why does each breath burn like her lungs are full of blistering sand? Foolish, she thinks as she is wracked by a rusty string of coughs that make her ears thump and sink a stitch into her side. Foolish to sleep here, where something has gone so badly wrong. Something that, she muses with an echoing, outside-herself calm, appears to be killing her, or at least about to deliver the coup de grace after a life not lived too gently.

You can't rest yet. Not here; it's not safe.

"Lo? I'm dreaming, aren't I?"

"No," says Loden, and it *is* her voice, smoke and spice and the subtle streak of wild good humor that always flashed just below the surface. "No, Heath, you're not dreaming – you're not the dreamer." Her words are as clear as the sound of bells, although not much louder than a murmur.

"Yes," agrees Heathcoat in a sleepwalker's voice. "The dreamer is going mad." She says this, then gasps as she feels the metal, smooth against her cheek in the darkness – and cold, so cold it burns. Loden's hook. It

15

trails down her neck, gentle as a lullaby. When it reaches the neck of Heathcoat's rough-spun shirt, there is practically no resistance; the fabric splits with a whisper and falls away, leaving her bare to the night air from the waist up. She shivers, although not from the cool of the air or the icy trace of metal on flesh. The hook continues downward, splitting the side of her pants with a purr. Within moments, Heathcoat is bare down to her toes. "Lo?" "*Ssshh.*" The cold tickle moves back up her body, down one arm until her fingers close over the hook.

Heathcoat lets herself be led like a child. The dust is like velvet under her bare feet; as she is pulled gently through the doorway, over the threshold, the dust underfoot becomes stone, coarse with grit. They travel without speaking; Heathcoat, possessed of the illogical logic of a dreamer, doesn't want to push this fragile miracle any further and risk its dissipation. Deep, they walk; then deeper, past vast rooms that hum and shiver like beehives, and other rooms that seem to be lit to brilliance, although not with light as Heathcoat understands it, but rather by a black and burning radiance that throws space into incomprehensible angles that refuse to align themselves in a way that makes sense. Down and down and down, until, at long last, they stop. Heathcoat waits. After a few long moments, she licks her lips.

"Lo?"

Nothing.

"Lo… Loden?"

"You should let go now," says the voice – a distorted voice that does not sound very much like Loden anymore.

ON THE ROAD TO MADNESS
by Armand Rosamilia

It's not often you're trapped in such a desolate place, but Big Charlie Watson preferred to be alone. Back east it was crowded streets and too much noise. You could barely see the stars when you looked up through the Bowery smoke, so thick it'd choke a man to death.

Speaking of death... Big Charlie had to do something about the dead man before it stank to High Heaven and had the locals and critters investigating.

Not that he'd seen locals stirring down in the valley below.

Maybe it was a ghost town. He'd seen a mess of them on his journey west, entire towns abandoned in the middle of the night. Cups and plates set for supper with rotting piles of food on them. Even the critters were staying away, and after the fifth ghost town Big Charlie decided it was safer for him to do the same.

The dead man was the first person he'd encountered in three weeks of travel.

He was down there. I seen him yesterday, Big Charlie thought. Does he live in the town, or is he like me... wandering through to get away from somethin'?

Big Charlie had amassed quite a collection of odds and ends in his trip so far: a couple of blankets, a tin cup and bowl, two forks, a dull knife, a pocketful of bullets but nothing to match them to, and a monkey coat that was two sizes too big but made for a nice comfortable spot at night when he put his head down.

He also had the gunny sack, filled with the bills he'd traded the silver and gold for: three hundred and eighteen dollars from the Williamsburg Bank. Legal tender he could use anywhere, even in the territories.

Except… there was nothing and no one to spend it on so far.

Big Charlie had been thinking about wine, women and gambling. It was what he'd come to find out west. He'd start a new life. Erase his past. No Marshal in their right mind was going to follow a fugitive into no man's land.

He looked at the dead man and sighed. After killing the crew of E.A. Martin, he'd sworn he'd never kill again. In less than a month he'd broken his promise.

This time, at least, it had been self-defense. The man was rabid. Foaming at the mouth. Screaming and yelling about monsters and death. His eyes were bloodshot but Big Charlie didn't smell any whiskey on his rancid breath. He was sober and insane, that was all.

I did nothing wrong. I was up on this ridge minding my own damn business when he popped out like a groundhog, Big Charlie thought. Scared the bejesus outta me, too. I had no choice.

He'd clubbed the man with a rock. One shot to the side of his head and he crumpled. Went down hard and slammed into more rocks, slicing through his darn neck and collapsing his chest.

Awful business. An accident.

Big Charlie knew he needed to carry the dead man away from the cave lest it draw attention. He still hadn't entered the dark opening. One thing he was missing was light. Nothing to make a fire with since the tree line was far below and he didn't spy two sticks to rub together.

Maybe the dead man had a lantern or firepot inside the cave.

Big Charlie hesitated. Without anything other than a rock as a weapon, he was loath to go inside.

It would be dark soon. He had three choices, none of which sounded fine to him: enter the cave and face whatever was lurking inside, head to the ghost town and face whatever was lurking within, or start walking to the west and face whatever was lurking out there.

Big Charlie sighed. It was gonna be a long night.

Marshal Isaiah Hicks had been following the trail of Big Charlie Watson for weeks. Sometimes he'd feel like it had gone cold, until he asked around.

If there had been a robbery or a woman of ill repute stiffed on payment, it meant Big Charlie had come to town.

He found the stolen horse hastily covered with some scrub a mile back, and knew he was only a few hours away. Big Charlie had ridden through wild lands, stopping at a couple of abandoned towns looking for food or shelter.

If not for the dead horse and the brand on the stolen saddlebag, Big Charlie would've been in the wind. There were no settlers to question. No hotels or watering holes to ask around or catch Big Charlie in the act of drinking or gambling.

This west of civilization, the world as Marshal Hicks knew was gone. As if a line had been drawn in the sand and everything on this side of it was dead. Decaying. Destroyed.

He'd heard of strange happenings out west, too: massive sandstorms, tornadoes and drought. The fella he'd arrested from New Orleans a few weeks ago had been running for his life, right into Manhattan, even though he had a warrant for rustling. He was trying to get on a boat to England and away from something.

Something he was scared of, but couldn't put into words.

Despite the warnings the Marshal was needed back in Manhattan, especially on the eve of what could be war between the north and south, he'd decided capturing the notorious Big Charlie Watson was more important. It would get him some notoriety, especially since he wasn't getting any younger. Most days he felt old. Plain and simple. He'd been on the trail of Big Charlie for years but had lost track of the man when he'd sailed off.

Marshal Hicks thought he'd seen the last of the man when he'd taken to the seas to escape the lawmen in Philadelphia. Big Charlie hadn't stopped breaking the law. He'd been able to do it in faraway places like San Francisco and Mexico.

When he'd returned, his pockets full of gold and silver coins, he'd spun tales in the taverns about his exploits. All about the women he'd bedded and the jewelry he'd taken from them as they slept.

Watson had murdered at least seven Marshal Hicks was aware of, and that was just those in his jurisdiction. Only God and Big Charlie knew how many more in his wide travels.

Marshal Hicks spit his last bit of tobacco on the hot sand and sighed. Even on horseback, he felt like he wasn't catching up to Big Charlie. Had he traded in his dead horse for someone's fresh one? He hadn't found a trail other than Hicks walking.

The sky was getting dark. There'd be a heck of a storm brewing ahead, and Marshal Hicks was afraid he'd be riding right into it.

A distant flash of lightning, so quick he would've missed it if he blinked, made him rethink going west tonight. Just for the night, though. By morning the storm would pass and cool the world down.

Hicks cursed and turned back east. There was a town he'd passed on the ridge to the north and he knew he should've stopped and asked around before following the tracks, even though he hadn't veered off.

Three hours later he'd arrived back at the town, night falling and the storm following at his back, the wind pushing him faster.

Only... the town was dark. Not a single light was burning. In another hour darkness would truly fall, and you'd have no clue a town spread across that land.

He felt trapped, caught between the onrushing storm and the strange abandoned town.

You can't stay out here on your horse, he thought. The marshal glanced at the storm at his back and sighed. He'd never outrun it. He was surprised he'd done it so far.

Or had he? He got a chill. It felt like the storm was pacing with him, leading him...

Marshal Hicks rode into town, found the dark hotel, and led his horse inside. He shut and locked the doors, calling out for the proprietor.

No one answered.

His horse, Maddie, which had been quiet, started to snort and pace in the lobby. Marshal Hicks tied Maddie to the door behind the bar, grabbed three bottles of whiskey and a glass, and made sure his weapons were loaded and ready in case of trouble.

With nothing else to do but wait, he pulled up a chair and put his back to the wall, placing one of his sidearms on the table next to the bottles.

And he waited.

Inside the mouth of the cave Big Charlie found supplies, which he was grateful for: a blanket, a cooking and coffee pot, a tin cup, a sack of rice and beans, and tied handkerchiefs with coffee beans. A set of boots with soles worn out and a faded gray hat.

He kept moving a foot further into the cave and then retreating again, scooping one item at a time until he had them outside.

The wind had started blowing fiercer now, and he knew a storm was brewing. He didn't have much time before he'd either need to get inside the cave or head to the town.

Neither choice looked promising.

Big Charlie walked quickly into the dark cave, the farthest he'd ever gone, and was about to turn back when he tripped and fell to the dusty ground, a puff of something earthy filling his nostrils. He cursed and squirmed, hoping his ankle wasn't twisted or worse.

It wasn't broken and he reached around for whatever he'd tripped over.

A small tinderbox. He grinned and prayed he'd find a lantern, which was a few feet away and could still be used.

Big Charlie rushed from the cave and held up his two prizes.

The first drops of rain, thick and heavy, fell from the sky.

He worked quickly, lighting the lantern and shuffling everything back into the cave.

When Big Charlie Watson held up the lantern, he gasped.

The cave went so deep he couldn't see the end, but that's not what had his attention.

It was the strange symbols and writing covering the entire surface of the walls and ceiling.

Marshal Hicks sat in the dark, sipping whiskey and listening to the thrashing of Maddie as the storm raged on. The doors and windows shook and rattled but held.

Maddie had managed to kick through part of the bar and shatter glass on the floor, but there was nothing to be done about it now. If Hicks tried to clean it up or calm Maddie, he was likely to get a kick in his chest from the horse.

Is anyone in there?

Marshal Hicks sat up and put a hand on his firearm.

Shadows, deeper than the darkness, flirted past the windows and door, creating curious shapes on the glass. When lightning flashed the shadows were still there.

Maddie was beside herself now, kicking with such fury Marshal Hicks knew she'd either hurt herself or break free and rush out into the storm.

Let us in. We want to calm your horse, mister.

He hadn't imagined the voice, just quiet enough to make him think it was nothing more than the wind.

"Who's there?" Marshal Hicks was ready to shoot, slipping his second weapon from its holster and standing. It was hard to hear with Maddie kicking up such a fuss. "Show yourself."

Open the door and we'll do more than that, marshal.

It was followed by giggling, not exactly a child but… what?

Like something trying to sound like a child, Marshal Hicks thought. Trying to sound human.

The marshal hoped the door held.

He finished the whiskey and overturned the table, pulling it back into the far corner, as far away from the door and his crazed horse as possible.

Come out and play, mister. We just want you to join our fun. Please.

"Go away," Marshal Hicks said, and crawled into the corner as tight as he could, praying to a God he didn't really believe in to save his soul.

Maddie broke free and slammed into the door, taking it off the hinges and letting the fury of the storm enter the saloon.

Marshal Hicks decided he'd use a bullet on himself if it came down to it, and tried to blend into the wall behind him.

Big Charlie had no choice but to ride the storm out inside the cave, exploring for a hundred feet until he gave up. The disturbing carvings and writing extended as far as he could see, and it left him hoping there wasn't something hiding down the tunnel.

At one point many people had been living in the cave. He found men and women's clothing in piles. A few children's toys. Several pistols and ammo, for which he was thankful. A shotgun with no ammo. Another six lanterns and a spot where the former inhabitants once built a fire, the smell still lingering.

The symbols seemed to pulse when he wasn't looking directly at them, and he kept snapping his head around. Was he imagining it? Big Charlie didn't think so.

He made a fire and tried to warm his body, but the fear made him shiver. There was something outside the cave watching him.

Big Charlie couldn't turn his back to the cave mouth but he knew if he looked directly out he'd go mad. Like looking at the cave drawings.

The voices came at the height of the storm, words heard and forgotten as soon as they dissipated in the air around him. With each word Big Charlie was sure the symbols on the walls glowed just out of his sight.

Despite the fire crackling inches from his arms and legs, Big Charlie couldn't get warm.

The ground shook with thunder and the lightning bathed the cave in wicked shadows, but Big Charlie refused to look outside to see if it was truly the end of the world.

Morning was heat and sunlight, although everything had a gray sheen about it.

Marshal Hicks was pleasantly surprised to find Maddie searching in vain for weeds or grass, wandering behind the saloon.

It was as if last night's storm had never happened. Nothing was wet and the air was drier than parchment.

Maddie was squeamish at first, bucking and scared when Marshal Hicks approached. It took him a full hour to calm her down enough to ride her, and by then he was covered in sweat and tired, the heat draining him.

Despite the storm he saw the trail he'd been on was clear as day. He rode to the very spot he'd gone furthest yesterday and stopped.

Maddie whinnied once before putting her head down.

To the north and south there were raging storm clouds, gray and black streaked with reds and oranges. Evil and unnatural, as if the world in either direction didn't exist.

Marshal Hicks thought it likely. No wind blew. No sand moved.

Follow the trail until I can't anymore, he thought.

It might have been a trick of the massive dark clouds on either side of him, but it felt like the trail he followed ran right between the ominous barriers, as if he had no choice but to follow the storm right to Big Charlie Watson.

He wondered if the man was even alive at this point. Had the tempest been too much for him? Could even Big Charlie Watson withstand that onslaught? Hicks glanced down at Maddie, who'd come through it alive, and thought he knew the answer. He then turned in his saddle and frowned.

The storm clouds were moving quickly, covering the vacant town he was now abandoning as well, and blocking his path the east.

But he knew better than to ride into them.

The town below Big Charlie was gone, covered in low black clouds that looked angry, despite no rain or wind.

It's not right, Big Charlie thought. Not natural.

He climbed up onto the top of the mountain, straddling a thin ledge twenty feet above the cave mouth, and caught his breath.

The view, under normal circumstances, should've been beautiful.

But now it was gray walls of solid clouds illuminated by lightning at regular intervals. The mountain itself was left alone and a small road coming from the east, the way Big Charlie had come, and lost on the horizon to the west.

One way in and one way out, Big Charlie thought.

Inviting. A way to escape from the cave and the symbols. A way to go… back the way he'd come, back to the chaos of his life in the east, or to a new life in the west.

The air felt heavy with rain now, and a gentle breeze started to stir on top of the mountain.

The outlaw grew fearful. A strong gust of wind might toss him to the rocks below.

He began climbing back down, wondering which of the three directions he would take: back east, into the unknown west, or into the strange cave.

Big Charlie got to the mouth of the cave and looked back just as the single rider stopped at the base of the mountain, looked him in the eye and went for his revolver.

Marshal Hicks watched as Big Charlie Watson ducked into the cave. The two men had seen one another and now there was nothing left to do but fetch the wanted man and head back east.

Into the clouds and chaos? If a road still existed, Marshal Hicks thought. He had a bad feeling the road narrowed behind him to a small path that petered out into nothingness and gray stifling clouds of noxious fumes.

He couldn't bring Maddie up the trail to the mouth of the cave. Too steep and loose.

"Good girl. Stay and find something to eat." Marshal Hicks glanced at the cloud wall, billowing but not moving an inch forward. "Stay away from whatever that is."

Maddie snorted in reply and began feeding on a stray weed sticking from between the rocks.

Marshal Hicks climbed slowly up the trail, weapon drawn and ready to shoot if need be. He only had to bring Big Charlie back to New York City, alive or dead, either way worked.

After the chase he'd given, Hicks wanted to see the man alive so he could talk with him and see how much damage he'd caused on his flight west.

On the other hand, dead men were quiet and didn't try to escape or make the journey hard.

"Mister Watson, why not make this easy on both of us, and come out showing me your empty hands? I promise not to shoot you where you stand," Marshal Hicks lied.

The cave mouth was dark.

"If you're not coming out, I'll have to come in," Hicks shouted. He didn't want to go inside. It looked dark. He had no light on him, and going back down for his lantern seemed like a waste of time.

Even now Big Charlie could've slipped out the backside of the cave and hopped on a horse heading west.

Marshal Hicks ducked down and moved to the right as he entered the cave, leading with his pistol. He kept shuffling from side to side, hoping Big Charlie wasn't going to shoot at him before his eyes adjusted to the gloom.

He waited a few minutes before taking tentative steps forward, side to side as he walked.

Marshal Hicks rounded a slight bend and saw the fire and Big Charlie seated in front of it, holding a shotgun in his arms and smiling.

"Please, marshal, have a seat and get warm," Big Charlie said. He glanced at the ceiling and Marshal Hicks noticed the strange carvings and drawings. "The storm should hit us with full force now that we're back inside safely."

"Why shouldn't I shoot you and be done with it? You'd never get the shotgun off of your lap before I plugged you," Marshal Hicks said.

Big Charlie shrugged his shoulders and put the shotgun on the ground. "Any chance you got any grub? There was a town down there but it got swallowed up."

Marshal Hicks remembered the town he'd spent last night in, and knew it was also gone. He sat down on the other side of the fire and placed his weapon in his lap. "What's going on here?"

Big Charlie shrugged. "I've been trying to figure it out myself. Maybe it's the end of the world. All around is nothing but clouds. A path going east to west. Leading us."

"To where?"

"Can't rightly say." Big Charlie tossed the last branch he had onto the fire. "I'm not even sure if I want to go further than this cave."

"Last night... there were voices. Beckoning me to come out into the storm," Marshal Hicks said. "What do you think that was about?"

"I think everyone else is dead." Big Charlie looked up at the carvings. "I heard muffled voices but couldn't make out the words. These markings are blocking the voices, keeping me safe." He looked back down at the fire. "Keeping me from plunging down the mountain into certain death."

"But the road…"

"It leads to madness," Big Charlie said and kicked off his boots. He glanced at Marshal Hicks. "Are you going to shoot me? I'm tired."

Marshal Hicks shook his head.

While Big Charlie Watson slept, snoring softly near the fire, Marshal Hicks stared at the raging storm just past the cave entrance.

The rain fell in sheets, but not a drop entered the cave. No runoff. No drips that splashed inside. It was as if the storm was forbidden to enter.

Whenever the lightning flashed or thunder shook the mountain, random symbols on the walls would briefly glow, only for a second and just within eyesight.

It was disturbing but Marshal Hicks knew it was some form of protection. He could still hear the strange voices but they were muffled, like they were underwater. He knew they were calling to him, trying to get Hicks to step foot outside of the cave and join them.

Maybe once the storm passed they could forage for food. He knew there was a town down there somewhere, hidden because of the storm.

There had to be.

"Morning," Big Charlie said with a smile.

Marshal Hicks jumped up and went for his weapons.

"Relax, marshal. I ain't touched your personal belongings." Big Charlie held up a tin cup. "I made coffee."

It was light in the cave but it was unnatural. Gray. A thin swirling mist played on the roof.

"Go see outside, but be careful," Big Charlie said.

Marshal Hicks stumbled to the entrance and stopped.

It was... gray. Cloudy. The entrance as if a blanket was covering it.

"Looks like we're trapped in the cave," Big Charlie said, coming up and handing the marshal his coffee. "We can't go forward. The world has ended except in this cave."

"How do you know that?" Marshal Hicks felt like he was dreaming. His mouth was full of grit and he sipped the strong coffee to get his head together. "Maybe this'll pass."

Big Charlie shook his head. "We passed. I'm starting to understand the carvings. What they do. How they protect us in what's left of this world."

"How?" Marshal Hicks asked.

Big Charlie smiled and tapped the side of his head. "I let them in. See? They wanted us to leave. Join them in the fog. On the road to madness. But I'm already mad. So I opened up and know what they need. What they want."

Marshal Hicks put a hand on his pistol and held the coffee cup with one hand.

Big Charlie drew his pistol. "I took your bullets while you slept. They told me to."

"I don't understand. We're safe in the cave," Marshal Hicks said. "We could survive."

Big Charlie shook his head. "It doesn't work like that. There's only room for one of us, and it's me. I gave

31

them my soul. They promised they'd let you go to find another cave. Another safe haven. To help spread the word." He glanced past Hicks. "See?"

Despite not wanting to turn his back on the crazy man, Hicks looked over his shoulder.

The clouds were receding, a path cut all around the entrance now. The sun was shining.

"Go on. Find your way. They'll protect you and your horse." Big Charlie smiled. "This is my cave and my new life, marshal. The world as we knew it is gone. Dead. Now there's only the two of us and whoever steps from the clouds."

Marshal Hicks walked out of the cave and onto the thin road leading only west, Maddie snorting at the base of the mountain and ready to ride.

THE HARD CASES
by Stuart Conover

No one witnessed the stranger as he rode into Pascola.

With the storm rolling at high noon it was darker than midnight. On a clear day, the clopping of the steed's hooves could be heard a mile away, but the thunder and rain silenced the sound of their advance. The storm was so forceful, the air around it crackled with unnatural energy.

The town's saloon was the only building visible, casting a faint glow that could be seen in the darkness. Even the lightning cutting through the sky couldn't pierce the pitch and illuminate the city.

Within the walls of the saloon, music played and men drank. They were giving into the vices usually reserved for the night while trying to ignore the building shaking around them. While there would usually be rancorous humor and laughter, it was almost still inside as many of the inhabitants of the town wondered what the Lord Almighty was punishing them for.

Punishment was surely what this was in their minds, as those that chose to live this far out had more than a single skeleton in their closets.

Rain seeped in through the walls and not a minute passed that conversations weren't interrupted by the storm. Anyone who took a glance silently swore that it must be the end of times.

In one corner, a group of four farmhands was playing a game of poker that no one seemed ever to win or lose. Money didn't change hands as the games flew from one hand into the next.

A few months back, there had been a fifth player.

He was found to be a bit too lucky though, and a careful eye had found him to be cheating them by using a marked deck of cards. These days he wasn't able to use one of his hands and was no longer to be found in the saloon.

A few ranchers and prospectors were also spread through the room. The mayor, local banker, and both of their wives had been in town when the storm had hit and opted to sit in the private room off to the side that was usually reserved for town meetings. The bartender was sitting in with the town's rich-folk to try and keep them happy. The rest of his patrons were mainly ignored aside from a lonely waitress who was halfheartedly keeping everyone else's glasses full.

For the past hour, she had been tipping herself a shot for every drink she served and was loose on her feet.

Only three men sat at the bar.

Pascola's sheriff, Steve, was there and slowly drank a warm glass of sarsaparilla. He seemed lost in thought and was the one person clearly out of place in this town. His job was to police these men who mostly couldn't read the law, let alone comprehend how it applied to them. He was constantly forced to find ways to negotiate peace among the various ranchers that went against his fundamental beliefs. Using bullets and brawn where he would prefer to use his brains.

He felt that things needed to be done the right way and would do whatever it took to uphold those values, even though doing so often meant compromising his own.

Steve had been in the army until his country had ordered him to do too much. There were lines that he would not cross and when he was told to rape and kill innocent Indians whose only fault was not leaving the area quick enough for his commander, it was time for him to leave. He had seen men go AWOL before and fortunately with his merits, he was able to walk away without any black marks on his record. The last thing he had wanted was to become a criminal himself.

His disgust, though with what was being allowed in the name of his country, forced him to leave regular life behind. People didn't see what was going on, so they didn't care. He couldn't change society where civilized folk wouldn't listen to what was happening, so he went somewhere where he could make a difference.

That's what he had told himself at least.

To his left was a young buck sipping Cactus Wine. It was a lifetime ago when he had raced into town on a horse that had been ridden hard into the ground. She was a young colt, and that was probably the only thing that had kept her alive through all the miles he had ridden her down. The young buck's name was James, and it didn't take long to see he was a man at the end of his ropes.

No one came to Pascola unless they were running from something and while no one could find out what James was responsible for, Steve quickly made him understand that he would have to either make himself useful or find himself on the long arm of the law. Days had turned into years and our young James, a finer shot than almost anyone Steve had seen before him, had turned from useless layabout to an excellent deputy.

To Steve's right sat a man named Bodaway Crowe, Boda to most who knew him, though not many did past his reputation. He was an outcast by everyone's standards, a half-white, half-Indian mix that everyone knew of and feared. He had seen more death in his life than most anyone here and looking into his eyes would cause a shiver to run down your spine.

The man drank whiskey as if it were water.

Before Steve had even come to Pascola, the bartender was nearly killed by a group of outlaws. They had decided to make this last ditch of a town their home. No one was able to stop them, but when one of them had tried to interrupt Boda's dinner at the saloon, things went south. The bandits had a gun in the bartender's mouth when Boda wanted a refill, and the story goes that he had pulled out a tomahawk and a long blade and killed all six men before they could hurt anyone.

Boda never had to pay for food or drink there again.

While not a man of the law, Bodaway had a code of honor that guided his life. With Steve being a man who held the law as his own personal code, he was a man Boda had come to respect. Even if they didn't always see eye to eye on what was right, they had come to tolerate one another over the years. It was a strange sort of friendship; a comradeship neither would choose to walk away from.

When the doors blew inwards, no one turned to look, as this wasn't the first time the wind had opened them. The sheriff, always watching the mirror above the bar to see what was happening in the room, was the only one to witness the stranger slowly saunter in.

A gust of air hit all the candles in the room. They didn't go out, but they cast a strange blue that caused the hair on the back of the sheriff's neck to rise. The stranger drew in the entire room in one motion; sizing up and dismissing everyone until he met the eye of the sheriff.

He tilted his head in acknowledgment.

The stranger briskly strode to the bar.

For a brief moment, the storm outside faded into background noise.

As he moved through the room, each man turned toward him and felt like someone had just walked across their grave. A few of the more religious townsfolk crossed themselves as he passed. The stranger seemed to enjoy the discomfort he was causing as he moved to where Steve was sitting.

An odor of ash and smoke followed him and started to permeate the room. In her drunken stupor, Jane the waitress couldn't keep her eyes off of him. They were filled with a mixture of terror and something else.

The quiet conversation in the room seemed to go entirely still as the stranger stood between Steve and James and cleared his throat.

"I would like you to fetch a bottle of your boss whiskey." His voice seemed to sound both eloquent and full of sarcasm.

The waitress unsteadily reached behind her for a glass and placed it before him.

"I'll be right back with that sir." Jane giggled while almost tripping as she backed away.

The stranger pulled out a case of cigars from his jacket pocket. Steve recognized the La Cosmopolitans as Cuban, which were surprisingly rare. Not only because being this far west put them in the middle of nowhere but before he had left the military and society in general, he had heard that Cuba's tobacco industry had nearly shut down.

He eyed the cigar with a sense of wistful nostalgia. Drinking dulled the mind and had never been one of his vices, but once upon a time, a fine cigar was the way he celebrated the good times and eased the bad.

The stranger seemed to watch Steve as he pulled out one of the cigars and clipped the end. While pulling it to his lips, he brought out a match. Slowly he puffed at it until it was fully lit and drew in a long breath.

A grin flashed across his face as smoke wafted from his mouth.

"Howdy there, sheriff." His nose curled up in contempt and it was reflected in his tone "My name is Samuel Faust, and it's a pleasure to meet you."

Between the smoke from Samuel's cigar and the brim of his hat, his face was hiding in the shadows. What must have been the lack of light was playing a trick on Steve's vision. Samuel's eyes seemed to have an unnatural shine and depth to them, but it was his face that was off. When visible, there appeared to be a rippling movement to it as if someone had dropped something into a barrel of water.

It twisted Steve's stomach to continue meeting Faust's gaze, but he wouldn't look away. It wasn't fear that kept his gaze upon the man but a primal need to show strength in the face of danger.

Steve knew his kind.

If he looked away, it would just invite a fight, and this wasn't one he was sure he'd walk away from.

"The name's Steve," the sheriff responded, "and I'd like to welcome you to my town as long as your time here is to be peaceful."

"My mission is the embodiment of peace. Tell me Sheriff Steve, has anyone new come into or passed through your little town in the last few days? Perhaps another who just couldn't help but get himself into trouble?"

Faust's eyes seemed to bore into Steve's soul and found it lacking as he asked.

Now what Samuel shouldn't have known, unless he was following the man, is that there was, in fact, another stranger in town. Right now, he was locked away in one of the three jail cells located in the back of the sheriff's office.

James was trying to subtly catch Steve's eye as the waitress came back in with a bottle of whiskey and an empty glass.

Faust slowly opened the whiskey and poured the drink without looking away from Steve.

It was apparent the man was here for the stranger, but Steve was torn. The young stranger who had recently shown up reminded him of James and how he had been so many years ago. The only difference was that James had been a cocky young buck while the man in the cell had ridden in on crow bait and was terrified for his life.

He couldn't, or more likely wouldn't say what he was so damn afraid of.

"No, Mister Faust I can't say we've had any strangers around these parts." The resolve was firm in his voice. "Aside of course from yourself."

Samuel stared at Steve. He took a long pull from his whiskey with a look that would have most men shaking in their boots. Steve shrugged off the cold chill running up his spine. His resolve restored as he knew that he had done the right thing.

"I see that you aren't going to cooperate," Faust hissed as the thunder once again sounded full force and shook the building. "A pity."

The man turned to the barmaid.

"I need a room." He puffed at his cigar. "You're going to show me one and keep me company."

He stood with a whiskey bottle in one hand and a cigar in the other. Brushing her hair back, Jane giggled while slowly leading him to the stairs in the back of the bar.

Steve reached out, "Jane, you don't have to stay with him."

She glanced back briefly with a look of annoyance before turning away to lead Faust to his room.

As Steve watched them leave, Boda spoke up for the first time.

"That is a man on the shoot." He gulped down a swig of whiskey. "He's the kind of man who long ago lost his humanity. He'll be trouble, sheriff."

"We cannot let him know about the kid in our cell," James grunted, "even if we have to force him out of town."

James meant what he said, but his voice was full of false bravado. While his deputy was usually a curly wolf, he was shaken in a way that Steve had only seen when they'd first met.

"Well there's not a whole lot we can do here tonight boys" the sheriff responded calmly, "why don't we take a stroll on over to the jail and get to know our mystery man. Maybe get an idea of what's actually going on."

As the three men strolled out of the saloon, no one looked up. All three were dangerous men, yet those in the room could sense that a real predator had been in their midst. And still was, the real fear was what did he want from their small town and what was going to happen when he got it.

The trio walked out into the storm and slowly pushed through the wind, rain, and darkness to the town's small sherriff's office. The wind pushing against them was strong enough to hinder each step. Even trying to hurry, the five-minute walk turned into ten. When they finally arrived, they pushed into the safety of the office. It might be cold, but they were out of the wind, and they all stood for a moment to gather themselves.

Before going in to talk to the prisoner, Steve stopped them as he needed a word with their unofficial deputy.

"Boda, I know we don't always see eye to eye, and while I appreciate your willingness to help, I need you to play this by the book."

Boda looked at the sheriff and instead of arguing as he usually would, nodded his head in agreement.

"OK, then," Steve acknowledged. "I'll take the lead. We need to know who the hell this Samuel is and what exactly we're up against. This man might be a criminal, but I'm sure that whatever Faust has planned will leave him in a shallow grave. Or worse, one of us along with him."

He unlocked the door to the back of the office, lit a couple of lanterns, and walked them past a small storage closet as they entered the jail. For a small town, having three decent-sized cells was a bit of overkill. However, having separate cells was a luxury they may soon require. Since Steve hadn't thought he would be back tonight, he had already put out the lanterns that were in the room.

Not that anyone could sleep through the storm that was ravaging the town.

As soon as the door swung open, it was clear that the prisoner was awake.

He begged for his life and for the light of God to protect him as he huddled against the back of the prison cell. It took time to calm him down enough to realize that it was only the sheriff, and no one was here to hurt him.

"Now son, I know you're on the lamb. You know that you're in jail. Let's quit beating around the bush. Why don't you tell me what's going on?"

It's not something that would work on a harder man, but the sheriff suspected it would work on the stranger who just wanted to keep running.

"There's nothing that you can do to help me, sheriff. They are going to find me, and they are going to kill me." His words were gasped out as if his very fear was choking him.

"Who's after you, son? Why don't you let me help?" He kept his voice calm with the same tone he'd use on a frightened mare.

The prisoner started to laugh, clearly at his breaking point.

"Help?" he cried "You want to help? There is no help left for Amos Wotes! My soul is forfeit for what I have done. For what I have taken. I only have death to look forward to!"

Steve tried not to show the frustration he felt for this sorry excuse of a man. He didn't hold it against him that he was in the corner crying into his hands. Some men were born weak; this one had no spine at all.

Still, he was making progress: the man was named Amos, and he had stolen something. It was a start but again didn't explain why Samuel was after him or who exactly he was.

"What is it that you took Amos? What is it that you stole, and why is it going to be the death of you?" Bodaway demanded.

Amos finally looked up with humor on his face. For the first time, his laugh didn't have a touch of madness to it.

"What did I take? Sure, I'll tell you. I'll tell all of you since none of you will even know what it is let alone what it's true worth is. Thoth's Ankh."

The three men looked at each other in confusion. It was clear that no one here had a clue what Amos was talking about.

"It's an ancient Egyptian religious relic supposedly from one of the Gods, if you believe such nonsense." He sighed. "I don't know what to believe anymore, but I know that the Ankh is not meant for human hands. The things I've seen since taking it."

He shuddered and tried not to remember, but it was always there behind his eyes.

"So where is this Ankh now?" James demanded. "And who is Samuel?"

The group of men had never actually seen someone go 'as white as a corpse' before. They'd all heard the expression, but the way Amos went pale was clearly what it had been intended for. "How do you know Samuel? Is he here? I must get out of here! You have to let me go!"

Further questioning was clearly going to prove pointless as Amos shrunk even further into the corner, blubbering for release or a quick and merciful death.

The three men finally gave up on him, and taking the torches, left him to the darkness as they went back to the front of the office.

"Well, he knows Samuel," James started out, "and he's terrified of him."

"I'm pretty sure everyone who meets Samuel will know fear if they have a pulse," the sheriff replied.

Boda chuckled at that.

"Amos said this is a religious artifact. Is this Egyptian that he mentioned a tribe leader? Why would a white man be hunting it down?" He grimaced before suggesting, "Why don't we get with the preacher to see if he can tell us what it is."

The town's priest was a preacher who had once lived back east in New York and had run a prosperous church. The rumor was he had been involved in scandal and to avoid the embarrassment of having been excommunicated had chosen to live the simple life on the outskirts of society.

He did not approve of Boda's half-white, half-Indian heritage and made sure to point it out at every chance possible.

"You're willing to find out what he knows about this Ankh that Wotes stole?" James asked.

"I was actually kind of thinking you might be willing to do that," Boda replied. "The preacher seems to have taken a shine to you."

Plans were made for all three men to stay at the sheriff's office that night. It didn't seem safe for Amos to be left alone.

As James would be trying to track down the preacher first thing in the morning, they agreed for Boda to take first watch and the sheriff to take second to be sure no one attempted to break in overnight.

The morning came, and there was stillness to the air that had not been felt for nearly two days. Though being greeted by the initial calm, it was quick for everyone to see that the sky was devoid of light. The darkness was still an oppressive force in everyone's mind.

Since the rain had let up, the town was a hub of activity. Everyone was trying to get their work in before another downpour prevented them from being outside.

After James had left to go meet with the preacher, Steve was leaning against the front of his office and watching the town. The prisoner was still whimpering in a back corner of his cell, babbling about his soul. Trouble had come to town, and he was waiting for it to rear its ugly head, knowing that his next move wouldn't happen until he heard from James.

Unless Samuel forced his hand.

Not even ten minutes had gone by before Boda ambled out of the office as well, having finally awakened from his slumber. It felt good to have someone else to rely on, especially when that someone needed less sleep than he did.

As Boda took up a position next to the sheriff, looking down the opposite end of the street, a shrill scream from the saloon pierced the air.

With guns drawn the two men ran across the street and flew through the front doors. At this early an hour, the saloon had been empty aside from a couple of people having breakfast and one lone drunk sitting at the bar. The screaming had come from one of the back rooms; one of the barmaids backed out from the guest lodging. She was sobbing and couldn't get a word out.

When no one could get her to clearly say what had happened, the two men moved forward.

With guns still out, they edged towards the back rooms, checking them one at a time. When they came to the fifth and final room, they were on edge. It was clear whatever they were about to encounter was to be found beyond this final door.

The men slowly moved into position to breach what might be a showdown. This must be the room that Faust had stayed in, and he was a man who clearly had no fear of the law and those who enforced it.

Boda motioned that he would enter first, crouched, and that the sheriff should be ready to come after him immediately. Without hesitation, they burst into the room and were both directly hit by the smell.

It was the smell which men who had done terrible things knew all too well. It was a smell that could not be explained, just experienced. Anyone who had been around death long enough has been in contact with the sickly smell that arises from the human body before decay begins, and the room was permutated with it.

Jane was laid out naked upon the bed, a sickly sheen to her now pale skin. It was hard to look away from her eyes, which were trapped wide open in the cold embrace of death. The look on her face was a mixture of ecstasy and horror.

There was no clear indication of what had taken Jane's life. Aside from a light bruise on her shoulder, there seemed to be no wounds on her body. By the looks of it, it was unclear if it had been murder or natural death, but neither man had any doubt who had brought about her death.

They summoned the town's doctor to help with the body and investigated the room. Samuel had left none of his possessions. Though hazy in the darkness, the sheriff couldn't remember him walking up with anything but the bottle of whiskey which now lay on the floor next to the bed.

Not seeing any sign of where the man was, they waited for the doctor to arrive before heading back to the sheriff's office to wait for James' return.

James had been riding to the outskirts of town where a makeshift church had been set up while the body of Jane was being discovered. It was run by a man everyone called 'The Priest', who was more of a preacher these days than the man of faith he had been in his youth. He still believed in God; just felt that God was wrong when it had come to what had happened to him.

His fall from grace had turned him into a racist and sexist to a degree that would make most honest men flinch, even in a time when that was the social norm. His sermons were littered with hate.

Half of the time he was drunk and the other half he was on a personal mixture of peyote, ginger, and soda. The concoction gave him visions which only strengthened his conviction that God had not forsaken him and had driven him to this hellhole for a purpose.

As James arrived, he crossed himself before entering the church. Not to ask for any kind of blessing but to ward off the evil from the twisted man he was about to talk to.

Assuming he was sober enough to speak, which is something you'd be able to figure out in less than a minute of talking to the hateful man.

He strode into the church, and the preacher was quietly standing with a bible in hand at the front of

47

where every Sunday's congregation would sit. How half of the town still came to the man's sermons was exactly why James couldn't stand most of the townsfolk he had been tasked to protect. The room was lit with candles and was almost bright after the darkness that still clung to the air outside.

He was praying loudly, eyes closed, rocking back and forth, and his shadow seemed to fill the room.

"Good day, reverend." James started, "I was wondering if I could borrow a moment of your time to ask a few questions."

The preacher's eyes flew open with a look of madness passing behind them. Even on the best of days, it was clear that the man had been touched. There was something clearly not right with him. When his eyes cleared, he focused on James.

"Of course, my boy, of course." He flashed a crooked smile, "How might this humble man of the cloth be able to ease your problems in these dark times?"

"It's not a spiritual matter of God that I need help with father," he responded, "but a spiritual matter of an Egyptian artifact."

He quickly sped through some of the high points of the night before focusing on a man having stolen a potential religious relic from another man.

"Do you have any idea what this Thoth's Ankh may be?" he ended with.

The priest took his time answering while nervously cracking his fingers as he appeared indecisive as to what he was willing to say.

"Well I can't say I've heard of a Thoth's Ankh in my years in the priesthood as a religious item." He paused at the crestfallen look on James' face. "However, Thoth was the name of a pagan god of knowledge in Egypt and

48

the Ankh was thought to be a symbol of life. It sounds like an item from another country and not Indians that your thief has with him."

Laughter suddenly filled the church as the door slammed shut. The candles along the walls all blew out aside from those to either side of the preacher, and the room was suddenly near pitch black with the two flames barely cutting the shadows.

Samuel's voice thundered in the darkness, and without being able to see him, it seemed to invade the thoughts of James and the priest.

"You do have the man or the item that I seek," laughing again, "and you came to the house of a fallen priest to the false God for help?"

The priest grabbed his crucifix and started to pray, his face ashen at the sight of the intruder.

Faust's laughter again surrounded them, and as he neared in the darkness, it became louder. James drew his gun and backed into the shadows trying to find the man who was stalking them.

"My Gods were old and dead before your false God was given a token divinity by the faith of his sheep. He has no power in my presence, and sheep are meant for the slaughter."

James was aiming his colt in the direction he felt Faust's voice may have been coming from.

"In fact, preacher, you have never held the faith to summon his power."

James whirled around as he heard the priest gasp and froze at the site before him. Samuel still blended with the shadows, but James could tell that his mouth was locked into the preacher's neck. He shakily raised the gun to aim at Faust when suddenly the priest was thrown at him like a ragdoll by the creature's inhuman strength.

The priest grabbed at his throat and tried to stand.

"Help me," he rasped with blood pouring from his neck. It was only moments before the man gasped his last breath and fell onto his side next to the deputy.

His young adult years spent on the lamb followed by years of training with the sheriff got James back on his feet and getting off a shot where Samuel was standing. Or where he had been standing as in the blink of an eye, he seemed to be across the room. Another blink he was directly in front of James.

He must have hit his head when the priest's body threw him to the floor. What had happened before his eyes wasn't humanly possible. Fortunately, his body reacted on instinct, and he fired again directly into the center of Samuel's chest as the man was on him.

Samuel's face registered the surprise of being hit. However, there was no pain or shock on his face, but humor.

The monster was laughing at him: His usually expressionless face drawn into a terrifying caricature of what could pass as humor on anyone else.

James' finger twitched to fire again, but his arm was pulled sharply to the side, bone breaking, and the hot lead dug harmlessly into the floorboards.

Pain flashed through his body and behind his eyes. The world went white. With agony coursing through his every thought he was aware of more pain flaring up and Samuel now on top of him.

The demon's mouth was on his neck, and teeth pierced his flesh. It was hard to focus through the pain and agony because of the underlying pleasure that also came from the bite. It almost was enough to cause him to stop struggling.

He tried to raise his hand to pull Samuel off him, but everything was moving so slow.

He could feel his strength draining from him, and by the time his arm reached Samuel, his punch was a light tap. As his arm fell back against the floor, the white pain that shot through his body turned to black, and the world slipped away.

Steve brought Bodaway back to the jail cell as it was time to finish last night's conversation. A bucket of water in one hand and a lantern in the other, he kicked the door open. Amos was passed out in a corner. The restless slumber was probably his most peaceful rest for the first time in months. Yet, the sheriff needed answers.

Steve put the lantern down and with both hands splashed Amos with a wakeup call from the bucket. The cold water snapped the cowardly Mr. Wotes instantly back to the land of the living, and he was on his feet shivering.

"Now that I have your attention," he growled, "you are going to tell me where you hid this artifact you stole and everything else that you know about it."

Amos looked at the sheriff and finally sighed.

"My saddlebag that you took when you brought me here." He seemed to deflate, "There's a hidden pocket on the left side. As to what it is, I can't really say. Rumor has it that it's a source of life, but as far as I'm concerned, it was supposed to be a way to live on easy street. I had a buyer lined up to take it off my hands until…"

He trailed off.

"Stay with us, Amos." Bodaway moved in front of him to grab his attention, "Until what?"

"Until Faust started to follow me." Wotes stammered, "I watched Samuel steal someone's soul when he was chasing me down. He kills with his hands and teeth. He's not a man."

Clearly he was delusional on top of being a thief and coward. The two men went to check his saddle. Within it, they found an object that they could not describe. It seemed impossible that this handheld object was religious or even from an Indian tribe. It was made of a kind of steel and glass that was more solid and smoother than anything either man had ever seen.

It could fit in their hands with the glass portion against the palm. It was impossible to tell what its purpose could be. Neither man could see how such an object could have any value short of its unique nature. It was another dead end. They hoped that James would return soon with an idea of what this might be and how they could use it to their advantage.

The day was mostly over when the sheriff started to worry that James was taking far too much time. Nothing the preacher could have to say should account for his deputy being gone this long. Another cursory search of the small town had Faust still unaccounted for.

A worry was steadily building in Steve's heart, and he decided that it was time to look in on the preacher. If Faust had followed James, there was only one way the man would be heading back into town.

Steve shared his plan with Bodaway. There was a canyon he would be passing through to return if he had ridden out. Steve had hope that James would pass through on the run though he knew this was likely their only chance to catch Faust alone. If they rode that way, they would either find the opportunity to dry gulch Faust on his way back to town, or they'd be able to ensure James had a safe return.

The two grabbed rifles and rode their horses hard to reach the canyon's edge, a lonely place with land perfect for the ranchers. During the right season, they would settle down on the opposite side. No one was quite sure why the preacher had built his church so far from town. Those who might have questioned it didn't want to entertain the reasons why.

The entrance had an outcropping of rocks that were positioned to give a birds' eye view to anyone who was going to be passing through it. In order to have the surprise advantage, they would need to be hidden up there before Faust passed through. Though it was an ideal spot for an ambush, they could be easily flanked if they didn't capitalize on their advantage.

Time was almost against them. As they finished setting up, a lone rider on a horse as black as the sky slowly appeared in the distance. The horse moved gracefully at a brisk trot and appeared to be an extension of its owner. Just as Steve had feared, Faust was the man in the saddle, which did not bode well for James. Steve knew he had to make a judgment call. He would have to do what he felt was the lesser of two evils and made a motion to Boda.

When Samuel was in range, two shots rolled out simultaneously, and the sound tore through the air. The monster flew from the saddle, and his horse stopped as if awaiting the fallen body to get back on.

The two men sat in the silent aftershock of the violence while the world went still. They both reloaded and waited for what seemed an eternity, though less than a minute, went by before they slowly rose up and started to walk towards Samuel.

Working their way down the cliff, they moved towards the body that lay motionless before them. As they moved in to make sure Samuel was truly down, his mare snorted. Its frame was at least two feet taller than either of the horses they rode, and its eyes seemed to glow. The horse's body was a mass of muscle that was barely held in check as they got closer.

Steve studied the dead man on the ground before them. Crimson was spreading across the dark shirt he wore. The man's mouth was frozen slightly open in what almost looked to be a grin, and his eyes stared forward.

If Steve hadn't been looking directly at Samuel, he would have missed what happened next.

The dead man lurched up and seemed to fly at Bodaway. The sheriff didn't even have a chance to call out before Faust had torn into his friend with fangs digging into his neck.

Boda's reflexes brought his hand up, leaving a blade in Faust's belly. The gunshots hadn't slowed the man down, and the blade appeared to be equally ineffective. The sheriff gave into his training. Heart racing with his mind on autopilot, the sheriff's hand was steady, and his aim was true. The first shot hit Samuel's chest dead center.

Still, the man didn't drop. Even with bullets having just pierced his body, the creature before Steve seemed unharmed and as strong as ever.

Samuel ripped Bodaway's arm loose from the socket, and as it dangled there, he moved the man in between himself and the sheriff, shielding him from the next shot.

Bodaway was conscious and screamed in pain and rage as he used his remaining hand to jab another blade into Samuel's side, stabbing him three times with the long knife. The shadowy man reached up with both arms

54

and twisted Boda's head until a loud snap could be heard. Bodaway's body went limp, and Steve wasted no time in lifting his six-shooter and unloading it into Samuel.

Samuel was nearly upon him by the time the sixth shot hit his body and Boda hit the ground. Steve was running on instinct, pushing away as the monster slammed into him. It was probably the only thing that had saved his life. He dropped his empty pistol and reached for the one strapped to his back, while his free hand pulled out the stolen artifact.

Samuel froze staring at the ankh, and for the first time, even in the dark, his features were evident. He seemed to illuminate the air around him; with his wounds, he resembled a bloodied angel that had fallen from the heavens. Calling him a monster earlier was more accurate than Steve could have guessed.

"Thoth's Ankh," Samuel whispered reverently, "5000 years ago you were taken, and now you are one of the last we need to be returned to our full power."

Eyes on the Ankh, he now had no interest in Steve.

To Samuel, nothing existed but the artifact, so he was clearly taken by surprise when a bullet left the chamber of Steve's gun and buried itself neatly in the center of his forehead. The look on his face was one of pure shock. Only instead of falling, the creature lurched at the sheriff who was again backing away.

Could nothing stop this devil? Steve fell against Bodaway to avoid being slashed by Samuel's claws. Covered in his friend's blood, the sheriff leaned against the corpse to aim as Samuel raced towards him. The air suddenly crackled with an energy that caused Steve's hair to stand on end.

The artifact seemed to be pulling blood directly from Boda's corpse. A brilliant light brighter than the sun shot forth from the artifact, straight at the advancing beast, and Faust's scream pierced the air.

Samuel's horse bolted at the sound of its master's agony.

The contempt had been wiped from his face to be replaced with pain and fear.

Through squinted eyes, the sheriff could see that the bright light spread over Faust, consuming his entire body.

The rage-filled scream quickly turned to an agonized wail as the creature began to burn. It took no longer than a minute, but when the monster vanished into the light, the artifact went dark. Its glassy surface glowed for a moment before it became inert once more.

Lying against his fallen friend, Steve looked to the sky. For the first time in days, the clouds were starting to dissipate.

The storm had taken more from him than he could have ever imagined.

In the days to come, his backwater town slowly returned to normal. As the sun returned to the sky, the sheriff was forced to bury the bodies of his friends. With the preacher gone he was the only one who was able to send them off, though nearly the entire town had come out to help.

They might not know precisely what he had done for them, but they knew that the sheriff had lost everything to keep them safe.

It was during the funeral that Amos slipped out of his cell.

The cowardly, blubbering man had been biding his time, waiting for a moment that he'd be able to sneak away when no one was looking. Disappearing with a horse, Thoth's Ankh was also missing.

With death no longer on his heels, he rode out of the town fast and hard with a smile on his face.

Never to look back.

STARLESS AND BIBLE-BLACK
by Lee Clark Zumpe

May 1, 1692

The sun's consoling glow extended beyond the reach of its direct light.

Miquel Josep Navarrete wept as his eyes traced the bed of the ravine. He had not believed such horrors could transpire beneath the watchful eyes of God. Those he had vowed to save lay scattered before him, their lifeless bodies bloodied and their souls enslaved.

Those who had survived admired him for bringing an end to the nightmare. They waited on the cliffs far above, too fearful to gaze down at the carnage. Navarrete respected their fear. He hoped their faith in his victory was justifiable.

He hoped faith alone could delay the ambitious darkness indefinitely.

November 1, 1888

"It's gone all black out there. Sky's lost all its color, like nighttime without moon and stars." Bitter Creek

McCallum shambled into the Cavern Saloon where lucky prospectors mingled with outlaws at game tables and unlucky ones frittered the last dregs of their ill-spent investment on whisky or worse. He carried a saddlebag in one hand and a six-gun in the other. Standing a few feet inside the establishment, his hands trembled. Looking down, he reluctantly holstered the smoke wagon in accordance with town regulations. "Bad storm coming."

Halfway between Tombstone and Long Home, the little mining camp of Dead Reckoning had mushroomed in the northeastern foothills of the Dragoon Mountains following the discovery of a rich vein of silver ore near Indian Grave Gulch. The lure of overnight wealth drew a horde of desperados and delinquents, including embittered soldiers fighting on either side in the War Between the States, hardened by the adversities and atrocities of military conflict.

"Storm?" Tulsa Sutton, a former Pony Express rider and stagecoach driver, spat tobacco into the spittoon near the end of the bar. The opportunity to serve as sheriff had lured him from retirement. "Never rains here."

"Rain or not, there's a storm coming." McCallum glanced over his shoulder at the menacing sky that had trailed him into town. Dark clouds descended, smothering the afternoon sun and conjuring illegitimate shadows throughout the town. "Ain't never seen nothing like this."

Most of the clientele, committed to wagers playing faro or poker, shrugged off the declaration – hellfire and brimstone could not turn their attention from the game. A few other patrons ceded their barstools, walked to the swinging double doors and followed old McCallum's gaze.

"Christ almighty," said Efren Ray, a preacher from back east. Midday had transformed into midnight in a matter of minutes. Stepping out into the middle of the street, he swept the boundary where sky met landscape. The raven mantle had all but consumed the heavens, leaving only a narrow band to the east. There, a dull red glow lingered like some meager memento of vanquished sunshine. "It ain't natural," he whispered, talking more to God than to any of his more recent acquaintances. "It ain't right."

McCallum had taken up residence at the bar, his uncharacteristic uneasiness temporarily diminished by the mere company of friends and strangers. Alcohol would surely reinforce his bravado.

"I was down to the gorge when it blew up, that storm," he said, tossing his satchel onto the polished oak. "How about some coffin varnish, Otis?" The barkeep – a fellow who worked for the Earps at the Oriental in Tombstone until their feud with the Clantons erupted into a full-fledged war – poured him a shot. "One minute the sun was blazing down hot as the devil's breath, the next I was cold as a corpse."

"Maybe you should see if your heart's still beating," Sutton said, eliciting sporadic laughter throughout the saloon.

"I ain't dead. Not yet, anyhow."

"What were you doing down in the gulch, McCallum?" Ray had retreated from the sinister skies brewing over Dead Reckoning. He hiked across the room, wary of the unnatural shadows congregating outside the establishment. Back in coastal Smithville, in his former occupation as a man of faith, he had seen things capable of putting fear into the bravest man – things that disparaged any logic science could muster and mocked any sanctuary religion could proffer. "That's hallowed land to the Indians. Ain't nothing there but bones from what I'm told."

"Sure, there's bones all right – plenty of 'em, too." McCallum patted the satchel, remembering his discovery. "But I found something else, something that ought to pay off right nicely." His tanned, leathery hand dipped into the cloth bag even as the gathering darkness infiltrated the saloon.

Lantern light illuminated the room, dispelling the bulk of the spreading pitch. Still, aberrant silhouettes populated the sheltered corners making more than a few patrons uncomfortable. The habitual afternoon hullabaloo dwindled to a hushed and anxious silence. "See here," McCallum said, bursting with pride and excitement. He held an ornate gold cross over his head. "Gold, and studded with black jewels."

"Fool." Kisto Azul, a Pima Indian, emerged from the obscurity of a private alcove partially concealed by a heavy curtain. Abandoning his cactus wine and the company of the Cavern's only saloon girl, the tall, gaunt man approached the bar. "Do you hold nothing sacred?"

"This here ain't got nothing to do with you, boy." McCallum's tone agitated Azul, though he had grown used to it from men of lesser intellect. Most townsfolk valued Azul's guidance and respected him as a citizen; a handful, though, would never see him as an equal. "This here's a cross. I know you think you're civilized, boy; now you mean to tell me you're a Christian, too?"

"That is a holy relic, placed in the gorge you people call Indian Grave Gulch two centuries ago – for good reason."

"Let me see that," Ray said, snatching the object from old McCallum's still shaking fingers. The former

61

preacher examined the artifact with a mixture of veneration and incredulity. In his hands he held a Crux gemmata – a cross inlaid with thirteen pieces of black onyx. The thirteen gems represented Christ and his disciples. At its heart Ray knew would be a sliver of wood, purportedly a fragment of the true cross. "Where did you find this?"

"I told you," McCallum said, downing his whisky in one gulp. "Down in the ravine where all them bones is."

"It must be returned. We are all in danger." Azul, generally a soft-spoken, levelheaded gentleman not given to fits of distress, pounded his fist on the bar to underscore his assertion. His aggravation and unexpected anger drew the attention of practically everyone in the saloon. "This is only the beginning," he said, pointing out the doors where powerful winds had begun to stir sand from the earth. The howling gale swept down from the mountains and surged through the streets. Outside the walls of the saloon, indistinct shadows began to coalesce forming corporeal forms. "You don't understand what you have done."

"It's mine, boy," McCallum said, seizing the object from the preacher's grasp. "Ain't nobody here can claim what's rightly mine."

"You've broken the seal," the Pima said. "You've doomed us all."

"What are you talking about, Kisto?" Ray tried to position himself between the two men, seeing the determination in Azul's eyes. "What was this doing in Indian Grave Gulch?"

Azul ignored the preacher's questions, acted without thinking. He knew that each moment spent arguing might cost lives – each second wasted the shadows would gain ground. Already, he heard the dreaded sound of malevolent voices muttering beneath the wind, voiced by wicked whisperers eager to stake new claims. The Pima ripped the ancient cross from McCallum's hands and bolted for the double doors.

McCallum, a man not known for having admirable principals, shot him in the back as he passed through the swinging doors.

McCallum found a half-dozen guns trained on him in the next instant, including the double barrels of the barkeep's shotgun. His Colt dropped to the floor even as the butt of Tulsa Sutton's pistol struck him in the head.

Ray knelt beside Azul as the black ceiling overhead pressed down on the town. As he rolled the Pima over, he knew the bullet had ripped through his lungs.

"Preacher..." Azul spoke softly, defying death. "You're the best chance this town has. Two hundred years ago, the Spanish Jesuit missionary Miquel Josep Navarrete, working from the Mission Nuestra Señora de los Dolores, used this holy cross to stop a storm like this one from spreading."

"But Kisto – it's just a storm."

"No, preacher – it's no storm." Blood painted the Pima's lips, trickled from his nostrils. "Listen: Water will seep into a crack in the mountain, wearing away at it slowly. Eventually, the mountain will disappear." Azul paused, his eyes glazing as he fought for a few more seconds of breath. "The place you call 'Indian Grave Gulch' is a crack in the mountain. Darkness is seeping through from another world – a world inhabited by horrors that roamed the earth long before the gods of men came into being. You've got to stop this blight from spreading."

"How's he doing?" Tulsa Sutton shivered as the wind excoriated his flesh. Ray shook his head silently in

63

response to his question expecting each moment to be Azul's last.

"I see them, preacher," Azul said, his eyes growing wide. "They're all around us, vultures ready to feed. Scavengers without form – insatiable shadows." Clouds of darkness flooded Azul's eyes. "Remember the words of God. Genesis…one…three."

The Pima grew still and quiet as death settled over him.

The stillness lasted only instants, shattered as gunfire erupted inside the Cavern Saloon and screams and angry curses spilled through the doors. Sutton stood, twin six-shooters in hand, expecting greedy McCallum to burst through the entrance with gun blazing, ready to recover his treasure. Instead, Sutton and Ray watched as dozens of willowy, sooty tentacles sprouted from the leadenness overhead and streamed into the establishment. Like amorphous inky feelers, each cluster of limbs sought warm flesh – living prey to seize and confine.

Saloon patrons ran into the street, joining other denizens of Dead Reckoning driven from their homes and businesses.

"Dear God," Sutton said, his deep-set eyes of blue watching the dark skies writhe with awful aspirations. The lawman blasted a few blind tentacles, his bullets bursting their black bulk and dispersing them into static shadow. "What do we do, preacher?"

"We've got to get this cross back to the gulch," Ray said, petitioning the lawman's aid. Sutton, who had faced both hardhearted outlaws and warring Apaches, shuddered as the blackness reeled in its first victim. Enshrouded in an ebon cocoon, the squirming sufferer shrieked as the dark appendages retracted, drawing him back toward nearby Indian Grave Gulch. "We've got to try."

"Sounds like a plan."

The ride into the foothills seemed like a descent into hell. Racing on horseback toward the source of the hungry darkness, the preacher and the gunman watched as the invisible enemy appropriated townsfolk one by one, dragging them over the rough and rocky terrain. Long before they reached the gulch, the victims' dying screams faded as their bones splintered and their bodies ruptured, ripping open inside the black bubbles.

"They aren't especially interested in us," Sutton said, trying to keep to the path in the darkness. Only the lingering glow of light from the east kept the two men from utter blindness.

"It's the cross. It's protecting us."

Windblown and edgy, Ray did his best to dismiss his fear. Back in demon-plagued Smithville, his forefathers had tussled with witch covens and self-indulgent cultists vying for control of the community. Even during his term as preacher, depravity and debauchery flourished behind closed doors, and unearthly evil manifested itself whenever the opportunity arose. Following a particularly vicious exorcism, Ray fled his flock and his faith – hoping the horrors at home in Smithville had no match elsewhere in the world.

He sensed the same authors he had confronted so often in the past behind this present wickedness – and while modern day religion might hastily attribute it to ethereal and supernatural entities, he had come to understand that its source came from more substantial beings with vast influence and dark designs dating back long eons.

In the area surrounding the ravine, darkness fermented and evolved, permeating the landscape, the air and the vegetation. Shadows cast shadows in a nightmarish transgression of nature. In comparison, night itself would have seemed as bright as day. Near the nucleus of the infestation, a blind man would sense the extinction of all light.

As Ray and Sutton drew closer, a few stray strands of shadow approached them inquisitively, threatening to impede their advance. Sutton's keen eye and gunmanship, however, managed to deliver them to the steep cliff overlooking the ravine.

Led by faith and an uncanny ruddiness radiating from the cross, the lawman and the preacher stumbled down the steep, narrow trail into the depths of Indian Grave Gulch. Amidst the scattered bones of long-dead Pima, the mutilated corpses of more recent victims rested in shuddering heaps on the floor of the ravine where famished shadows feasted on flesh and blood and entrails.

Drowning in a sea of shadow and choking on the ubiquitous gloom, Ray held the cross high above his head where its flickering light seemed to falter.

"Do something," Sutton said, firing blindly at the shadows. His bullets vanished almost as they exited the guns' barrel.

"I don't know what to do." Ray considered a handful of rituals he had utilized to banish spirits and cleanse souls and bless homes, but none seemed applicable. Then, he remembered the Pima's dying words. "That's it."

"What?"

"Fiat lux – let there be light."

The blackness convulsed, rippling with anger and frustration. Immediately, the shadows thinned as the eventide began to recoil into the rift. In that instant, the dwellers in darkness emerged from the obscurity, their hideous forms revealed as the dark matter which spawned them diffused. Lingering over their prey, gorged on the carrion meat of slaughtered innocents, the resentful entities pitched their weight upon the two whose actions had fettered their incursion.

"Blasted monsters!" Sutton fired indiscriminately as they piled atop him. Seconds later, the lawman found himself sprawled over stones and bones and a pool of gummy, black tar.

Far above, blue sky and sunlight replaced the blackened heavens.

"It's over, Sutton." The preacher offered him a hand. He placed the cross in a crack in the rock where the darkness had blossomed. The incident had reacquainted the preacher with his own faith, reminding him of the mystical power of ancient icons. Nothing men had devised could defeat the entities Smithville elders called the Great Old Ones; but some signs and symbols, bolstered by the legends that accompanied them, managed to patch the seal and restore the partition that kept them at bay. "That will hold them for now."

"And what about the next idiot that comes along and takes that cross?"

"Well," Ray's eyes scoured the steep sides of the ravine. "Seems like we'd be better off if this whole place became less accessible."

"We got plenty of dynamite back in town – a few well-placed sticks would bring those walls tumbling down."

"Sounds like a plan."

67

February 26, 2006

Post-graduate student Emma Stanley, assigned to oversee the excavation at Indian Grave Gulch, could not believe her eyes. Though the recovery of dozens of bones had been the focus of the expedition, a number of religious artifacts – mainly of pre-Columbian origin – had made the semester remarkable and had drawn the attention of many scholars in the field.

The cross she held would not only earn her prestige at the university – it might well lead to her first publication.

"What in the world is this doing here?" Her academic curiosity blinded her to the shadows that had begun to leach into the recently cleared ravine.

THE HARVESTMEN
by Aubrey Campbell

R ue Loveday hadn't seen another living soul in two years, seven months, and nineteen days. The *living* part was the catch. A slew of vacant souls wandered the desert, wasting away in the heat until the buzzards picked their brains out while they were still standing. They weren't dead, but they weren't alive either. Not when their will to live had been sucked clean out of them.

Ever since Jesus and the Devil rendezvoused with temptation in the desert, the barren landscape had been a hotbed of supernatural activity for one creature after another. Nothing good scurried around in those sands when the sun went down – demons and banshees, wraiths and specters, chimeras and hobgoblins. The list grew longer with every passing moonrise. Towns had long since sunk into the desert, swallowed by dust and destruction. Cities attempted to fortify themselves only to fall in the night if they weren't deep into the forest or clinging to the ocean's shoreline.

There was something about the desert, the dry heat, bareboned tumbleweeds, and lonely expanse of desolate emptiness that attracted the ugliest, nastiest, meanest monsters alive in countless hordes.

But monsters didn't worry Rue. Humans did. In this hellish landscape, desperation knew no bounds, worse than any monster looming on the horizon.

The stars had barely winked themselves awake when she stumbled upon the scrap of a town. Pieces of it protruded from the whirling dust like broken teeth. A roof perched on the desert presumably above a building worn away by wind and sand. A few paces to the south, a crudely carved sign on a pole read STABLES.

Rue kept going, steering her horse around the rubble. Spending the night near ruins was a bad omen and a risk not worth taking. There might be supplies she could use if she dared to waste time scavenging. With dark closing in, if she stopped, the town would become her grave. No amount of supplies would do her any good after that.

As she passed the stables, movement out of the corner of her eye made Rue grab for the gun strapped to her back. In one smooth motion, she pulled it from the holster, took aim, lining up that blue fire beginning to buzz in the barrel of her rifle.

Two grizzly old men crouched beneath the crumbling eaves of a shack's remains. They held up their hands in surrender.

"Easy now," the short and stocky man said.

"We made camp here first," the other man said. He was tall and lean, a bit younger, with a mean look in his eye.

"We don't have much," the short one said. "But there's plenty of lizard jerky to go around if you'd like to rest awhile. I'm Nash. This is my brother, Shane."

Before she could respond, Shane's gaze dropped to her rifle and hunger blew his pupils wide.

"Must have seen some serious trouble in your time, lady," he said. "Nobody but a Saint packs a Last Rite."

Rue gritted her teeth. She'd tipped her hand. Now she had to distance herself before Nash and Shane started asking questions she didn't want to answer.

"The Saints are dead," she replied in a flat voice. "And you will be too if you spend the night in this hellhole."

Nash shrugged. "We're old. Tired of runnin'. Heard El Paso fell a few days ago. It's only a matter of time before we go down, too. Thought we might as well make peace with that."

Shane snorted. "El Paso was on its last leg anyway."

"They had the army behind them. We've got nothin' out here."

"A handful of washed up, worn out soldiers ain't an army."

Rue glanced toward the horizon but the darkness was thick and smooth as ink. Though she saw nothing, the desert was likely swarming already. El Paso was only fifteen miles away as the crow flies. And monsters traveled faster than crows.

"Well, aren't you a ray of sunshine," Nash said.

"Just bein' practical," Shane countered.

"Put that on your tombstone."

Shane snorted. "When the Harvestmen get here, there won't be a tombstone for either of us and you know it."

The echo of that word—*Harvestmen*—resounded in the stillness, accompanied by a chill of dread that even the desert heat couldn't chase away.

"With the two of you jawin' as loud as you are," Rue said. "They'll have no trouble finding you."

She holstered her Last Rite and steered her horse off into the dark.

"Then do something about it," Shane called after her.

71

Rue stopped. Her spine went rigid and she seethed through her teeth.

"With a piece like that," Shane added. "You could take out those things comin' this way."

For a split second, Rue considered turning around and lighting into those bickering old men, waiting for death, giving up without a fight.

Instead, she nudged her horse forward and didn't say a word.

Shane's scratchy voice drifted through the shadows as she rode away.

"It ain't right, Nash, I'm tellin' you," he said. "That woman has no business hauling around a Last Rite like it's nothing more than a pocket knife. Sure as hell doesn't deserve it when she ain't gonna handle it proper."

Rue slowed to a stop. The Last Rite was a sleek weapon with a burgundy handle, green ivy detailing, and silver filigree worked over the barrel. Instead of bullets, holy blades were locked into the clip, rimmed with spines that bit into flesh and seared through bones. With such a pretty weapon, someone was bound to steal it for themselves. She could make a run for it, but galloping in the pitch black was never a good idea. It wouldn't be hard to ditch Nash and Shane on foot, but she had a feeling the sight of her gun had breathed new life into them. Besides, she never liked being chased. Having her back to the enemy made her uneasy.

Rue slid to the ground, tied her horse to a saguaro a short distance away. After surveying the area, she selected a spot hidden in the shadows and waited.

Hardly two minutes passed before Nash and Shane were creeping by her, just as she had expected. Rue kicked at Shane's knee, cracking it like a tree branch.

He dropped with a strangled yelp. Nash whipped around, a rusty old rifle in hand. He must have hidden it earlier, fearing she might rob him. Rue swung, knuckles colliding with his jawline and he stumbled. She stripped the rifle out of his grip and flung it into the darkness.

"Thought you gentlemen were smarter than that," Rue said.

Shane, huddled on the ground and clutching his broken leg, glared up at her. "If you're going to flaunt that weapon, you better have the guts to use it."

Rue met Shane's stare and stepped closer. As she leaned over and grabbed his collar, her necklace slipped loose from her shirt. The white glow of the holy crystal on its gold chain gleamed in the dark like a star.

"A Saint," he whispered.

"Probably the last one alive, too," Rue replied. "So, whether I choose to use that gun or not, it's got nothing to do with guts, buddy. Out here, it's every man for himself."

Rue walked away, leaving Nash and Shane to the desert's mercy. At the back of her mind, an echo of disappointment resounded.

A Saint never walks away from those who need protection.

Two years ago, the earth cracked open and the Harvestmen came boiling up from Purgatory. A massacre of Saints ensued, staining the sand red. If the holiest order of lawmen couldn't withstand the Harvestmen, lowly sheriffs and deputies didn't stand a chance. Since then, any semblance of law in the desert was thin at best, turning it into a frothing pit of monsters, cutthroats, and bandits.

Rue's fingers strayed to the crystal around her neck. Inscribed along the stone's edge, it read, *Saint Isaiah*

Longfellow. She had loved him once, what felt like a lifetime ago, when they stood side by side and faced the things that lurked in the dark.

You're better than this, Rue, he would have said, ever her moral compass, guiding her true north. Saints protected people, warding off the shadowed creatures that stole the light. Saints stayed behind and stood their ground when others ran away.

But Isaiah was gone and Rue was not. In the desert, there was no true north, no right or wrong. Only survival, brutal and merciless.

Rue kissed the stone and tucked it back in her shirt.

"I was never very good at this Saint thing anyway," she muttered.

Rue guided her horse at a slow, silent pace, listening for signs that Nash had followed. She wasn't in the habit of killing people outright if they didn't try to kill her first. But she had clocked Nash in the face hard enough to knock him off balance. Some men might take that personally and come after her.

Rue was so focused on what was behind her that she didn't notice what was ahead until the child careened out of the dark.

Rue's horse startled, sending Rue into the dirt flat on her back. The child—a girl, barely seven years old—latched onto the Saint. Her hair was a ratty, filthy mess. She wore a paper-thin nightgown stained with blood and dirt and hell only knew what else.

Rue attempted to pry the girl away but she held on tighter with a whimper.

"Get off," Rue growled.

The girl shrank back, shoulders hunched like a kicked puppy.

"What are you doing out here?" Rue said.

The girl ducked her head, mouse-brown hair shielding her face. She crossed her arms and scrubbed the back of her calf with one foot.

Rue stifled a groan. She'd seen kids like this before. Families lost. Living off of whatever they could get their hands on, whether that was from begging or stealing.

"Fine, I don't want to know anyway," Rue said. "How about a name then?"

"Sadie," she whispered.

"All right, Sadie. I'll be straight with you. Turn around and get out of here. Rely on yourself and no one else, just like you've been doing. It's better that way."

"But—"

"Don't ask me for help. You won't get it."

Sadie cast a wary glance at the horizon and huddled closer to Rue, her grimy fingers grasping for Rue's hand.

Rue would have shaken her off. Physical contact formed a bond that only made it harder to break. But Rue knew the look of a hunted rabbit when she saw one. She followed the line of Sadie's gaze.

For a moment, there was only darkness. Monsters were born that way, wreathed in shadows where light never touched, nightmares surged in veins instead of blood, and a tangle of black horrors served as a heart.

Then a flash of lightning slashed the sky and Rue saw them. A hulking horde fanned out across the desert, thirty strong, and towering fifteen feet high.

Harvestmen, they were called, after their strong resemblance to daddy-long-legs. Thin, grey legs speared the earth as they moved with a rumble like thunder. Their heads were mangled human faces, dented, misshapen, with stringy, greasy hair that dripped oily blackness to the desert floor. Where it landed, it sizzled and burned, leaving a scorch mark like a footprint.

The Harvestmen shifted as one, gliding over the dune. Their heads turned in Rue's direction and each distorted face held twelve golden eyes, shining in the dark.

Rue swore under her breath. The Harvestmen advanced toward her, one graceful stride after another. Her horse was nowhere to be seen. If she wanted to stay alive, she would have to find terrain too tricky for the Harvestmen's massive bodies to navigate.

"Take me with you," Sadie said in the wisp of a voice. "Please."

Rue gritted her teeth. The chances she'd make it out of this alive were slim as bone already. A child would only slow her down.

In the distance, the Harvestmen began to chant, a guttural, mindless hum to hypnotize their prey. The sound echoed off of the dunes, amplified in the dark until it pounded in Rue's head, vibrated in her bones. Her instincts went soft and gummy at the edges, slowing her desire to run.

Sadie yawned and sank to the sand, curling up with her head pillowed on her arm. Seconds ago, she had been willing to claw her way to survival, whether Rue wanted her around or not. Now, the Harvestmen were putting her to sleep, rendering her an easy target.

Something inside Rue snapped. Her lethargy sloughed away and without thinking, she scooped Sadie into her arms.

The Harvestmen covered more ground in one stride than Rue ever could on horseback. Attempting to escape on foot was pointless and hiding wasn't a better option. The Harvestmen could chant for days without pause, rendering Rue and Sadie immobile. If monsters didn't kill them, starvation and dehydration would finish the job.

Rue ducked between dark pillars of saguaros, skidding in the dry scrub. She knew this terrain, every shift of sand and cleft of rock, but it wasn't enough to buy her the time she needed to get Sadie awake.

The earth shuddered as the Harvestmen closed in. The chant grew louder, thunderous, until Rue's ears began to bleed. She pushed harder, breath aching in her lungs, to gain a few more inches, a few more minutes.

"Wake up, kiddo," she said. "You have to run like hell."

Rue climbed the crest of a sand dune, clutching Sadie to her chest. Then she slowed to a stop.

Scattered across the desert were standing figures, human, frail and tired. They milled around below the Harvestmen's feet, jaws slack, posture as limp as if their spines had been snapped, the pupils of their eyes as milky white as the moon.

"A nest," Rue whispered. "This is a breeding ground."

She glanced at Sadie, sleeping soundly in her arms. The chanting went silent.

Then Sadie was ripped away, rising upward on a pool of darkness. Her head fell forward, mouth hanging open, and the soft brown of her eyes clouded over. Up above, a Harvestman loomed, spinning a silver thread of soul out of Sadie's back.

Rue had no right to call herself a Saint anymore. She had stopped fighting, wrapped up in herself, as if she was the only one who mourned the Saints' death. The desert was overrun because no one had the backbone to look a monster in the eye and pull the trigger.

Rue drew her Last Rite. She carried it only in remembrance of her fallen comrades. Their bodies had been strewn across the desert in pieces, shredded by the Harvestmen, but she was the one left standing. She wanted the world to remember what they had lost. Good people, brave and selfless, beings of light in this world where darkness ruled with a death grip.

For the first time in two years, Rue fired. Holy blades whirled from the rifle's barrel, spinning into the night. The blades swung wide, slicing along the Harvestman's leg. Gray flesh oozed yellow acid, searing the desert floor. Hardly enough damage to slow the creature down but she wasn't aiming for a kill shot. Not yet. She needed a distraction and she'd hit her mark.

The Harvestman shrieked and dropped Sadie. She slumped to the ground. Rue grabbed the back of her nightgown and hauled her away. She kept the Last Rite trained on the Harvestman.

Sadie mumbled, eyes slowly beginning to regain focus and color. The thread of her soul still dangled from her back like a wisp of smoke, gradually curling back inside her.

Rue pushed Sadie behind an outcropping of rocks and grabbed her wrist hard enough to make Sadie yelp. Sadie's gaze cleared a little faster, sharpened by the sudden jolt of pain from Rue's hold on her.

"No matter what happens," Rue said, "stay down. And if anything comes near you—"

Pain bloomed through her body, igniting every nerve all the way to her fingertips. Rue looked down. Protruding through her chest was the long, spear-like leg of a Harvestman. Blood gleamed against the sickly gray skin. Her blood. The leg was hard as metal, more of a weapon than a body part.

Somewhere in the back of her mind, she thought of Sadie.

Everything will be okay, Rue wanted to say. *We'll get through this.*

But she couldn't bring herself to manage more than a groan. A monster had kicked through her lungs, with a dozen more monsters waiting in the wings. Precious seconds remained before she suffocated or bled out.

Sadie didn't need placating words. She needed a Saint to fight for her.

Rue raised her rifle, the weight of it causing her fatigued arms to tremble from the exertion. Her finger curled over the trigger. The holy blades inside hummed with power and light.

The Harvestman bared its yellow jagged teeth at Rue's defiance. With one twitch of its leg, it yanked Rue into the air. The rifle fell from her hands as fresh pain blurred her vision. The Harvestman drew her up to eye level, letting her hang there for a moment.

Then the cold came, icy pinpricks burrowing through her heart. Something tugged at her ribs, as if attempting to pry them apart and she knew her soul was unraveling. A moment later, she saw it, a thin pale thread winding away from her body. With every inch that left her, a dark desert of nightmares bled like poison across her mind.

A gleam of light on the Harvestman's back caught Rue's attention. She struggled to raise her head and get a better look. It hurt to breathe, to think, to move. The nightmares in her head were screaming, clamoring for her attention like restless spirits eager to possess every waking thought.

"Eggs," Rue croaked.

Nestled between the Harvestman's shoulder blades were thousands of round egg sacs. Squirming lumps of flesh twitched inside, black and twisted creatures that would soon hatch and patrol the desert. Each fleshy lump was attached to a ball of soul thread, gradually sucking it dry.

One egg sac drew her eye, a faint, familiar voice emanating from it.

Rue. Rue. Rue.

Isaiah's voice. His soul—the remnants of it—was trapped in that egg sac, feeding one of those baby monsters soon to be born. The light of his soul was nearly gone, desiccated to a firefly's dying autumn glow.

Rue grabbed for it, flailing on the Harvestman's leg. She missed, fingers swiping the mucous-laden covering of the egg sac. The Harvestman reared its head, spinning her soul from her body faster. Rue knotted her fingers in the Harvestman's greasy hair and wrenched its head to the side. She reached for the egg sac, straining against the leg impaled through her body.

There.

Her fingers punctured the sac's covering. Green fluid gushed over her hand and the parasite flopped to the ground, squealing like a piglet.

Let me go, Rue, Isaiah said.

Rue cradled the last of Isaiah's soul in her hands. She had held his failing body in her arms once before in the aftermath of the Harvestmen's massacre. It broke her last time. She couldn't watch him die again.

"No," Rue replied. "I won't. I can't."

I'm too far gone to bring me back, sweetheart.

Rue closed her eyes. He was right. The nightmares hovering at the edges of her consciousness grew thicker, a horde of horror ready and willing to swallow her whole. For two years, she had given up, over and over. It would be easy to do it again now, to let the darkness take her under where she didn't have to fight anymore.

The wisp of Isaiah's soul coiled over her wrist with a burning grip.

You're a Saint, Rue Loveday, he said. *End this. Bury these monsters, once and for all.*

For the last time, Isaiah slipped through Rue's fingers. His soul dissipated, finally at rest, no longer consumed by the maggot of a monster.

A crack of gunfire split the air.

Rue glanced down to see Sadie clutching the Last Rite. The rifle was bigger than her, the butt resting on the ground. A holy blade's blue arc sailed off into the night, soaring over the Harvestmen's heads.

Sadie was too small and Rue was too high to reach the rifle, but a gun at close range wouldn't do much good anyway.

Rue pointed to the writhing larva on the ground.

"Kill it," she croaked.

Sadie fumbled with the Last Rite, dropped it. She picked up a rock and smashed it against the Harvestman's larva. It flashed its circular sucking mouth of teeth but Sadie didn't flinch and she didn't stop, even when acidic blood burned her hands.

At last, Sadie stood, the mangled body at her feet.

The horde of Harvestmen screamed, a wild, banshee's cry of grief.

Rue wrenched herself free from the Harvestman's leg and she plummeted, hurtling to the ground.

The Harvestmen descended on Sadie, a little girl armed with only a rock in the middle of the desert night.

Rue scrambled for her Last Rite. Her legs were numb, too weak to hold her weight. She half stumbled, half crawled until she flung her body over Sadie, raised the Last Rite and turned.

Three Harvestmen's faces peered down at her, mouths wide, vengeance shining in their many gold eyes.

Rue jammed the muzzle of her Last Rite into the nearest Harvestman's mouth, buried it so deep her hands were slick with saliva.

"Go back to hell where you belong," she said.

Rue pulled the trigger. Everything exploded black.

Sunlight seared Rue's face, flooding her world with heat and light after a cold, merciless night. Slowly, she opened her eyes, wincing at the burn in her chest and the screaming ache in her bones. She touched the tender skin only to find a makeshift bandage wound around her ribs.

Rue carefully turned her head to the side. She didn't dare move – not when every breath sent a fresh wave of white-hot pain through her lungs. Beside her, the remnants of a campfire smoldered, thick with ash, a few low coals warm and red.

"You're alive."

Sadie emerged from the underbrush, two rabbits slung over her shoulder. She crouched beside Rue with a small smile.

"I feel like roadkill," Rue groaned.

Sadie said nothing as she stoked the fire.

"What happened?" Rue whispered.

Sadie went still. She set the rabbits aside and inched over to take Rue's hand. Despite how admirably she had fought the night before, she was still human, a little girl seeking the comfort and reassurance of touch.

82

"The Harvestman you shot," Sadie said. "He was burned alive by blue fire. It worked through him from the inside out. The other Harvestmen got upset. They started taking those egg-shaped things off of the dying one's back. Then they left."

Rue stared up at the sky. This was only the beginning of a fresh wave of Harvestmen. They had retreated for the sake of their young but when they found safer nesting grounds, the monsters would need a source of food again.

"I saw where they went," Sadie said. She pointed to the west, toward the gentle slope of a dune. "I followed them. They went down a hole, over there."

Rue swore under her breath. "Where's my gun?"

Sadie reached for it, propped up against a saguaro. She handed it to Rue. The gun felt good in her hand again but too heavy to lift with her tender, abused body. She gritted her teeth, easing it down until it rested across her chest. If she was lucky, she might have enough time to heal before the Harvestmen returned. But she didn't like relying on luck. She needed backup.

"Do you know what a Saint is?" Rue said.

"You," Sadie replied.

Rue nodded.

"I used to be. And then I wasn't. I thought I could hide. I thought I could look the other way when the monsters came. As long as I stayed alive, I didn't care what happened to anyone else."

Sadie was quiet, listening.

"You made me a Saint again," Rue said. "But even Saints need help."

She slipped off Isaiah's holy crystal and looped it around Sadie's neck.

"It's time you learned how to shoot," Rue said.

AUBREY CAMPBELL

The Harvestmen were coming. This time, the Saints would be ready for them.

TAKE THE DESERT WITH YOU
by Joanna Parypinski

I am the desert. Harsh and unforgiving, with nights so cold they can freeze you where you stand. I am vast, quiet, stark. I feel within me every creeping lizard and windblown particle of sand, and I wrap the sandstorms around me as protective covering, disguised by death.

Dusk. The low plains here are almost picturesque against the red mountains. I can't recall how long I've been out riding but the sun is almost to the ground, and there's still not a soul in sight. My horse, Betsy, is growing tired, I can tell; we must rest.

No dinner tonight. The wind howls across the desolate plains, and I set up camp among the scrub. From my rucksack I pull out some old photographs, and I ponder them by the fire that I light from chaparral and other kindling. These last vestiges of an old life.

Lucky for me I've got a wineskin, so instead of sitting here thinking how hungry I am, at least I'll have a drink. Bartered it off a mean fella trying to set up an establishment in the wasteland to the east, a sorry place plagued by sandstorms and other unlucky weather, aside from, of course, the Darkness. We haggled over it, but in the end he accepted my offering of one pound of meat although you could tell he'd rather kiss a cactus than make a fair deal with the likes of me.

85

While the stars come out I sip and tip my head back. There is nothing like a pleasant warmth—wine in the belly, the heat of fire on the face, and in that warmth, the attempt to think nothing at all. I almost manage, too, until there is a cry from out of the dark. I sit up, clutching the wineskin in one hand, the other finding the knife in my boot.

There's the cry again—and, off in the distance, footsteps, pattering haphazardly over the dirt. Frantic panting. It is a woman, by the voice, being chased, by the sound of the following footsteps. Betsy snorts and swishes her tail disapprovingly. "Shh," I say. "S'alright, Bets."

The running people draw closer. "Please, please," the woman's voice rings out, half-blubbering. Then, a more chilling sound: laughter, a man's. He isn't running at full-tilt, I realize; no, he is teasing her, slowing when he needs to, tiring her out. Enjoying the hunt. He will chase her down until she falls.

"Come on, darling," he says in a low throaty croak. "I ain't gonna hurt you. Hell, I think you'll enjoy it."

"I told you," the woman pants. She doesn't finish her sentence. She's drawing awfully close to my fire, so close she must have seen it by now even if I can't see her yet.

He laughs again, sand in the wind, sand raking over vocal cords, a sound I think may drive me over the edge until the woman stumbles into my firelight, falls to the ground, and looks up at me, pleading with desperate eyes. Her hair is wild, matted; sweat has slicked over her face and likely through her threadbare and dirtied clothing. "Put out the fire," she whispers, having the nerve to start casting sand onto the hissing flames, which fight against her attempt to douse them. "Put it out, he'll see! We have to hide!"

It is too late, though; he has seen, and now he steps casually into the light, a figure in dusty black. His boots stomp into the dirt on the other side of the fire, and I look up to his craggy face shielded beneath the wide brim of his hat.

"Well, what have we here?" he says. "My lucky day? A two-for."

"Go on. You don't look the type to like dark meat," I counter. My hand hovers over my knife. "I won't stop you. Have your way, but leave me the hell alone."

The woman stares, scandalized, at me. "Are you fucking crazy?" she snaps, then looks up at the man with terror. "No, no, please—" But he has yanked her up by the hair.

"Much obliged," he says. "But you've got me wrong, there. I think I'll have the both of you."

Here's how it goes down: in an instant, or what feels like one, I'm on my feet; I've pulled the knife out of my boot, and it's at the man's throat. That might have been enough to put someone off, but I can tell it won't do for this sonofabitch. Just as the woman is choking out a sound of pure animal relief, I slice the blade in one clean motion. An eruption of blood showers my front, and the man's black eyes go wide, their inner darkness flickering in the firelight behind me and releasing his ghost from those vast pupils. He sputters, claws momentarily at his split neck, and collapses.

"Serves you right," I say, and spit on him.

The woman stands slowly, comes up beside me, and looks down at him. She wipes her brow, then her hands on her jeans, but I don't think it did much of anything to cleanse her, not in the way looking upon his dead body has cleansed her soul. "Mary," she says. "My name's Mary."

"Quaint."

She's pale and sickly, an anemic look I recognize as starved for protein, with dark rings hugging her eyes. "We have to go. He's got friends. They'll be on their way. And they've got guns."

So we kick sand over the fire, and over his body to boot—I hesitate before doing so, but good riddance to the bad meat, let him rot—and then I help her onto Betsy and we ride off into the vast unsettled dark with the moon making ghosts of cacti and scrub.

After a while we figure we're safe, so we get off the horse and walk from there, making a show of looking for somewhere to camp although neither of us wants to stop.

"How'd you survive out here on your own?" I ask.

"I was with a group for a while," she says. "We were doing okay. Living in this cave, which was perfect because of the natural shielding. Whenever the Darkness came, we just retreated, and we hardly ever saw those things. Mostly kept to ourselves except to go out for trading. But..." She sighs. "It never lasts, does it? Wasn't my first group. It's always the same. Someone gets brave. Someone gives up. Someone runs off. Someone gets mean. Someone brings trouble. Someone gets left behind."

"And which someone are you?"

Mary throws me a playful smirk. "Wouldn't you like to know?"

Betsy gives her head a little shake; she's getting tired. We slow down just a bit. "Sorry I almost gave you up back there. But you know how it is. Every woman for herself."

Mary shrugs. "So what's your story, mystery woman?"

"No story," I say. "Or, same story you always hear. Lost everyone when the first Darkness came. Figured a way to fend for myself."

She gives me a look, then keeps to herself. We talk lightly of our location for a bit, sharing wine and arguing over the constellations above, and then she says, "You know, we'd probably better get ourselves out of the desert. There's cannibals here."

"Oh?"

"Well, it's just a rumor, but… I don't know. Things the way they are. Could be true." She shrugs as if to show how foolish she is being. "It makes sense, though, doesn't it? No food for miles, not like you can just up and go to the grocery store… God, I miss the supermarket. I miss the rows of avocados and bell peppers and tomatoes. I was only twelve when it happened, but damn, I can still remember. Twenty years, and I can still remember."

I say nothing. Then: "I was eighteen."

"There's a lot I don't really remember, though. I wish I could remember a time when I wasn't afraid of the sky," she goes on, nostalgic now. "When I could look up and enjoy those stars without worrying what might come and blot them out. What might reach down…" She shudders. "I've only actually seen them twice. It's a miracle, really. But even twice was about enough to make you…" She trails off. "How many times you seen them?"

Dirt crunches beneath my boots; it's too dry here for much to grow. I think Mary would be better off heading east, where it rains some, to find one of those farming communities I've heard about, or maybe to the tech centers on the west coast working on building massive shields, so I hear, if it ain't all just rumors. I think she would do better in civilization, or what passes for it these days, and leave the desert to me and my kind. I think it's a wonder she's survived this long. I think it's unfair that she has, when my own husband, my own little boy—

"Too many to count," I say.

There, in the distance—a gleam of light. Fire. Shadows around it. "There's a camp up ahead."

Mary bites her lip eagerly, her eyes catching the glow, filled with hunger. She craves human connection, I can tell. She needs other people, and I am not such good company. How strange, to be so desperate for other people when these days, they only ever seem to weigh you down. Liabilities. Like she said: someone gets mean. Someone brings trouble.

I wonder if she's thought to ask herself which someone I am?

"Let's get closer," she says. "See who it is."

Imagine! How desperate she is to start a new group when she was only just lamenting that each group she's been with has always dissolved in the worst way, leaving her alone to fend off the beasts who roam this wasteland, both human and otherwise.

Closer. We can make out, now, that there are three around the fire, two adults and one child. A mother, a father, and a little boy. Mary seems utterly relieved that there is a woman and child there, and hell if I blame her after what she's been through tonight.

We're creeping closer, still trying not to be seen or heard just yet, when her stomach lets out a wrenching growl. She throws a hand against it and murmurs, "Maybe they have food."

"Don't worry," I say because I have the strange desire to comfort her, this creature who seems so ill-equipped for survival. I make a promise to myself that I will feed her, even if it is the only kind thing I am capable of, after all.

When we're close enough, I call out, "Hi there, friends," and we walk forward with our hands raised, Betsy hoofing just behind us. The man shoots to his feet, and the woman grabs the child and wraps her arms around him protectively.

"Who's there? Show yourself!" he calls.

We step into the firelight, and after a quick assessment, he lets his guard down.

"Just two weary travelers, looking for a respite," I say, then lower my hands to put them in front of the fire, enjoying its warmth, maybe the only thing that passes for pleasure these days. Mary takes the initiative to tie Betsy to a gnarled tree that provides some meager cover to the campsite, where there is otherwise not much plant life or protection, just an endless black sky reaching from horizon to horizon. The stars are still out, though, which means it's a friendly black, for now.

The woman lets go of her child, and the man introduces the little family: "Jorge," he says, with his hand on his chest, "Gabriella," he points to his wife, "and this is Angel," and they both look at their child, who is perhaps eight years old, young enough that he has never known a world before this one. I wonder how they managed a pregnancy and a birth in this place with no hospitals, no doctors, no technology—nothing from the old world. Why they would even want to bring a child into this world? But then I realize that humanity has done it before, under different circumstances no doubt,

91

but they have survived, and will again, I suppose. Like cockroaches.

Mary smiles. "Hi there," she says to the kid, who looks wary of her, his eyes wide and haunted. He says nothing.

"Mind if we sit by your fire for a bit?" I say. "It's cold out tonight."

"Please." Jorge spreads his hands. "Our fire is your fire. We are happy to share what little we have, and are blessed to share your company."

Too nice. No wonder the kid looks so scared. How many close calls have they had, welcoming everyone so readily into their midst? He'll grow up keen, but his parents still have too much of the old world in them, the kind old world with its kind old religions.

I share my wineskin with them, and we toast beside the fire for perhaps an hour before Mary's stomach gives another terrible growl, and she clutches it dejectedly.

"I'm sorry," says Gabriella, sounding truly apologetic. "We don't have any food."

Mary manages a smile. "It's all right. I'm sure we'll find something tomorrow. I am tired, though."

From my rucksack, I unroll my blanket and give it to her; she lays it beside the tree and is breathing deeply in minutes.

"What about you, little man?" I turn to the kid. "Are you tired?"

He shakes his head.

"You don't say much, do you?"

Gabriella ruffles his hair feebly. "Be nice, Angel."

I can tell in his eyes he doesn't trust me. His parents are too relaxed, too comfortable, but he knows better. There are ghosts in his eyes. I wonder how many times he's seen the things that come with the Darkness. More times than Mary, I reckon.

"She's right, though," Gabriella continues. "Time to sleep for you. Go."

Angel stands, looks at me inscrutably, makes his way to their tent, crawls inside.

"I want to thank you for your hospitality," I say. "You've been perfect hosts."

They are so somnolent, so contented, they don't even notice when I come up behind Jorge, reach around, and slit his throat. He falls forward, sprinkling the fire with his blood. Gabriella screams, but I silence her with the palm of my hand and lift my blade for her.

She is trembling, tears running from her eyes, breathing short panicked gasps under my palm. In another moment, she has joined her husband on the ground.

I've barely decided where I'll make my cuts when I notice Mary standing on the other side of the dying fire. Its flames light her haggard face from below—a face fixing me with unbearable horror.

"How..." she murmurs. "How could you?"

"Don't be like that," I say. When I stand, she takes a quick step back. "Come on, Mary. We're together now. I can provide for you. You're hungry." I kneel down again, planning my cuts by miming where I'll make them on Jorge's body. "This is good meat."

"You... you..." Her body and her voice both are shivering. "You're a monster."

"Oh, darling," I say, wiping blood from my hands. "There's scarier things than me in this world."

As I begin to filet the fresh slabs of meat laid out before me, soaking the ground in red, Mary turns and flees. She doesn't even try to take the horse or my bag, the fool, just runs off into the night, blind and terrified.

And then the darkness grows queer—more absolute. I look up to find the stars are winking out in waves. Something is moving over the sky, covering them up with its enormous body, blacking out the world below.

The fire has burnt itself to embers now, casting a low red glow over my work. The only light against the Darkness. Against those vast, impossible things floating over the sky.

The meat can wait. I sit myself against the tree and hold very still.

The hairs on the back of my neck prickle. In the dim glow, I sense more than see the creatures releasing their feelers. Impossibly long, thin tendrils reach down from the sky, searching the ground, dragging over the sand and caressing the outlines of cacti. I slow my breathing. In and out. Don't panic. Don't move.

Mary, poor Mary, who has only seen them twice, doesn't know what to do. She is still out there, running terrified from me, from the monster that saved her, thinking stupidly that running will save her. I don't want to hear it but the desert is quiet, and her scream echoes hauntingly through the unnatural night, as excruciating as if it were ringing inside of me. My body hums in sympathy. Her scream flies upward into the sky and abruptly stops.

I wait. A roaming tentacle draws near—so close it nearly rakes itself over the moribund fire, black and twitching. It drags along the dirt toward my feet. I wonder belatedly if this is my last moment on earth, what I want my last thoughts to be, but the thing continues on past me. I hold my breath until it's gone.

Slowly, the stars come out again, and the Darkness gives way to a more natural dark, a friendly dark. I resume cutting the meat from Jorge's body. By morning I've got quite a few sizable steaks wrapped in cloth and stored away in my bag. Their filleted skeletons lie on the ground near the ashes, bits of gore clinging to that which remains. Pale morning washes over the desert, and the sky is turning a grim faded blue.

I find myself missing Mary already, so I pull out my old photographs and look at them. A smiling, happy family. I can almost pretend it's real.

Angel emerges from the tent.

I put away the photographs.

"Are you hungry?" I ask.

His breathing is deep and even. Slowly he looks from his dead parents to me and nods. I am jolted by a fierce tenderness for the boy, and a long-buried grief that springs up unexpectedly.

"We've got plenty to keep us going."

"You're the Cannibal of the Sonoran," he says.

"I see my reputation precedes me."

He walks carefully around the bodies, then approaches me with those haunting eyes and takes my hand in his. "We were going to Los Angeles," he says.

I have spent so very long roaming this desert that it has become me, and I it. I am the cold craggy moon cast ghastly white on cactus thorns. I am dirt the color of dried blood flaking off into a deathly wind. I am the Cannibal of the Sonoran. I will take the desert with me wherever I go.

But maybe it is time to get out of this desert, after all. "That's a long way. It'll take us weeks."

"I can make it," he says.

And we do. We make our way across the desert. Sometimes we are hungry, sometimes not. He is a clever kid. I teach him how to wield a knife, how to make the right cuts. He still doesn't talk much, and that suits me fine. The less he talks, the more I can imagine he is mine.

Living in the desert, you can almost pretend the rest of the world is still the same as you left it so long ago. As if it's only you, only the desert, that has returned to the primordial wilds, but that civilization still exists, somewhere, even if you're not a part of it anymore. The hardest part is not the journey, but at last beholding the truth of the destination where it becomes clear that whatever you left in the desert never really left, at all.

Los Angeles is a burnt-out husk of abandoned buildings, cracked freeways, and desert scrub slowly reclaiming the remains of mankind's golden age. But there are people here—living in the subway tunnels, in the basements of destroyed buildings and below the wild array of overpasses. The Darkness comes as we approach, and from our vantage point, scaling down from the mountains, we have a magnificent view of the creatures casting their uncanny twilight and lowering their long fine tentacles down to the city. It is abjectly beautiful, and we watch from our covered perch until they pass on.

It is not what the boy had hoped for—but then, whatever he had expected was only a fantasy, after all, a dream. It is different from the desert, anyway. There are people surviving here—a fair few at that, and Angel looks up at me with a smile and says, "At least we won't be hungry."

HENRY RAIN
by Cassidy Frost

"**W**hy are you so cynical? " Callahan asked. "You should be too. Now, kick out his chair boy!" the deputy instructed.

"I didn't know that this was part of the gig."

"Well," the deputy let the word ring out, brushing his boot on the back of his pants. "Now you know. For all I care you can pull it out like yer sittin' down for dinner. Just get rid of it!"

Callahan focused on the man at the mercy of the noose. A thick woven bag covered his face, but his hands, tied together, were without calluses. Earlier he had pleaded for his life, crying over who would take care of his mother. He told them that his crime was committed to insure her comfort, robbing his neighbors to buy her some food. If Callahan could, he would untie the rope at once, but he knew where that path would lead. It would set in motion his expulsion from the Lawmen, or worse, he'd have a rope appointed to his own neck.

"You really are just a fancy mustache, no guts," said the deputy.

Callahan tucked his hair into his hat, and looked at the ground. "I'm sorr-" pain pierced Callahan's chest.

He fell onto his back, groping at the dirt. He tried to comprehend; to slow down his racing panic, as this was

97

worse than the pain. Another gunshot rang out, but Callahan felt nothing more. He turned his head and watched the deputy land stiff. That bullet was not for him. Callahan's ears rang over the sound of approaching hooves. Biting into his lip and blotting at the hole in his gut, he watched a woman untie the man from the noose.

Callahan would die knowing that his intentions were honest. That this prisoner would have been dead by now, if he had kicked the chair over when the deputy had instructed. He would die knowing that he had never taken a man's life. Callahan smiled. "I am an honest and noble man," he breathed out.

He began to blackout as the woman looted his body.

Gus heard the gunshots and wet himself. Two. One to his left, and the other to his right. He gagged himself with each frantic breath, sucking the woven bag into his mouth.

"Please! Don't shoot," he croaked. He felt a presence at his side and began to shake, hearing the subtle sawing sound of knife on rope. Headfirst, he released, clumsily falling off of the chair. A stranger straddled him, cutting his hands free. He threw the bag off his head, and took a deep breath.

The sunlight stung his eyes as they investigated his surroundings. He spotted a grey horse with a braided tail and felt the stranger's hands still steadying him. The prisoner turned to her just as she let go and jumped off the chair.

She walked to the dead men and began digging through their clothes, squatted over their bodies with the stance of a gorilla. She swayed powerfully back and forth in her high buckled boots. Her hair was piled on top of her head like a large beehive.

"Thank you for saving my life," Gus said. The woman kept quiet and busy. "Could I bother you further for a ride back to town?" he asked, stepping behind her. "My home is close by, but not by foot, and your gunshots scared off the other horses."

"Some weak horses," she grunted, walking towards her own. He waited for her to answer his question. Instead, he watched her pluck a newborn baby out of the tall grass, like she was harvesting a crop.

"Is that *yours*?" he said.

"Where do ye' live?" Her voice was odd for a woman's. Not deep, but unmannerly.

"Past Silver Springs. The house by the saloon. Do you know of it?"

She pulled a piece of fabric out of her horse's saddle. "Swaddle him and hop on."

He let her wrap her child around him. The warmth of the small living being at his chest made calmness wash over him. That, along with his adrenaline crash. His eyes were heavy, and his head felt full of lightning. He watched the woman mount her horse. She reached out for his hand. "Careful," she said, helping him up.

"Please don't take this the wrong way," Gus said, once the horse was in motion. He fought back nausea. "But why did you save me?"

"I needed someone to hold my baby, and today I trust any man who pisses his pants."

"Any man who stares at death would piss his pants!" he yelled over the horse trotting.

"Maybe so, but yer' also plenty small," she replied. "I was surprised to see a man's face under that bag."

"Yet, you knew! You knew that by law I am considered a bad man."

"No badder' than I is, Mister."

"My name's Gus, and what may I call you?"

Silence, and that's how they rode the rest of the way. Gus cradling what remained of his pride along with her child. He pondered over her intentions. If this strange woman really *was* going to drop him off, then why did she need him to hold her baby? Wouldn't she hold him herself?

Carriages and other signs of life were starting to ride past them. They had reached the smaller town that lead into his. This path was familiar to him, and he took that as a sign of hope. Then she made an abrupt stop at a small house, and Gus's hope faded.

"This should be quick," she said, tying up her horse to a porch railing.

"How about bringing me home?" he moaned, still sitting on the horse. He realized how ridiculous he sounded, like *he* was the helpless infant. Ashamed, he wrapped his arms around the child, holding him closer.

"This first," she said, sliding a sheathed knife into his boot. He looked down in alarm. "Now get inside before he sees ye'!"

Gus cautiously slid off the horse and let her rush him inside. The home was very small, but it was inviting in a lived-in sort of way. It had woven baskets that held fresh fruit, and the shelves were packed with plenty of canned goods. Quilts and animal furs draped the chairs. The woman went to a shelf, taking down a glass bottle filled with an amber-gold liquid. She then setup two cups and poured. "In case of any pain," she said.

"Is this your house?" Gus asked, accepting his drink.

"Not anymore. This is the devil's house."

She was a rough woman, Gus knew this, but her eyes were a comforting bright blue, and her smile was kind. She threw her drink back, and slammed the glass down on the table. Gus tasted his, it was quality drink.

She removed two revolvers from their crisscrossed holsters. They were large, but didn't look odd in her hands.

"Can't we lay low?" he said. "I'll bring your son to my mother. The baby will be safe there." He waited, but her expression remained unaltered. "You killed two men this morning! Can't death wait another day?"

"I've waited nine months," she said, looking at the baby in Gus's arms. "And this child will grow up to be nothin' like his cursed bloodline."

"You're killing his *father*?" Gus squeaked.

"Yes," she replied, heading towards the open door. "By the way, the name's Helga. Helga Hardknock. And another bad man's about to meet his end," she said. Helga stepped out into the evening light.

Gus looked out the door. The man he saw waiting in the distance was nothing more than a figure standing tall down the dusty road. He jumped away from the door and prayed that he hadn't been seen. Holding the baby tighter, he scanned the room for cover. He thought the cupboards looked big enough for a little man like him.

Gus realized he was cradling an alarm. If he could make the boy comfortable, and keep him happy enough, maybe he wouldn't cry. Bundling up his jacket, Gus put it into a large pot, then tucked the baby into it. He fumbled to fit his body into the cupboard with him, and closed the door. The two of them sat in the darkness.

"We don't need to worry," he whispered to the baby, but more to himself. "Your mother's coming back. She saved me once, and she'll save us both again." Yet the anxious voice in the back of his mind knew better. Seeing the man had frightened him. The way his dark hair blew in the wind like the streams of a shadow, and how steady his stance was, even as a silhouette.

Hardly any time had passed before Gus heard the gunshot rip through the wind. Quiet, he pushed the pot holding the baby into a far corner. His mind was cloudy, under the stress of his raised blood pressure. He fought to keep his vision from blotting over. Slow breaths. He pulled out the knife that the woman had given him, now thankful for the gift.

He heard booted steps on the deck, and then throughout the entranceway. *Helga's boots*. He relaxed his grip on the knife.

A deep throat sound filled the room, followed by the sound of a loogie hitting the floor. Gus broke out in a cold sweat while strange heels dug side to side. These weren't Helga's boots.

Signing the cross, Gus listened as the winner of the shootout thrashed through the house. Tin was clanging against wood as he threw things from the kitchen shelves. He didn't sound like he was leaving this victory without his prize.

Gus wished he was the sort of man who could use the child to negotiate his freedom. Could this stranger help him? Maybe he was a man who could put the lawmen in their place, or a man wealthy enough to help buy back Gus's freedom. The old Gus would have come up with a way to use the child as a bargaining chip. Anything to see his mother again, but now his priorities had taken an unsuspected detour.

Besides, this was all a fine fantasy, but if this man could kill the mother of his child, what difference would one more body be? And why should Gus mean anything

102

to him? He looked at the child, who hadn't moved or made a sound. He was angelic, tucked into Gus's jacket with the slightest smile on his sleeping face.

Gus's mind cleared. He put a pot on his head, wearing it like a helmet. He readied the knife in his right hand, and a frying pan in the other. Then the cupboard opened.

He saw a black boot, thin leather. Before the man could look down Gus threw out his left arm. Stabbing hard, the blade went through the boot and into the man's foot. He heard the cry, and then bullets rained into the cupboard. They hit the frying pan Gus was using as a shield and ricocheted.

Gus pushed all his weight off the knife's handle, and the blade went into the floorboards. He brought his body upward, slamming into the man's crotch. The gun went off again before falling onto the floor and sliding away from them. Unbelieving, Gus forced his body to move, throwing himself on top of the weapon.

Gus stood up. He was alive, and *he had the gun*. He steadied his aim at the man, and their eyes met. The man's whites were now filled with broken blood vessels. His face was grey, like meat beginning to spoil. He screamed out in anger. Gus watched him pull the blade from his foot.

Heart racing, Gus dropped the pan. The clanging sound of metal hitting wood rang out, but the baby in the cupboard did not cry. He stabilized the arm that held the gun.

With a stagger the evil man pointed the bloodied blade at Gus. A pool of blood was forming around his foot. He swayed forward. Gus took a step back.

"I'm not sure what *that bitch* told you, but a son needs his father," said the grey face.

That was when the baby laughed. After all the uproar, he didn't cry, he *laughed*. A sound so small and gooey that it would melt even a cold man's heart, but this child's father wasn't a man. Gus watched his hand tighten around the blood-soaked knife. He saw the hate in his eyes and decided then to shoot him.

He shot him until the rounds were emptied. Bang!-Bang!-Click.

Gus had never killed a man before.

Without taking too long to observe, Gus stepped over the man's body, reaching into the cupboard for the baby. He held him close, giving his soft forehead a kiss. *Thank you, for being good.* He was hoping that he could still return the baby to Helga. Clinging onto his last shred of hope, Gus walked outside.

When he saw her lifeless body, he covered the baby's eyes. Even though they were too young to truly see, he was afraid that they might somehow remember.

"Damn it," he whispered. The child felt heavy in his arms.

Her body lay beside the steps. Her chest had clotted from the gunshot wound. By her sides, and still held in her grip were the guns. Gus removed them from her solidifying grasp. "For when you're older," he said to the child, and realized that he didn't know what his name was. "Damn it", he said again. "Damn it all to hell."

Gus approached Helga's horse, stowed the guns, and took a piece of fabric out of the saddle bag. He swaddled the child to his chest. Helga wasn't there to help him this time, so it took longer, but he made out just fine. After all was secure he went back to collect Helga's body. She had saved his life, so he would bury her properly. With her corpse slung over his shoulder he took one last glace at the house, wondering if the father should also be buried. "No," he whispered, tying Helga to the back of the horse. He carefully mounted her grey beauty.

Gus and the baby rode until sunset. He wanted to be far away, to avoid any lawmen in case they were looking for him. When darkness fell, he stopped at a field, admiring its abundance of flowers. He decided to leave Helga's body there. He didn't have a shovel to dig a proper grave for her, so he poured a few handfuls of dirt over her and prayed. Remembering Helga, the craziest mother he'd ever met. The wind picked up. Gus, thankful for his luck, was sure that it was now spent. That it would all blow away.

It began to rain, and the chill droplets sent goosebumps down Gus's neck. He was nervous, but excited. Excited to be alive, excited to eat. He was hungry, and he was sure the boy was too. He imagined how good a homemade pot of his mother's stew would taste. He thought of his mother, Henrietta, and how she always cooked in an old dress, stirring stew in an ancient clay pot. The rain came down stronger, and the baby began to cry. Natures release. Gus surprised himself by crying too. He looked down at the child and whispered.

"It's okay Henry," he watched the rain droplets run down his little face. He pulled the swaddle over to block them. "Little Henry in the rain. That's what I'll call you. *Henry Rain*."

Gus could now see a clear image of the boy, and knew it was something that he could look forward to: Henry, a strong boy running around the deserts, riding his stick horse and firing his toy guns.

DOUGLAS SMITH

MEMORIES OF THE DEAD MAN
by Douglas Smith

You are done for--a living dead man--not when you stop loving but stop hating. Hatred preserves: in it, in its chemistry, resides the mystery of life.
-- E.M.Cioran, *The New Gods*

You ask me of the Dead Man. What kind of man was he?

Good question. But not the right one.

Some call him a murderer, a cold-blooded killer--or worse. Some call him a hero. Jase and I made it through those days only by his hand in our lives, so you'd think I'd know where I stand on that one. But even after thirty years, I'm still not sure.

I had dreams once, beyond living another day, but they'd died when I was twenty, died with my husband and daughter in the Plague. For ten years after that, I did what I had to, to feed Jase and me, to survive. That meant taking what we needed and staying in motion, one step ahead and not looking back. Not getting involved. Not trusting.

I made an exception with him, with the Dead Man. No--not that name. You call him that. They call him that. I won't. To us, to Jase and me, he was Bishop. He said his other name was John, but we just called him Bishop.

Yeah, I made an exception with Bishop. But then he was an exception to a lot of rules, even before the Merged Corporate Entity rebuilt Earth under its own rules.

It began in a shantytown, squalid and squatting on the edge of the Alberta Badlands. Began at 4 a.m. on a chill May night, under a moon as bright and cold and pockmarked as the chrome on the old Buick I'd just hot-wired.

Jase and I left some pissed-off locals in the dust, including Lizard, the skinny boss-man who'd proposed a business deal earlier I hadn't wanted to consummate. They ran after us down the broken asphalt right to the crumbling ramp onto the old highway until we faded into the night. I'd trashed the alternators on the two other cars in town, so I wasn't worried about pursuit. I planned to drive all night and hide out in the hills come first light.

Jase slept in the back as the road climbed into foothills lying like rumpled sheets on the bed of night. The town fell two hours behind, and an eastern light began to wash away the holes that stars had poked in heaven's black canopy. I began to relax, humming an old lullaby I used to sing to Sally and Jase when Sally was still alive and Jase didn't think he was too old for lullabies. Some of the words even came back to me just before the Buick coughed once, twice. Then it stopped coughing and just stopped period.

It sounded like we were out of gas, but the gauge showed three-quarters of a tank. I popped the hood, as a suspicion grew along with a cold lump in my gut.

They'd rigged the gauge to move no lower than three-quarters. At least I had the two hours head start, and they had no wheels. That hope died as I looked back to the flatlands below. Two pairs of headlights bobbed along the broken highway.

It looked like they kept spare alternators.

My earlier bravado blew away with the cold night wind. I could take whatever they did to me--I'd been ready to die a long time ago--all except for Jase. He was what kept me going on. And these people wouldn't limit their retribution to me. Even if they spared Jase, what would happen to him if I were dead?

I looked around for a place to hide, but we were a good mile from any cover the still-distant hills might provide. Trying to convince myself that maybe we could make it, I checked the headlights below again. The highway started weaving about where they were as the terrain got rougher. I was just figuring we had maybe ten minutes when a black shape following the two cars turned off the highway and cut across the rocky desert, straight for us. A third car, running dark. And the lack of a road didn't seem to be slowing it down much.

Straight for us. Shit. Too late, I remembered I still had the Buick's lights on. "Why don't you just send up a fucking flare, bitch?" I swore at myself.

I ran back to the Buick. Jase was awake and sitting up in the back. He always knew somehow. "Mom?"

"Out of gas, and we got company." Yanking open the driver's door, I killed the lights as Jase jumped out. He threw my bag to me then ripped his open and began pawing through it. I pulled my gun from my belt and thumbed off the safety.

"How close?" he asked, standing again, his own gun in hand.

"Two minutes tops," I said, looking at him. Small for his eleven years, calm and sure, thin sandy hair blowing in the night wind as he scanned the terrain for a place to hide. Ready to fight. Are you ready to die, Jase? Do you know that's what this is about? Do you blame me for this life?

I pointed at some rocks about a hundred yards east. Jase nodded, and we ran. We were about halfway when the growl of an engine leapt over the rise behind us. I turned to see a black shadow launch itself over the ridge of the hill we'd climbed in the Buick. Airborne for a full breath, it landed far more smoothly than any car should, then immediately spun towards us.

I stopped, putting myself between the car and Jase. Jase ran for another twenty yards before he noticed. "Mom!" he cried.

"Keep going!" I yelled, but he stayed put, gun out, one eye on the car. I raised my own gun as the car swerved around me and slid sideways to stop between us. It had an oversized Caddy body but this was no Caddy. Tinted windows hid the inside.

The night held its breath. All I could hear was the dying rattle of rocks the car had kicked up and my own hard breathing, louder than the engine in this thing. Both back doors *shooshed* opened. I tensed and sighted along my gun, but no one emerged.

"Get in!" An amplified voice, metallic and cold, boomed from the car. Jase looked at me. I shook my head. The driver's door opened with another *shoosh*. A man stepped out. Dark hair, slim, six foot. Long coat covered in black chain mail, probably crysteel loops, light and strong. Gray T-shirt and faded jeans. Black, finger-less gloves, and a short heavy chain around his neck with metal balls hanging from it. Smaller metal balls decorated the chain mail and the back of the gloves.

Arms raised, he stepped away from the car. I could see a knife sheath strapped to each of his forearms. His movements seemed casual, but he kept his weight low, knees slightly bent. The gravel barely crunched when he moved. He looked from Jase to me, both our guns on him, and he grinned. "Two minutes, and your friends from your car rental will be here for payment." His voice was calm, bantering.

"Why would we trust you?" I said, aiming my gun at his chest.

He shrugged. "Me or them."

I bit my lip. I could hear other engines climbing the rise. "We could shoot you. Take your car."

He nodded. "You could try."

I sighted along my gun at him. His grin faded, and he opened his hands, still held above his head. Two shiny balls like the ones decorating his coat and gloves seemed to hover above each palm. I heard a metallic clicking. What the fuck?

"Mom!" Jase called. I could see him out of the corner of an eye, but I didn't want to take my eyes off the stranger.

"What?" I snapped.

"Mom, he's okay." The approaching cars, now much closer, almost drowned out Jase's voice. "Mom, look at me!"

I hesitated, then shot a look at my son. Jase was smiling at me, running towards the man. "It's okay, Mom. He's okay."

Back then, in the Fall of Earth that followed the Plague, before the Entity and its empire, the world consisted of those who survived and those who died. Survivors learned fast what their skills were. Me, I could fix anything on wheels. Jase, he knew people. Just knew them. Could size them up just by looking at them. Got a feeling, he said. I'd learned to avoid people that made him nervous and to trust the ones he said were okay.

The man dropped his hands and waved us to the car.

Jase scrambled into the back seat before I could yell at him to stop. Cursing but committed now to trusting the stranger, I ran to the other side and climbed in as two cars crested the rise and pulled to a stop fifty feet away from us. I squinted out the back window into their headlights.

Two men unfolded themselves from each car, all four carrying short-stock M18 rifles.

The stranger still stood beside our car. Unarmed--I thought. Pointing his arms at the men, he opened his hands. The spheres he held blurred then disappeared. A whistling shriek cut the night. The gunmen jerked as if shot, then crumpled to lie motionless. More men piled cursing from the cars. The stranger reached toward his necklace. One of the larger metal balls leapt loose from the claw that held it and into his hand.

Again he held the ball in his palm, and again it seemed to blur. I'd figured out that somehow he could launch these spheres like projectiles. But now he held only one, albeit larger, against four opponents. Thinking he needed help, I clambered out of the car, gun in hand-- just as the night exploded, and I went blind then deaf. A blast of heated air punched me in the chest, and I fell. I blinked my vision back as pieces of dirt, flaming car, and body parts rained down around me.

At least I knew why he only needed one sphere the second time. C-4 with an impact fuse, I guessed. Strong hands pulled me up and into the front seat. The stranger slid behind the wheel while I checked on Jase in the back, his face lit through the back window by the flames of the destroyed cars. "Holy shit!" Jase exclaimed. "How'd you do that?"

"Telekinesis." The man put the car into gear. "Got what you need?" he asked.

"Our bags and us. That's it," I said, still shaking from the explosion. The stranger nodded as if he approved.

"What's tele... keesis?" Jase asked as we drove away.

He smiled. "Telekinesis. I can move things with my mind."

"Oh," Jase said.

I couldn't think of anything intelligent to add so I just stared at the road, struggling to make sense of what had happened. It took a moment for the weird lighting of the scene ahead to register. The windshield was an infrared viewer. I checked out the dashboard, which had more instruments than a small plane. I checked them again before I was certain. "Jesus Christ! This is an urban Hummer." The man just smiled again.

After the Plague had initiated the first stage of the Fall, the feds privatized domestic militia and police duties to the Entity. The Entity had introduced a scaled-down version of the military Hummers--looked just like a full-size car on the outside. Now I knew how the stranger had arrived ahead of the others--this thing could handle practically any terrain.

"Thanks. I mean, for back there," I said, not knowing what else to say but wanting to break the silence.

"No problem. I pulled into town as they were heading out."

"Why'd you help us?"

"I knew Lizard," he said. "Anyone he'd go after needs help. And usually deserves it. And..." Some inner struggle played itself out across his face. "And I had a wife and son once. If they had made it through the Fall instead of me, I'd have wanted someone to help them out."

Jase leaned over the seat. "I'm Jase. This is my mom."

"Mary," I said, holding out my hand.

He took it in a warm, strong grip and held it a little longer than he needed to, giving me a good once over while he drove. "Bishop."

I smiled, feeling no threat from his appraisal, and checked him out as well. He was lean but muscular, with a face of sharp lines and edges around a mouth out of place in all that hardness. Our eyes met, and I caught my breath. Black as old secrets, young-old like a child who has seen things a child should never see. They held me and made me want to hold him, to make those secrets, those things go away.

He looked back to the road. Released from the hold of his eyes, my breath returned, and my gaze fell to a thin chain he wore below the short necklace of metal balls. From it hung a chess piece, a black bishop. But under the traditional bishop's miter, a skull with two ruby eyes grinned.

I stared at that death head as random figures of rumor, legend and out-right lies jostled and danced themselves into patterns and finally into realization.

"My God," I whispered. "You're the Last Dead Man."

Behind me, Jase fell silent and still. Bishop kept his eyes on the road. "I've had a lot of names, Mary."

A lot of names. A lot of stories. You've heard them. Pick just one and try to settle on it. I tried, as I sat there beside the man who was either the most cold-blooded killer to emerge from the Fall or its greatest hero. But he saved our lives, I told myself, and Jase trusted him.

"Where are we headed?" I asked, just to say something.

Bishop just shrugged. "Why? Someplace you need to be?"

113

Jase laughed, and I joined in. "Anywhere but here."

"You're in luck. I'm heading there myself," Bishop said.

I thought of the life Jase and I led. I thought of the past, a husband and daughter long dead. I thought of the future and of Jase, and how this man could protect him better than anyone. And I made a decision. "Mind if we join you?" I asked.

He looked at me, and I knew then that my life, Jase's life had just taken a new road. "You already have," Bishop said.

The Dead Man wound the Hummer through the jumbled terrain as if each dry riverbed was a familiar road and every rock formation a street sign. "You ever heard of the Priests of the Night?" he asked after an hour of silence.

"Sure," I said. "Major bad news. We steer clear of them. Started out as a network of bike gangs before the Fall, I think."

He nodded. "When the Plague broke, the Entity used the Priests as militia in Alberta, a last gasp at keeping control before it all fell apart. They've grown into a small army in the prairies and upper mid-west states." He looked at me. "You run into them lately? Or heard of them around here?"

I shook my head. He looked disappointed. From inside his vest, he produced a photograph, faded and creased in a clear plastic pouch. "Calls himself 'The Pope'. Ever see him?"

I stared down at the picture. Shaved head, lots of skin piercing, and the inverted crucifix tattoo of the Priests on one cheek. Hawk-nose splitting eyes like diamonds, bright and sharp. Nasty grin wrapped around bad teeth. I shook my head. "Nope."

"You're sure?" This time his disappointment was obvious.

"Not a face I'd forget." I showed it to Jase, and he shook his head too. "Why?"

Bishop just stared at the road ahead. "I'm looking for him," he said, stating the obvious, and I knew that asking again wouldn't prompt any more information.

We drove until sunup, then Bishop pulled into a cave he seemed to know would be there, and we slept. Well, Jase slept. Bishop and I made love, slept, made love, slept. There were no awkward discussions, no bargaining or maneuvering. Just an unspoken agreement. And in truth, I found him attractive--and a gentle but passionate lover. It had been a long time for me, and the sincerity of my own passion soon caught up to his.

When night fell, he built a fire, and we sat around it eating canned meat cooked on that fire. I couldn't identify the animal, and I'd learned long ago I generally didn't want to.

"So how do you move things like that?" Jase asked.

Bishop smiled. He seemed to genuinely like Jase. And me too, but I assumed that was sexual. "Do you tell everyone you meet about that switchblade tucked in your boot?"

Jase's jaw dropped, and he pulled his jeans down to cover the knife. Bishop chuckled.

"Meaning you don't trust us?" I asked. He just shrugged.

"But why didn't you just pull the guns out of those guy's hands, instead of..." Jase's voice trailed off, but I knew what he was thinking. Instead of killing them.

"My power has limits, Jase. They were too far away."

I knew he wasn't telling us everything, but it didn't bother me. Survivors learned to keep their secrets to themselves. Trusting was another word for dead.

"What did you do before the Fall?" Jase asked. I cringed. You didn't ask people that--too many memories for survivors, all of them painful. To my surprise, Bishop answered him.

"Worked for the Feds. Covert op called the Office."

"Were there others like you?" Jase asked.

He nodded. "Eight in all. We each had a unique...ability."

"And the Office called you the Dead Men?" Jase asked.

"No, Jase. That name came later. The Office used the names of chess pieces. I was the Black Bishop." He fingered the piece that hung from his necklace.

"So Bishop's not your real name either?" I said. He just smiled.

"What did you do for the Office?" Jase asked.

The smile disappeared. He didn't answer right away. "I killed people for them, Jase. We all did."

"Oh," Jase said and looked at me. I swallowed.

Bishop stared into the flames for a long time before he spoke again. "They'd raised us from kids, as a team, trained us as an elite assassination squad. There wasn't a soul on Earth we couldn't get to. At first, we told ourselves we were patriots, that our targets deserved it, that the world was better, safer without them. At first, I think we were right. Then the targets started becoming...questionable." The shadows of the flickering fire, or of long buried memories, writhed across his face.

"Then on one target, we said no. We wouldn't do it. They sent another team after him. We took them out. They sent a team after *us*. We took them out too. Then they sent Father. We called him Father. He'd brought us together. We'd served him all our lives it seemed. He stood before us that day and said 'You're dead men. Each and every one of you--you're all dead men.' I said, 'Good--*you can't kill a dead man.*'"

Bishop threw a log on the fire. "After, we took that name. Not strictly correct--three were women. And one was my wife."

We all fell silent for a while. Then Jase spoke again, his voice low, cautious. "That last target. Why'd you say no?"

"He was just a kid, Jase. Younger than you. A reprisal against his father. They weren't above killing families." Bishop stared at the fire, and I knew he saw more than flames twisting in its depths. "No, they weren't above that at all."

I thought of the wife and son he mentioned, but it would be months before I had the courage to ask that question. "What happened to Father?" Jase asked.

Bishop tossed a last log onto the fire then stood. "I killed him." He walked to where his sleeping bag lay and crawled into it, while I sat wondering what sort of man I had tied us to.

Over the following months, I came to realize Bishop's claim of having no planned destination was only partly true. Much of the time we indeed just headed for the next known enclave, usually a remnant of a town guarding stockpiles of gas and supplies. But once there, a pattern soon emerged. He would ask anyone he could find two questions: had they news of any Priests in the area, and had they seen the man in the photograph. Any answer in the positive would prompt more questions and determine our next destination.

So our lives changed but stayed the same. A life of wandering still, but with a lover for me, a father figure for Jase, and a protector for us both. A life less lonely. And safer--most of the time.

If we remained too long in any town, Bishop would attract attention. Attention from young bucks looking to carve out a rep by taking down a legend. They would try. And they would die.

Through those incidents, I learned of his ability--and its limits. The closer he was to an object, the more easily he could affect it. It followed the inverse-square law: if he halved the distance, his control increased four-fold. Best was touching something. He said he transferred some of his power into objects, then used that to animate them, like drawing on the potential energy stored in a battery.

Time offset distance. The longer he could work with something, the more energy he could store in it. He could control an object from across a large room if he'd been in contact with it for a while.

He'd use that as a defense. He'd walk into a place, pick up a glass or ashtray or bottle, hold it a moment, then put it down and wander across the room, repeating the process. Sometimes he'd leave one of his metal balls in some part of the room. He'd do this before he'd take a seat. He wanted objects he controlled spread around the room, ready for his use from whatever angle he might need.

But not just any object. He couldn't transfer his energy into living matter. Even with a non-living object, the more organic material it contained or was in contact with, the less control he could exert. Metal worked the best. And the greater the mass, the greater the life force

118

required to move it.

That was why he couldn't have taken the guns off our attackers: they were distant objects never touched by him, and in contact with another person. It also explained why he wore the balls and knives: metal, in contact with him, with stored energy from long exposure, giving him instant and total control.

So some of my questions found answers. But with Bishop, questions were like nesting boxes--I opened one only to find another inside. And each box lay in a darkness deeper than the one before, until the one that hid within all the others--the box I would not open, the question I feared to ask--dwelt in a blackness no light could penetrate.

We'd been together for three months before I found the courage to open that last box. With Jase sleeping in the back of the Hummer, Bishop and I made love outside one warm August night. After, lying under him and prairie stars, his body growing heavy on me, his breathing deepening to sleep, I asked him. Asked him of his wife and son, of the Priests, and how his hate was born.

I felt the muscles in his back tense. Then he rolled off me and reached to where his vest lay. From an inside pocket, he pulled a leather pouch, larger than the one in which he kept the photo of the Pope. He sat up and looked at me. I propped myself up on an elbow, held his stare, and waited.

Finally he spoke, his voice soft and low. "Her name was Tess. She was four years younger than me. A lot like you, tough and soft all mixed up together. Our boy's name was Daniel. He was just five when..." He stopped and turned away.

After a while, he spoke again. "Tess and I were

surprised when they let us marry, said we could have a kid. Looking back, I figured they wanted to know what abilities our offspring would have. Tess could make you see things...things that weren't there." He laid the pouch down and ran his finger around and around its edges as he spoke.

"When we rebelled, the Office came after the Dead Men hard. We were easier to find together, so we split up. The rest went their way into deep cover, and Tess and I went ours with Danny.

"I figured we were safest not moving around. Too many probes and cameras in cities and checkpoints. So I bought a secluded cabin near Kananaskis. Paid cash.

"By now, the Feds had given the Entity local militia powers, and they'd hired the Priests in Alberta. Finding the Dead Men was a high priority." He swallowed and picked up the pouch.

"And they found us. Or found Tess and Danny. I'd gone into town that day. Tess and I always prearranged an 'all clear' signal. That day it had been the right front window, raised partway. I came home in the evening. The window was down. The Priests were waiting for me, but I'd been warned."

He paused, jaw muscles working as I pictured him descending on the Priests like a hound of hell. "I killed every Priest there, but I was too late. Tess was..." He stopped. "Danny died in my arms." Bishop stroked his arm as if smoothing his son's hair. A sad smile lived briefly on lips that suddenly hardened again. "The Pope himself had left before I arrived, but he'd staged the...events where our security cameras would catch it all on film. Thoughtful of him--I didn't have to miss a thing. That's where I got his picture. And these souvenirs."

He tossed the pouch in front of me, where it lay untouched--the final box, a container for nightmares--until at last, like Pandora, I reached to open it.

To release the horrors within.

The pictures, arranged it seemed in perfect chronological order, depicted the progress of the bondage, rape, and torture of Tess--the progress from a beautiful frightened woman to a thing in that last picture barely recognizable as human. That last picture--the one I threw from me, that made me cry out, sent me crawling on my hands and knees trying not to puke. That thing of blood and flayed flesh, limbless, a lump that must be a head.

"They tied Danny to a chair," he said. "Made him watch." His words fell like dead leaves, lifeless and brittle, waiting to be blown away.

When I looked back to Bishop, he was carefully putting the pictures back into the pouch. "Got to be careful with these. They're the only pictures I have of my family, the only..." He broke down then, sobbing on the ground. My mind clawed at words that skittered away from my mouth, from the memory of that picture. Finally, I said nothing for there was nothing to say--just crawled to him and held him close to me.

"You know what really scares me, Mary?" he asked after a while as we lay there. "I'm starting to forget how Tess really looked." I held him until he slept, no doubt trying to remember how she looked, while I lay awake trying to forget.

We never spoke of it again.

But I still remember that picture.

The pattern of those first months continued unchanged,

except now I knew the demons that drove Bishop. Looking back, the taste of that time lies bittersweet in my memory. In many ways, I have never been happier. Three years we were together, an impromptu family assembled by fate and held together by necessity--and love. Yes, I came to love Bishop--even more than I had loved Jase's father. That love lay like a safe harbor within me, a place I ran to when the horror that strode the Earth like a beast in those days passed too close.

But a different beast dwelt deep within Bishop--a thing of grief and bitterness and hate that lived with him always. And sometimes I didn't know what I feared more: the horrors outside or those inside Bishop.

I was happiest when we had no goal but to reach the next huddling of humanity. Days of ignoring the world, of just being together, the three of us. But as we approached an enclave, my tension rose as if we were climbing to a precipice where mists hid what lay beyond. We'd arrive in the town, and I'd balance on the edge of that precipice while Bishop asked about the Priests. If he heard no news, then the mists and my fears would blow away, and I'd gaze down into a sunny valley of our next days together.

But if he heard of Priests nearby, then that valley became a place of eternal night where dark shapes lurked half-seen in shadows. Dangerous shapes. And one was Bishop.

He never took us to the towns with Priests. He'd leave us behind and come back for us after.

After. I just called it that. *After* he killed whatever Priests he found, and did God knows what else, for he always came back with more information on the Priests. And I don't think they volunteered it to him.

But for three years I pretended I didn't know the

122

things he did. Then one day we were in a mountain village mapping our next destination. Winter was dropping hard and cold out of the high peaks, and a blizzard had closed the pass behind us. We'd be trapped for the winter soon. The only road still open led down the mountain--through a Priest town Bishop had just visited.

I could see he was uncomfortable about it, but we had no choice but to drive through that town. No choice but to see, for the first time, the corpses he left on his visits. No choice but to notice they weren't only men crumpled in the streets, on steps, against walls. Staring at Jase staring at the bodies, I resolved to finally confront Bishop at the next enclave.

That turned out to be an ugly two-story building crouching in the shadow of the foothills, a refueling spot and hostel. The lower level was one huge room with a bar to the right of the door, an open kitchen on the left, and rough-hewn wooden tables in the middle. A balcony ran around all four sides upstairs, forming the sleeping quarters. Closed in only by a flimsy railing, it provided just enough room to lay our sleeping bags.

A scrawny, greasy-haired man named Blinder ran the place. Bishop traded him guns taken from the Priests, redundant to Bishop, for gas, supplies and lodging. Blinder wore an eye patch, which I assumed was either payback or motive for his rumored target in fights. His good eye spent a lot of time leering at me, but narrowed when Bishop mentioned the Priests. Blinder said he hadn't seen any for months. I relaxed a bit but knew I still had to confront Bishop.

Blinder left as Bishop spread our much-used map on a table. "I don't trust him," Jase said. "He's lying about something."

"He lies by habit," Bishop said, shrugging but frowning too. He'd learned to trust Jase's feelings. "If he *is* lying about the Priests, they could only be ahead of us, down the mountain."

Because you've already killed the ones behind us, I thought.

"We stick with normal procedure," Bishop said. "I'll check out the next town. You're still safest here." He nodded at an ancient CB rig on the bar. "Call me if you need to. Remember the code phrase." The current code was "Bishop takes Queen". If we *didn't* use the phrase, something was wrong. Jase nodded.

Now's the time, I thought. "Jase," I said quietly, "could you please get me a beer?"

"I thought you said it tasted like--"

"Jase," I interrupted. "Please." Jase shrugged, reminding me of Bishop, and left.

Bishop leaned back, his eyes locked on me. "What?"

I didn't have the courage to look in those eyes. Instead, I stared after Jase. "He was just two when his dad died. He can't remember him."

"I'm sorry."

"He was a doctor. A good man."

"I don't doubt that. What's this about?"

"He saved people." I looked at him. "You kill people."

His jaw tightened. "I've tried to protect you."

"I'm not talking about self-defense. I mean your obsession with the Priests. That last town--Jase saw that."

Bishop said nothing, just looked away.

"He worships you, Bishop."

"Mary--"

"I can't let my son worship a killer." My voice rose,

and Blinder and Jase looked over. Bishop reddened and swallowed. I lowered my voice. "You have to choose: the Priests--or Jase and me. Your hate for them--or..." I didn't finish, didn't say 'your love for us'. Bishop had never said he loved us. "Jase loves you. I...I love you. But I can't go on like this."

Jase was coming back. Bishop carefully folded the map. "We'll talk about this when I get back."

"We may not be here," I said quietly.

Bishop stood as Jase rejoined us. "I hope you will be, Mary." He bent to kiss me. I turned away. He straightened, then walked out, not looking back.

Jase watched him leave, then glared a mute accusation at me. "I'm going to bed," he said, plopping the beer I didn't want in front of me. You couldn't hide things from Jase. And he sided with Bishop a lot lately. I felt a pang of resentment at that. Jase went upstairs as I heard the Hummer drive off--both my men leaving me.

My conversation with Bishop played in my head through the night and the next morning. Then just before noon, I suddenly had other things to worry about.

Jase and I were sitting upstairs on our sleeping bags, reviewing his math lesson for the week, when he brought his head up. "What's that?" I didn't hear it right away, had to wait before I caught a low growl, like a pack of angry dogs approaching. I wasn't far wrong. The growl rose quickly to the thundering roar of motorcycles. A lot of them. We ran around the balcony to the front window.

Priests. At least forty, I figured.

"Downstairs. Out the back. Now!" I rasped under my breath.

"Our bags and--" Jase began.

"Now, Jase!" I snapped, pushing him towards the stairs. Scrambling down to the main floor, we turned to the back door.

And stopped. Blinder stood at the rear exit, pointing a shotgun at us. "Don't think so, folks. Chino's gonna wanna talk t'ya, you bein' friends of the Dead Man an' all."

Bishop had been wrong. The Priests weren't in front of us. They'd been behind us, following us down out of the mountains, following us for weeks. A special hunting pack to take down the Dead Man. Seems like the Pope was getting worried.

Flanked by two Priests, Jase and I stood in the center of the room before their leader, a small mountain named Chino. He had a big round head, cropped black hair, and a smile I would have called warm under other circumstances. About twenty Priests lounged around us, with ten more upstairs and the rest outside.

"So you're the Dead Shit's pussy," Chino said to me.

Snarling, Jase lunged at Chino, only to be punched hard in the side of the head by the nearest Priest. Jase fell to one knee, and the Priest grabbed him by the hair, holding him there.

"Stop it!" I snapped, turning to Chino. "What do you want?"

"What do you think? Where's the Dead Man?" Chino asked.

I hesitated. Chino shrugged and nodded to the Priest holding Jase. The man flicked open a switchblade.

"All right!" I said. "He's gone down to the next town."

"Mom!" Jase cried.

Chino smiled and looked at Blinder. "So we hide the bikes and wait till he comes back for these two." Blinder

126

nodded, his head bobbing like a chicken.

I bit my lip. Bishop would die, walking into a trap. Then, of no further use, we'd die too. "Bishop's not coming back," I lied. Chino spun back to me, and I swallowed. "We had a fight," I said. "All he wanted to do was fuck me. I told him we were through." Jase stared at me wide-eyed.

Chino turned to Blinder, who started shaking. "They had a fight, for sure. Didn't know he wasn't coming back," he mumbled.

Chino picked him up with one hand. "So we sit here, while he gets farther away. And you didn't think I should know that?"

"Couldn't hear," he whined, "Just knew they was fightin'."

Chino tossed Blinder to the floor then turned back to me, his broad face creased in a frown. "Now why would you tell me that? You're worth keeping around only so long as Bishop gave a shit about you. Now..." He shrugged.

"If he didn't show, we'd be dead anyway," I said.

Chino tilted his head, as if reappraising me. "So what's the deal?"

"I can bring him back," I said quietly, "if you let us go." I could feel Jase's eyes burning me.

Chino's eyes narrowed. "How?"

"He's got a CB radio. I'll call him on Blinder's rig."

"Why would he come back, if you two are through?"

"*I* told *him* we were through. Now I'll say I changed my mind." I put a hand on one hip, trying to look like a woman a man didn't walk away from easily. It must have worked.

"Blinder," Chino called. "Crank up that rig."

"Not so fast," I said. "Jase and I go free if I do this."

127

"Once we have Bishop, sure," Chino said.

I knew he was lying, but I had to play along. "Why should I believe you?"

Chino chuckled. "Cuz you got no choice. Cuz you're buying you and the kid a few extra hours. And who knows?" Looking around the room, he raised his voice. "Maybe the famous Dead Man will pull off a miracle and rescue you." That prompted hoots of derisive laughter from the Priests.

Just what I was thinking. "All right," I said. "I'll call him." Jase stared at me as if I'd just pumped a bullet into Bishop. Jase, I thought, this was the only way to warn Bishop, give him time to prepare. Time was important with Bishop.

And he was our only hope.

"Mary, is everything all right?" Coming over the battered tinny speaker of the CB set, Bishop's voice seemed a small fragile thing, and suddenly so did our hopes.

"Everything's fine," I said. "I just wanted to say I was sorry we argued. That I've changed my mind. I want you to come back to us." I hadn't used the code phrase. I bit my lip and waited. A Priest held a shotgun on Jase.

A silence followed. And grew. "Bishop?" I said.

Then Bishop spoke again. "Who's the head Priest there, Mary?"

Now the silence came from our end, as Chino's face purpled with building rage while I tried to look surprised. Chino grabbed the handset from me, shoving me aside. "The name's Chino, asshole," he snarled.

"Always glad to meet a new Priest, Chino," Bishop replied. "Kind of a hobby of mine. Here's the deal. I walk in. Mary and Jase walk out, unharmed. Me for them."

"You walk in clean. No weapons. Nothing," Chino said.

"I walk in clean. Deal?"

Chino looked like he'd just found a cockroach floating in his beer. A man like him needed to control situations. Bishop had taken over this one, and he'd done it in front of Chino's people. "Deal," Chino said, as if spitting out something he wished he hadn't put in his mouth.

"Bishop..." I sobbed.

His voice came soft and low from the set. "Mary, I've been ready to die since Tess and Danny were killed. Been wanting it. This way, I can save you and Jase, something I couldn't do for them. You take care. Give Jase a hug for me."

"Bishop!" I cried, while the Priests hooted behind me.

"Unharmed, Chino. You don't touch them," Bishop said.

Chino flicked the set off and turned to me. "Don't know how, but I know you tipped him." Without warning, he backhanded me across the mouth, knocking me to the floor.

"Mom!" Jase cried. The Priest drove the butt of the shotgun into Jase's belly. He doubled over and fell to his knees. I lay on the floor, head ringing, tasting blood, feeling with my tongue for broken teeth. "You said you wouldn't hurt us," I mumbled.

Chino shrugged. "I lied." He motioned to two Priests. "Strip her and strap her to a table." He grinned down at me, and Bishop's pictures of Tess suddenly seemed superimposed over this scene. Chino raised his hands to the crowd. "Party time!"

Tess's face drifted through the mist of pain and shame of that night, now looming frightened and huge before me, now tiny and distant, now multiplied a thousand times on jagged shards of some shattered cosmic mirror. And through the rape, I kept telling myself I wouldn't die as she did, that they needed me alive until Bishop arrived.

But they made Jase watch.

Morning. Huddled on floor. They left me finally. Blanket over me. Jase must have done that. He's beside me, arm around me. Try to move. Pain. Like a fire inside. The smell of them. The taste of them. Shame. Nearby laughter. I feel anger. No. No word for what I feel. Yes. There is.

Hate.

I had never known hate. Fear, yes, after my husband and daughter died. Anger at their dying, but that had been an unfocused, futile, impotent anger, a raging against a world gone mad, a fury with no target. It was hard to hate a plague.

But now I had a target, faces, names. Now I could hate.

Jase felt me stir and helped me rise, wrapping the blanket around me in now pointless modesty, as the Priests ate breakfast and laughed. I walked with him to the crude shower stall in the back, under the watchful eye of a Priest. In the shower, I tried to pee but I was too swollen and when it finally came, the pain dropped me to my knees. I stared at the water spiraling to the drain, tinged with dirt and urine and blood, wishing I could wash away last night as easily, wash me clean. Jase helped me dress, and the Priest brought us back to wait for Bishop.

Jase and I sat alone at a table, his arm around me. We didn't speak, and I realized Jase hadn't spoken all morning. Concern for my son, for what this had done to *him*, pushed through my self-pity. "Jase," I said. He didn't respond. I put a hand on his knee. "Jase," I repeated gently.

"I'll kill them," he said in a voice I barely recognized.

"That won't change anything," I said, not believing it, wanting them dead myself. Wanting to kill them myself.

"I'll kill them," he whispered, his voice a dead thing. I pulled him to me, the victim now the comforter, the mother again.

And in that moment, in Jase's hate, in my own, I began to understand Bishop.

About noon, a cry came from a kid named Fly, younger than Jase, standing at a front window up top. "He's here!"

"Scan him!" Chino called.

Fly nodded and squinted through some sort of scope out the window. A few seconds later, he lowered the device. "He's clean. No guns, no knives."

"None of them metal balls?" Chino asked.

"He's not carryin' nothin'. Except..."

"Spit it out!" Chino snapped.

"He's wearing that mail coat. Black, shiny loops all over."

Blinder squinted his one eye. "Tell him to lose the coat?"

131

Chino snorted. "What's he going to do? Throw it at you?" That brought laughter and a chorus of comments: "Can't protect him...Not from all of us...I'm going for a head shot anyway...Me too...The *Dead* Man...The *dead* Dead Man..." More laughter.

Chino held up a hand. Silence fell. "Positions!" he cried, pulling Jase and me to the center of the room. The Priests fell back to the wall facing the door and the one that held the bar. Made sense. They could shoot from two angles but not be in their own crossfire. Upstairs, more lined all four sides of the railing, aiming down at us.

Forty of them, all with guns, waiting for Bishop. Waiting to kill the man who hunted them.

"Wait till he's with 'em in the middle," Chino shouted. I hugged Jase and lied to him that we'd get out of this. "Fly, open the door," Chino snapped. Fly swung over the railing above and dropped lightly to the floor. Jerking open the door, he scampered back upstairs.

And I could see Bishop.

He walked from the Hummer with a slow easy gait towards us, framed by the door, dark and lonely against an empty blue sky, dust devils stirred by a chill wind dancing around him and nipping at his heels like mongrel dogs.

His coat reached almost to the ground, its black covering glinting and glittering as the sun caught each loop of the mail. His head was bare. Our eyes met--and he grinned. God damn him, he grinned. Grinned that grin that always seemed so out of place, even more so now, like a happy face sticker on a corpse.

Time seemed to slow then, and I felt as if my heart was drumming out its final beats, in time with each step of some obscene ballet, with each step Bishop took toward us.

Step.

He was almost at the door, still grinning, his long coat flowing around him like a black mist.

Step.

Inside, Chino backed away from Jase and me to the side wall as forty guns rose in forty hands. I held Jase tight.

Step.

Bishop came through the door to the sound of the metallic chink of his coat and the clicking of weapons. The room sucked in its breath and all I could hear was the chink, chink, chink of that coat as he walked toward us.

Step.

Bishop began to...*blur*. I blinked tears from my eyes but no matter how hard I blinked, the blur remained. Someone shouted. The blur got worse. Bishop seemed to expand outwards, his outline growing more and more indistinct.

Step.

He spread his arms. An opening appeared before us in the blur surrounding him--and I understood.

"Run!" I yelled, pushing Jase ahead. There in the center of the room, the Dead Man embraced us, while around us a whirlwind rose and spun and screamed, enveloping us like a force field--a whirlwind of tiny loops of crysteel, tiny loops that moments before had covered his coat, not as a network of links but each held there--unconnected and individual--by the power of his mind.

Jase and I pressed ourselves to him. Bishop was shaking and soaked with sweat. The Priests were firing now but the whirling cloud of crysteel shielded us like an impermeable cocoon. The bullets died as bright flashes in the cloud, and the shriek of the tornado about us washed away the sound of the shots. Washed me clean. I felt powerful, invincible, immaculate.

"Hold me," he rasped in my ear. I braced myself against his weight. His body tensed and then spasmed like an orgasm. The cloud of crysteel loops, each harder than diamonds, exploded outwards from us in all directions--and through anything and anyone that got in their way.

And then it was over.

The whirlwind was gone, its shriek gone, the gunshots gone. And the Priests lay dead around us on the floor, slumped over the bar and tables, above us on the balcony, pierced and riddled. Light bulbs destroyed, a thousand pinpricks of sunlight lit the room from holes in the walls and roof--a heaven of stars shining into hell.

Bishop surveyed the room, then walked shakily to the nearest body, stooping to retrieve a handgun. Chino was dead, but some Priests still lived, twitching where they lay. Bishop started turning over bodies, and I knew he was checking for the face that haunted him, a face he wouldn't find. He stopped beside Blinder.

Blinder looked up at Bishop. Blood trickled from a wound on his forehead, and two more red blotches blossomed on his chest. "Help...me," he croaked. "Hurt...bad."

Bishop stared at the gun he held, then at the man lying at his feet. "Mary, take Jase outside," he said quietly.

I stared at his gun too, and at Bishop. I stared at the dead and dying before me, realizing then that he had not returned just for us. Suddenly I felt as if all the dead of the Plague, of the Fall, were crawling into that room. My

134

Sally, my husband. Tess, Danny. Every Plague victim. Every Priest ever killed by Bishop. Corpse scrambling over corpse, piling themselves higher and higher, choking the light from the room, from my life.

I realized then that still more awaited me--those I would add to the pile if I took the same path as Bishop. A path that lay before me at that very moment.

In that moment, I chose.

My hate remained, and perhaps, like Bishop, I would never lose that hate, never forgive. But unlike him, I would choose a different path. I'd had enough of death. "Bishop," I said. "Don't. We can help them. The next town--"

"Take Jase outside, Mary," he repeated.

"Hurt...bad," Blinder cried.

"Don't do this, Bishop."

"Mom?" Jase whispered.

"Now, Mary," Bishop said.

"No, Bishop. Don't!"

Bishop shrugged. "Suit yourself." Turning to Blinder, he raised the gun.

"No!" Blinder gasped. "You gotta help me!"

"No problem," Bishop said. And shot Blinder in the head.

Jase stiffened beside me. I grabbed his arm, and we ran to the door as if we were just two more things Bishop had thrown from himself. Another gunshot sounded as that room spit us out into cold sunlight. Still pulling Jase with me, I ran past Priest bikes onto the road. I think I would have just kept running if Jase hadn't twisted free. I stumbled and fell, scraping the skin from my palms on the broken asphalt and landing hard on a knee. I stood, ready to run again. And froze.

Jase was walking back to the building, with slow stiff

steps, like an animated corpse.

"Jase!" I cried.

He stopped but didn't turn. "He's doing it for us," he said, his voice a dead thing, flat and lifeless.

A chill rode my spine. "He's doing it for himself, Jase."

"No. For us. Because of what they did to you."

"He doesn't know what they did to me." He didn't even ask me, I thought. "He's doing it because he hates them."

"I'm going back." He started walking again.

I can remember that scene so vividly. It lives in me like a thing immortal, never changing, never fading, never dying: Jase walking away from me, that building squatting dark and ugly against a washed-out sky, the dust in my mouth, the wind cold on my face where it dried my tears. And the crack of Bishop's gun, repeated again and again and again.

But one thing I can't remember--what I called to Jase, screamed at him, cried to him before he stepped back inside. Maybe I didn't say anything at all. Maybe I just stood there, waiting. Waiting for the sound that would tell me I had lost my son after all. The sound that finally came.

The sound of a second gun, joining with Bishop's.

Bishop and I didn't talk that night. We slept apart. In the morning, he was gone. He'd left us the Hummer.

We never saw him again.

The Fall bottomed out the next year. The Entity had established some power bases, rebuilding the Earth under its rule, consolidating local warlords into itself or eliminating them. Jase and I were living in a mountain enclave when the Entity hit it. They separated us, put me on reconstruction teams, maintaining vehicles. I heard they sent Jase off-planet.

I never saw him again either.

You asked me of the Dead Man. And I have told you.

Now, do you want to know the question you should have asked? The question I've asked myself every day since then?

Why did he walk in there that day? Was it to save us, or kill the Priests? What drove him? Love? Or hate?

Both, you say?

Yes, I suppose. But that's not the answer I wanted.

You say he's dead now. You say they finally caught him.

I don't believe you. *You can't kill a dead man.*

So if you see him, tell him...tell him I forgive him. For Jase. For everything. Tell him I've learned what hate is. That I finally understand him.

And tell him I still...

No. No, damn him. I won't say it.

Just tell him I still think of him.

THE BRIDE'S ROAD
by Hawk and Young

Report and inquiry from Terran Custodian:
Subjects moving to fiftieth generation of inbreeding.

Feudal hierarchy-based ability to breed shows no signs of improving. Requesting permission to cure medical condition among males to enhance diversity, and guarantee crop survival.

Response of inquiry:
Records show Terrans have survived with 20 females and two males through past crop purges.

Standards and regulations have clear parameters regarding interference.

436:1 reads - No medical treatment can be given to a subject if even one member of the crop possesses that standard of medicine (knowledge). Therefore, since one group of Terran subjects possesses a solution to the breeding problem, Custodians are not allowed to administer treatment.

 bald-faced renegade steer nearly made it to the safety of the underbrush when Billy Jack's old

138

lasso drew tight around its neck. Billy's mare squatted her hind end, and the girth and saddle leather were put to the test as the steer flipped backwards. Before the steer could regain his hooves, Billy Jack's old mare was dragging him back to the herd.

"Good toss, hoss! I thought he's gone get away." A lazy-eyed Cowey they called Whiskey Dan whooped.

Billy shook off the compliment, tucked his billowing afro back in his hat, and drug the steer.

An egg-shaped robot as large as a barrel of whiskey, called a Custodian, flew up next to the cowboy, not even spooking his horse, and quickly scanned the roper. It found no injury and flew off. The Coweys were so used to the Custodians that nobody ever paid them any mind. They had been there all Billy Jack's life. The Preacher said they were Watchers sent by God after the great 'pocolips. They would render medical aid and sometimes enforce the Great Law. The Great Law was that no man could harm another man by using an object on him. Coweys and the city gang, the Macys could fist fight, but if one of them used a weapon, the Custodians would make sky sparks that burned the attacker like a sausage on a campfire. They'd be dead as winter grass. He'd only seen it happen once, with an old Big Macy and his own Pa. Preacher said it had to happen every so often so's the youngen's could bear witness to the Lord's power.

A third Cowey, a mid-thirties man named Culky Bainbridge said, "Let's get these beeves in that arroyo a'fore supper. I ain't et since lunch yusterdee."

Billy knew why Culky hadn't eaten. It showed in his weathered, sunburnt face, and in the way he kept looking to the Bride's Road for Sheila Jean to come riding through. Billy reckoned she would look a mess with her long hair something like a rat's nest and her makeup smeared six ways to summer. She'd walk like she just broke a spring colt, and there wouldn't be enough of her dress left to cover her love-bit teats. Unlike the New Moon Brides, Sheila wasn't trying to pay a debt for the Big Macy's seed; she already had three kids by him. Culky had once said in a crying fit that took him, "She ain't no bad woman, she just got needs. She 'ill hold long as she can, then it just takes her. She really is a good woman."

Billy had to spit the taste of bile out of his mouth, as his stomach heaved with the thought of his own sweet Lucinda on her eventual trip down the Bride's Road come next New Moon. His chest burned like a heart-a-stop and his stomach threatened to bounce up his cracklin' pork breakfast as his mind made an image of her naked, sun-kissed skin lying under the huge, muscled frame of the Big Macy. He had seen studs breed mares, and he knew some were gentle as a baby. He also knew some studs were as abusive as they were stout. The Big Macy was the rough kind. The brides who came back after their first breed were as likely to have a black eye and a busted cheek as they were to have a littlen in the oven.

The angry scar on Billy Jack's cheekbone was a firsthand witness to the Big Macy's power. The rangy cowhand knew there must have been a secret to the Big Macy's magic. Granted, the only thing he or anyone that lived in Tumbledown Town knew about breeding they learned from the livestock, or Sheila Jean. She was the only woman who would talk about what happened at the end of the Bride's Road, and talk she did. He remembered when he was just a little kid with his first pony helping his ma carry washing clothes to the creek, and Sheila had come back from her first breeding. She was going on and on to the other girls about how her body felt like it was being stretched apart, but she never wanted it to stop. She hoped she didn't take so she could go back. If she didn't turn up pregnant, she could go back next new moon. Culky's face was as red as a 'Gittle' bird 'cause she was saying all this just in his earshot. He just loaded up the wash with his head down. His ma finally put a stop to it, telling her to hush up 'cause she was scaring the little 'uns.

The Big Macy who bred Billy Jack's mother wasn't the current leader of the Macy Rex gang. The gang was made of its leader, the Big Macy, and about ten to fifteen thugs that were all waiting their chance to become the head honcho. They did very little besides patrol the area around the building they lived in. It was a fortified old block structure at the edge of a burned out metropolis. An old sign with some letters missing read -Macy RX above it.

Every so often, Tumbledown Town had to send five girls to them. Once they were worn out and worked to near death they would send them back for fresh ones. The gang kept about eight women who cooked, slaughtered livestock, and tended to the Macy's beck and call. The Little Macys congregated at a building called the Gold G. Sheila said they mostly exercised by lifting heavy steel discs. The smallest Little Macy was still very muscled but nowhere near the leader's size.

When Billy was about six, the old Big Macy, Macy Red, rode into town with two near-worked-to-death girls and demanded replacements. When nobody stepped forward, he grabbed Billy's mother, who was a real beauty in her day with her ebony skin and green eyes, and snatched her up across his saddle. He turned to ride

141

out with a handful of Little Macys behind him, but Billy's dad blocked the road.

"Put her down. She ain't ever gonna be yours again."

The man was a skinny little gnat compared to the giant they called Macy Red. No one knew exactly how the Macy magic worked, but once a Little Macy was promoted, in about six months time they would put on around a hundred pounds of muscle. Sheila said the magic was something called "Anna ball licks." He wasn't sure who Anna was, but her life sounded far worse than a Cowey's.

"I'm gonna count to three and if'n you ain't out my way, I'm gonna beat you to death in front of your family. One!" Macy Red threatened.

He never got to two. The skinny, hook-nosed man's leather cattle whip sailed through the air and split the brute's neck like a razor. He dropped Billy's blood soaked mom and grabbed at his gushing throat like he was trying to button up a shirt. He was dead in seconds. Almost as fast, the Custodians, who were always hovering, watching just at the edge, shot sky sparks that disintegrated Billy's dad.

Billy was brought back out of his recollections by a new voice.

"You ought not be so rough to that steer, neither one of ya'll's pecker works. Ya'll are almost like brothers," called a thug named Ike, who had rode up on them unnoticed in the commotion.

"Easy Macy, we're just Coweys trying to get our herd in. We ain't looking for trouble," Culky said.

Whiskey Dan caught Billy's eye and shot him a raised eyebrow that said a fight wasn't all bad.

Billy flipped the rope off the steer to let him run back into the herd, spit a black wad of chew out of his mouth towards the bully, and said, "Don't pay him no mind, Culky. He don't want no trouble either. One Macy and three Coweys. He's as scared as these cows."

"Who said I was alone?" The bullying Macy they called Ike, waved a hand and two more toughs came out from behind a stand of scrub brush.

Ike rode a mighty steel gray stallion that Billy remembered having to send as part of the gang's yearly tribute a few summers back. He sure hated sending such a fine horse to hands that couldn't hardly ride, at least by any Cowey's standard. Any kid from Tumbledown Town could have told Ike his feet were too far back, his weight was too far forward, and he had too much slack in his reins.

Billy goaded him, "Culky, they always want to point out there ain't a working pecker in Tumbledown Town, but there it'n but one working pecker at the Rex, and it ain't Ike's."

"This pecker 'ill be hard as that head of yours when I become the big cat in our outfit."

Billy let out a laugh so hard that it spooked Ike's stallion a little. The Cowey thought, *The colt's still skittish, that's why we used to call him 'Fraidy Cat.*

"You'll never be the big man. 'Afore that happens, Sheila will become the preacher, Dan here will start liking women, and my prick will get so hard a Custodian will kill me for usin' a weapon."

Whiskey Dan didn't take offense, instead let out a laugh 'cause the big-bearded, lazy-eyed Cowey was known for his peculiar fondness for men.

With eyes narrowed and teeth gritted, Ike said, "Ya'll won't be here to see it."

The two muscled toughs behind him dismounted for the fight, but before Ike could dismount, Billy slung his

143

arm out, unfurling the deadly twelve-foot leather whip. Every muscle in the Cowey's dark-skinned arm was tight as a saddle girth.

Two Custodians flew to the edge of the action.

"You'd never hit me with that. You ain't as dumb as your pa was."

"I ain't gotta hit *you*. Sorry, 'Fraidy Cat."

With that he swung the big whip just inches from the fractious stallion's face, and cracked it louder than a sky spark. The big horse reared straight up, and a second crack sent the terrified creature over backwards and running for his life.

When the dust cleared, Ike was squalling like a hill cat. One of his legs was bent completely backwards, and a bone was poking through his jeans.

"See Ike, that whip never touched anything, it was just like you, making noise."

The two Custodians flew over and went to work resetting and casting the ruined leg.

Ike yelled to the toughs who were already mounting up, "Where are ya'll going? Get 'em!"

Billy coolly replied, "When the big man dies and ya'll fight to see who's next, remember bigmouth's bum leg. It won't hold up in a hard scrap."

As the Custodians were spraying the plasteel cast on Ike's leg, he spat, "The Macy is gonna take that little lady of yours for his own."

"He can't do that. The rules say he can't take a bride for his own."

"No, but he can have any widow he wants. He said he's going to beat your skull in on your wedding day. He's tired of playing with you."

Off in the distance a spotted night stalker let out a bone chilling squall, and Billy smiled, "You better get moving. That sounds like a big cat. You got a long way to limp 'fore dark."

"You can't just leave me here to die."

"Oh, I can. You came here to kill *me.*"

"We weren't gonna kill you. We were just funning."

"How funny is it gonna be when that spotted cat comes down and tears your arms off real slow. She ain't gonna try to kill you straight off. This time of year she's got young ones. She's gonna hurt you real bad and let them kittens practice on killing ya. Might take em' all night."

"Please don't."

"I tell you what, you tell me how the big man's magic works. How does he get so big, and how does he get the lead in his pencil? Ya'll live in the same damn building, you gotta know. Tell me that and I'll put you up on my horse and lead you to the Rex."

The Cowey thought he had him good and scared, close to cracking, but Ike wouldn't say another word. He just awkwardly got to his feet, tested the cast, and limped down the Bride's Road.

The Coweys finished herding the cows into the arroyo and Billy Jack, who had been in deep thought through the whole drive, pulled off his boots and tucked them in his saddle bags.

"I'm gonna run back to Tumbledown. If what Ike says is true, I'm gonna need to be lean and fast. The bride's moon will be here in three days."

Billy unsaddled his horse, slung the saddle over his back, adding thirty pounds to his lanky frame.

"Ya'll go on without me; I ain't leaving the herd alone with that big cat out there." Culky called out. They knew Culky was staying to watch for Sheila riding home down the Bride's Road.

145

Transmission to Terran Custodians:
Interplanetary mainframe calculates a high probability of crop loss. The crop is highly likely to create a disruption that will upset the delicate balance between the 'Macy' and 'Cowey' factions, ending in sectarian violence.

Response from Terran Custodian:
Do we have permission to intercede, facilitating prevention of crop loss?

Transmission to Terran Custodian:
You have been warned previously for interference. Although central oversight could locate no evidence of rule violation, central mainframe calculates a 99.978 percentage of likelihood of Custodial tampering. Any other infractions will result in a complete data wipe, and replacement of Terran Custodians.

Billy Jack loved to run. The feeling of pushing his body to the limits took his mind away from the consuming problems in his life. He worked his tail to the bone and owned the finest herd in Tumbledown. He went to church every Jeday, and could read and do sums. Where was the Preacher's God when he needed him? Obviously, the Watchers were seeing everything.

There was one time that really made him wonder about the Custodians.

The only books in Tumbledown Town belonged to the church. There were only four, and they all dealt with religion, but his ma's ma had told him there was a place just past the Rex in the metropolis called Jack's Son, that

THE BRIDE'S ROAD

was filled with more books than a man could read durn near his whole life.

Ma called it the Lil' Berry. She said there were a woman's name out front and Billy memorized it for when he got big. Her name was Eudora, and the Lil' Berry was dedicated to her.

He was sixteen years old when he asked Lucinda's pa if he could court her. It had been a long three years.

Thinking of their first courting made him laugh because it reminded him of a conversation he had with Whiskey Dan.

"If'n you kill the Big Macy and become the hard dick round here, you reckon you could teach me the magic?"

"Why would you need it? You ain't looked twice at no woman. Ya ain't haven' no kids."

The lazy-eyed bearded cowboy blew raspberries at Billy and said, "Just 'cause I ain't havin' no youngens don't mean I on't want to be with somebody for real, like a man and a woman. Sex ain't just to make babies, look at Sheila."

Billy laughed and told him he weren't right.

"Hell, there is bound to be one of those muscled up Little Macys what would love to have a big, hairy Cowey to treat em right." Dan said wistfully.

"Dan, I on't reckon I seen none of those boys that looked like they had sweet feet."

Dan smiled and said, "I wouldn't be sure, that good looking Ike looks like he might have a little sugar in his shoes."

"Oh Lord, anybody but him."

"I on't know, I got a thing for the cocky ones."

"You're terrible Dan."

"I try my best."

A spotted nightstalker let out a cry in the distance and the runner's hair stood up.

Whiskey Dan, following behind on a horse and leading Billy's mount at a brisk trot, said, "Seems like they are moving closer every year. Wasn't but a few years back nobody had ever seen one."

First time Billy had ever seen one, was also the first time he had ever been to the dead city of Jack's Son.

He took the Bride's Road south making a wide berth around the Macy Rex, and it took him most of the night to reach the once bustling necropolis. He couldn't ride his horse inside the city because the ghost town's only inhabitants were the descendants of the former attractions of the state zoo.

The only thing he knew about the place was what he had learned from Sheila. She had never been there, but the Big Macy had sent his cronies there many times. She said they were looking for buildings that said Rex on the outside.

According to the Macys there were two types of big cats that roamed the city. The sheep-necks were the most common, and they had a strong smell of cat urine that acted like a warning when a group of them was near. They were huge cats half the size of a horse, with razor-sharp claws.

The other cat was the spotted nightstalker. One had killed a Macy with one swipe, and they never saw it coming. It was a solitary killer that hunted alone. The only warning was from the tree monks who lived in the canopies of the massive trees weaving in and around the myriad of dilapidated structures. The monks were everywhere; the place was lousy with them.

Billy spent what was left of the first night sleeping inside a locked closet of what he figured must have been a boarding house. He knew there were dangerous predators, but he felt confident that he could scare anything that came after him with his twelve foot whip, if he saw them first.

This was a dangerous trip, but he had a dangerous plan. He was going to marry Lucinda, but he was not going to let her carry the Big Macy's child. Even though all the males in the world were impotent except for the leader of the gang, he was going to find a way. He was going to fight the leader for his magic.

The Big Macy was around three hands taller, and pure muscle. Yet he had seen banty roosters kill big cocks three times their size, 'cause they knew how to fight.

He was going to learn how to fight, and for that to happen, he was going to the Lil' Berry. There had to be a book like the Preacher's 'cept 'bout fighting. The Preacher said before the 'pocolips that wicked people used to put people in cages and make them fight. They would gamble on it. There must have been a book about it.

Out of the corner of his eye he caught the first glimpse of a Custodian he had seen since passing the Rex. He knew that sometimes they would fly so high that they weren't visible, but this one was definitely observing him.

He remembered his ma telling him that the Lil' Berry was on a place called North Street. It had taken all morning but he had found a concrete building that had North Street carved into both sides, so he must have been on the right road. Several times he had smelled the cat piss scent of a sheep-neck and held his whip at the ready, but there had been no other signs.

149

As the day drug on he sipped from his canteen and started feeling nauseous and fatigued. He finally got a little dizzy and when he went to one knee, blood poured from his nose. That was when the Custodian who scanned him and sprayed a solution in his nose did something peculiar. It blocked his path. He tried to go around and it kept blocking his path. He had seen this exact floating robot before, because one of its rivets had rusted, making a stain on its carapace.

"Look here, Rusty, you need to get the hell out of my way. I'm going to find Eudora's Lil' Berry if I have to die doing it."

Then the robot did something he had never even heard of: it answered him.

"You are in a highly radioactive area. You have less than two hours before exposure will be deadly."

"I don't care; I'm finding that Lil' Berry."

Then it spoke again, "The Eudora Welty Public Library is not in this direction."

"Then where is it?"

The floating robot did not respond immediately, instead it paused like it was having a private conversation before answering, "I am not allowed to render you aid for anything that is not life threatening."

Before he could walk away, a telescoping arm extended like a finger and beckoned him to follow as it floated back down North Street. He followed briskly on weak legs trying not to vomit till the radiation weakened. At the point of his near exhaustion the robot stopped, and Billy fell to his knees and puked. When the gagging subsided, he raised his head and saw through tear-filled eyes: Eudora Welty Public Library.

"Damnit, Rusty we made it!"

The building was tall, four or five stories, and ringed by trees whose canopies brushed against and even outdistanced the roof. The tallest story had massive windows inset into each side.

Billy walked into the library and barely closed himself into a closet before darkness took him.

He awoke twenty hours later with a raw throat, bloodshot eyes, and aches in places he didn't know he had. He pulled himself from the closet and drank from one of his canteens. He had to be careful with his water, because the water near Jack's Son was filled with huge trap-jaws. They were murderous creatures that would eat man and horse both. If they didn't get you, the river cows would. They were three times the size of a horse and had four massive tusks the size of a man's arm.

He started in on the barrage of books in the Lil' Berry, but the problem was that he hardly knew what any of the words meant. If there had only been a book that said what words meant, his path would have been easier. Alas, no book existed so he had to do it the hard way.

On the third night, dangerously low on water and almost out of the jerky in his backpack, he ventured to the fifth floor of the Lil'Berry. He had been hoping to find a fighting book on the first four floors because he had heard noises upstairs that made him uneasy. He tried to convince himself that there were just big rats up there, but deep down inside he feared something more sinister.

He had always approached every problem like his pa had taught him: task, condition, and standard. The task was to find a book on fighting. The condition was given a dead city filled with predators and one rusty semi-helpful Custodian. The standard was to return home with a book that would help him defeat the Big Macy. Well, sometimes luck will save a man if his heart holds.

The first book he opened on that dead quiet fifth floor was a fighting book about Kenpo Karate. Every book on that shelf was about fighting. He had so many books in minutes he had to leave some behind. On his way out the door he passed by a broken window and saw the most beautiful moon. Even though this was the highest point he had ever stood at, Billy Jack wasn't scared of heights. He leaned out the window to get a better look at the rising blood moon when a spotted cat rose out of the darkness and leapt at him. The blow wasn't true, but it wasn't gentle either. The window, whose glass had long since been lost, was only a metal grate on a large hinge. The big cat cut through his clothing, leaving four long, bone-deep slashes in his ribs. The blow tumbled him out the window and he fell ten feet smashing on a ledge one story below. His body gave momentum to the window and it slammed back shut. The big cat showed razor-sharp teeth from above through the impassable grate, hissing at the broken book borrower. Tree monks in the canopies of the massive trees were going crazy with alarms, and Rusty the robot just hovered next to the ledge uselessly scanning him.

"Thanks for the warning, you rusty cookpot."

His body was banged up but nothing felt broken, and the bag full of books was still intact. As he started to get to his feet, still unnerved by the nightstalker's threats from above, something touched his elbow and he almost fell off the narrow ledge on the fourth floor. There in the darkness, huddled on the ledge were three nearly-hairless kittens. They were skint up and as bad off as he was. They tried to huddle against him in the dark, whining for their mother above. He noticed one was missing a toe on his front pad, and another was missing an ear. It was hard to imagine that those sweet little things would become the death machine just ten feet above him. He deduced that they must have fallen from overhead and the mother couldn't get to them.

"Well toeless, one-ear, and you, pretty-girl, are just gonna have to come down with me. No help from you, Rusty."

He took off his jacket, making a bundle and slung all three crying kittens over his back. The mother was calling for his murder. He walked around the entire building on the narrow ledge and there was no way back in, not that he would go that way anyway, and no way down. He didn't know if he was more annoyed by the tree monks howling, the killer cries from the nightstalker, or the damn Custodian just hovering there. He was out of options. He couldn't climb back up. He couldn't just sit on the ledge and die, and most of all he couldn't jump four stories down to the rubble below. He had no other choice.

With a sweep of his arms, he jumped off the ledge onto the Custodian like he was mounting a wild bronc. The startled sentinel bucked and swooped with everything it had, but couldn't shake the cunning Cowey. Rusty finally stopped and simply hovered in the air, and Billy figured he was about to be fried with sky sparks. The tamed tin can lowered him to the ground.

He opened his bundle to check on the kittens and fear paralyzed him as he raised his head and stared into the eyes of the angry nightstalker only a few feet away hissing from the darkness. The kittennapper's hands trembled as he slowly placed his purring partners before their murderous mother. She snarled at him making his blood run cold, but instead of attacking she curled up and began nursing, while he slowly limped away.

Instead of following behind him, Rusty led the way through the necropolis, back to the field where Billy had left his horse. It took him awhile and a lot of whistling, but eventually it came trotting up.

That had been three years back, but it felt like a lifetime to the relentless runner. He had studied boxing, kenpo, and Taekwondo from his hoard of books. He trained every night using a padded up Whiskey Dan as his sparring partner. Dan wasn't as muscled as a Macy, but he was as big as a grizzly. The gang had tried to recruit him, but the allure of being a ladies' man held no sway over Dan. Finally, Billy's skills at martial arts had progressed to where he felt he could defeat the Big Macy almost at will, and he decided to act. One year into his training, he travelled the Bride's Road and called out the Big Macy.

Billy Jack had oiled up his dark skin, to keep the monster from grabbing hold of him and shorn his wooly afro down to the scalp. The big man came out wearing nothing but his small clothes. Sheila, who had been a runaway for three days at the time, came out behind him, wearing nothing but a small shirt that came to her navel.

"I don't appreciate, a wormy runt like you interrupting my humping."

"I'm here to challenge you for your magic."

The Macy's laughter made Billy's heart drop. Muscles that would have made full grown bulls jealous rippled.

"I accept your challenge for my authority. If he kills me boys, give him the stuff."

Before the Macy could continue, Billy flew through the gap between them and landed a roundhouse kick on the side of the monster's head that would have knocked down Whiskey Dan. However, he wasn't fighting Whiskey Dan. The muscle-bound mauler caught Billy's foot before it found the ground. He used the foot like the handle of an ax chopping wood. Billy flew through the air three times, each time crashing on the ground. He was broke and barely holding onto sight when his opponent stood over him.

"Come back when you need another beating."

As if being swung like a child's toy wasn't enough, the victor stood over Billy and pulled out the first erect penis he had ever seen.

"This is as close to a hard prick that you'll ever get."

Oddly enough what Billy thought after seeing the angry blood engorged member was, *Why are his balls so small? Those look like little kid balls.*

That was the last thing Billy thought before he was kicked in the face and the big man split his cheek like it was an old shirt.

Big Macy grabbed Sheila and finished with her in three mighty strokes from behind. She squealed like a pig as he hefted her, both hands crushing her ribs as she rode out his success.

"Get outta here, you washed up heffer! I'm done with you." He sent her back down the road clad only in her small shirt. Whiskey Dan tried to give her his shirt to cover with, but she just held up her head and walked.

The worst part of his first defeat came three days later on Jeday. The Preacher sentenced the Cowey to the punch post. That was a harsh punishment where the convicted was tied to a post and every person leaving the church was required to punch him. The Macys were part of the way the world was designed. He would be punished for going against the will of the Almighty

Creator. He held on through about fifty people till it was Dan's turn.

"Sorry BJ, but if I go soft on you, Preach will make me hit you again."

Dan's mighty right knocked him unconscious and the Preacher declared the punishment paid in full.

The jogger came out of his recollections and looked up at his bearded buddy with a great appreciation for their friendship.

"Bad news BJ; ain't gone be no training tonight."

Billy saw what had changed their plans. On the porch of the Cowey's farm house was the lovely bride-to-be setting out pies to cool.

Billy's heart sank, but Dan reassured him, "You been training for three years, if you can't do it now, three more days ain't gone make a bit of difference. Please, she made pies!"

Lucinda stood on the porch in her sundress and bonnet. She was such a contrast to her young beau.

Where he was without an ounce of fat on his lanky frame, she was as plump as a harvest calf. Her skin was a whiter shade than a fish hook moon, and Billy's was a moonless midnight.

He ran up on the porch and had to bend over to brush back the corn silk hair of his betrothed. Caught up in his embrace she wrapped her thick stubby fingers around his sweaty back.

She pulled back and said, "Oh my! Gee, you are filthy. You better get to the crick and bathe before you sit at my table."

In confusion he asked, "*Your* table?"

"Billy Jack Hawkins, you spend too much time with them cows. The next three days is our briden' days."

He still looked confused until Dan said, "Hoss, it's where ya'll live together afore her trip up the road. Her family prolly moved all her stuff in 'bout daylight."

"Thank you Dan for educatin' this heathen for me. Please, let me pay you back with the supper I been cookin' all day. Of course your gone have to hit the crick too. Ain't muddying up the house I spent all day cleaning."

Dan rinsed the stinging lye soap out of his beard, and asked his friend, "B.J. you sure this is what you's lookin' fur?"

With a smile that made his bright white teeth glow, Billy answered, "More than anything else in the world."

"Well just in case it on't work out like we's praying, there's other ways a man can please his wife."

"Now Dan, you old hugger," (hugger was slang for homosexual), "what you know about pleasin' women?"

"Now first off, ain't no man ever called me no hugger to my face without gettin' an ass whoopin', but since it's your briden' days, I'm a let you make it. Second, I know that I on't like whisker fish, cause I once et whisker fish. I mean that both as an example and the fact. So's I'm saying if you on't win this last fight. It on't mean ya can't still have a damn fine life with that plump pie cooker."

"You know as damn well as I do that if Jeday don't end with my dick as stiff as a corpse, I'll be a stiff corpse. I fought him twice, but it wernt at nothing like what it's gone to be. No Dan, it's all or nothing," Billy lamented.

Before Dan could finish his last attempt to dissuade him, Lucinda showed up at the creek with washed and pressed clothes for her betrothed and his dinner guest.

"Dan, I found these in the guest room. I reckoned they must have been yours, so I washed 'em."

The Coweys dressed and had the finest meal they had ever eaten before Dan went home.

The only naked woman Billy had ever seen besides his ma was Sheila. Sheila wasn't a bad looking woman, but there wasn't anything about her that made Billy's heart skip a beat like the first sight of Lucinda standing in that doorway wearing what she came into the world in. Unlike most girls who had some extra weight, Lucinda had small, undeveloped breasts. Her dewy white skin muffin-topped over her hips, but her legs set him on fire. The curves of her thighs and legs did something to his innards that made him want to eat the flesh off of her bones. She lay back on his moss-stuffed mattress and was lost in caresses that rosied her milk-white cheeks. When he lowered his head down to her tiny vee of corn silk curls, her hands held his curly afro like a Cowey gripping a saddle horn. He felt in her final twitches and bucks of release, that she was willing to forgo any torment at the end of the Bride's Road for her man.

Report and inquiry from Terran Custodian:
Tension between feudal factions of the current crop are becoming increasingly volatile. The events of the custodial enforcement of the weapons ban may lead to total crop loss. Requesting permission to intervene.

Response to Custodian:
Galactic Mainframe predicts that it is a 70% likelihood the current crop is at an evolutionary junction. They will either elevate the basis of their society to a greater societal norm, or fail.

There will be no intervention.

158

Billy was up before daylight with his horse fed and saddled when Dan rode up.

"So how was your first night of briden'?"

Billy sashayed over to the Cowey like he was walking on cotton, and said in a quiet voice, "Lemme just say, I knew before yesterday that I'd eat a mess of whisker fish, but I know now, I like the yella ones best."

Dan pantomimed vomiting and then slapped him on the back with a guffaw.

They laughed and teased each other without a care in the world till they saw the buzzards. They cleared a ridge and saw their herds spread as far as they could see. There was no telling how many would be lost and scattered, but they spurred their horses into a dead run to investigate what the feathered undertakers were feasting on. The Coweys dismounted and ran into the high grass scattering the red-headed Gittle birds. Billy had seen Macy Red and his own pa die before his very eyes, but nothing could have prepared him for the sight of Sheila's mangled, half eaten body. Her entrails were spread around the ground and her head was almost completely gone. Billy ran a dozen yards away and uncontrollably vomited up two helpings of biscuits with bacon and fried eggs.

Dan was an expert tracker who could read the spore surrounding the carnage like a bellicose bible.

"Was a pack of cats all over this place."

Still hunched over with his eyes watering, Billy answered, "Must have been a bachelor pack of sheep-necks."

Dan said, "Sorry buddy, but these twernt no sheep necks. They were nightstalkers."

"Nightstalkers don't travel in packs. How you know it ain't young males?"

"I know cause I seen this three-toed track before. It's the cats you saved, the ones that et my horse."

He was referring to the second time the Cowey had challenged the Macy. Billy had studied Muay Thai and Capoeira, believing the loose style would give him the advantage of speed. The fight ended rather quickly, but that time Billy had broke the Big Macy's nose and blacked an eye. The Big Macy almost crushed the Cowey's ribcage. It took Billy two months to heal up enough to go to the punch post. When Dan helped the bloodied Billy back to where the horses were tied, three nightstalkers were eating Dan's best horse. One of the adolescent cats charged and Dan fell on his back with Billy. The nightstalker showed its teeth, then took a leisurely swipe with a pad that was missing its front toe. Billy didn't flinch as the paw made a small slit on his shoulder. Instead of attacking, it just went back to eating. Billy's horse, tied nearby untouched, was out of its mind with fear.

Dan would never forget that missing-toed nightstalker if he lived to be a thousand.

Billy, who had finally stopped dry heaving from the remains of Sheila, saw something just a few hands in front of him and said, "It wasn't no cat that killed Sheila."

"I'll be damned if it weren't no cat! I see the claw marks where they ate her."

"They might have ate her, but Culky killed her. Come look."

In the grass was the body of Culky, burned to a crisp by sky sparks clutching a bloody rock.

160

"I didn't see any remnants of clothes in that mess. The Big Macy prolly made her walk back buck nekked, and Culky had finally had enough."

The day of the ceremony was an overcast mess where the clouds wouldn't make up their mind if they wanted to rain or just make the whole world depressed. The Preacher had pulled the grooms aside and explained to them how they shouldn't be ashamed of handing their girls over to the Big Macy. It was how God had wanted things, or he would have had his Watchers stop it. Billy kept his right hand in a fist the whole time, spinning it in a counterclockwise motion. That little spin was the secret behind all of his dreams. He had been bested twice after training for over two years, but each time he had landed at least one blow. The only way for him to end it all was to win it in a single blow.

The last two books in his collection were Bruce Lee's Jeet Kune Do, and Dim Mak, the Art of the Chinese Death Touch. He had combined the powerful one-inch strike with the five finger death punch of Dim Mak. His prowess with the technique was amazing; he could punch through boards like paper. He could even split bricks and flat sandstones. He knew that was how it had to happen. The Preacher said that the Custodians were watching, but wasn't it a Custodian who brought him to the Lil' Berry? He knew it had to be the will of God.

After the ceremony, the grooms were the first to travel down the Bride's Road to deliver the tithe: eight cows, three horses per bride.

The brides traveled a couple miles back on their best tithe horses. According to tradition, they walked home.

The husband was not permitted to come get them; they had to wait at home for their brides to return.

"You still reckoning on going through with this?" Dan pleaded, while the Macys were looking over the groom's tithe.

Billy knew they would be impressed by his tithe because he had the finest herd in Tumbledown Town.

Finally, the Macys had taken his herd and there were six grooms left in line, with the brides just appearing over a ridge two miles back. There were ten Little Macys making demeaning comments, but they all quieted and parted when the statuesque shirtless Big Macy appeared. He walked straight to Billy Jack and said, "So, you finally gave up? It'll all be over soon. Ya'll go on home."

The grooms turned to ride off; Billy didn't budge.

The Macy added, "'Cept you Billy, you'll walk on home. You walk home like a bride, leave that horse here."

When Lucinda, in the distance, saw her lover step down she bolted her horse to a dead run, but she had too much ground to cover to stop anything.

The groom stepped back into the fluid stance of the Jeet Kune Do fighter.

"I was hoping you'd choose this route," the big man goaded.

The Big Macy charged in with a flurry of blows, but Billy's sidekick to his hip bone jarred the brute and stood him up. That was the only chance he was ever gonna have. Like a cobra, the cunning Cowey slid inside, and with the prowess of a Shaolin master, with every fluid muscle of his body working in concert, he delivered the Chinese death strike. He felt the ribs crack as his fist turned counter-clockwise. For a split second, the Macy's face was a mask of fear, but the second passed. The giant

162

didn't die. He hit the Cowey with a horrendous haymaker, and as Billy spun he spit out two front teeth. The monster was on him with his arm around his neck choking the life out of the bridegroom. The Little Macys were all screaming and cheering in the background, which was slowly fading into nothing. The little man fought with elbows and fingernails, but the iron grip of the Big Macy was unbreakable. The screams around him had grown to a fevered frenzy as his life and energy faded. He remembered thinking that he had wasted his entire life only to die here, when the choking arm of his attacker just fell away. He had no time to judge the reason, as they both fell over backwards. Billy spun around and started beating the Macy with all the power his fists could manage. It only took a few seconds for air to rush into the Cowey's lungs and his wits to return enough to survey the surroundings.

The Macy's arm had fallen away because it had been severed at his shoulder. The cries of the Little Macys weren't cheers for their leader, they were screams of horror. Three adult spotted nightstalkers had leapt into the crowd and were laying waste to the Macys. The scene looked like a slaughter house with body parts everywhere and the big cats still mauling Macys. He saw all the cats turn toward Lucinda as she rode up with Whiskey Dan jumping in between her and the cats.

Billy yelled at the top of his lungs and all three cats, covered in gore, snarling and vicious, turned towards him.

Well I won. I killed the Big Macy. Now I'll die at the claws of the cats I saved. He thought to himself.

The biggest of the three was the one-eared male and he jumped with full claws right onto Billy. His paws connected with the Cowey's shoulder and he was prepared to die, but the cat just licked his bruised face. In the next few moments, all three killers were around his feet purring like housecats.

There were two Macys left alive, despite the Custodians who were trying to render aid. Ike had used the cast on his leg as a shield and fought off the majority of the attacks, but he was still in no shape to challenge Billy Jack. The other Macy was sobbing like a child deep in shock, crying for his mother.

The last words the Big Macy said were, "He did it. Give him the pills."

"What are pills?" Billy asked.

Ike limped inside and Billy motioned Dan to follow him.

When they came back out Ike spilled all the gang's secrets. He brought three big bottles of little blue pills. He told them that they were the secret to the Macy's magic. The building they lived in was really called a Pharmacy Rx, but the other letters had fallen off long ago. The Macy sent them out looking for other buildings all over the land with the same writing. They believed that they had raided every single one within a ten day's ride. The pills he handed over were the last. There were a couple hundred, but when they were gone that would be the end of the human race. He also handed over another bottle that said 'anabolic steroids' on the side, and explained this was how the Macy grew so big.

On the ride back to Tumbledown Town, Billy threw the anabolics in the river, believing no man needed that type of power. He poured a handful of blue pills in his pocket and gave some to Whiskey Dan.

"Bring the rest to the Preacher and let him decide what to do with them."

Dan raised an eyebrow and asked, "And what if he decided to become the Big Macy?"

"I'll kill him, too."

"Well, that's easy. Where're you going?"

"If the world is going to end at the end of that bottle, I'm planning on catching a whole mess of whisker fish first."

Dan chortled, then turned to Ike, who had been riding silently behind them. "Where're you going?"

"I figured y'all might need a Macy's word to back up yer story?"

"And then after that?" Dan asked.

"I ain't give it much thought."

"Well I got room at my place."

"You sure?"

Dan winked at Billy who smiled and they rode their separate ways.

A hovering Custodian with a long rust stripe down its torso sent a message.

Report from Terran Custodian:
Supply of reproductive aid has been distributed amongst the lower faction. Estimated time of depletion is one week.

Response to Terran report:
When last pill has been consumed, take medical action to correct reproductive problem. Current crop has exceeded expectations.

BAD AIR
by Jack Lothian

arshal Frank Reeves would have disliked Harold Baylis even if he hadn't known the man's crime. Some people just had a bad air about them, and Harold's was worse than most. They sat in the third passenger car as the train cut across the dark plains, a blanket of stars overhead, Harold's gaze fixed on the world outside the window. Frank checked his pocket watch, more out of habit than purpose, knowing they were only halfway there.

Harold was handcuffed to Ethan, Frank's deputy. Ethan was barely a day over twenty, and next to Harold he looked like a boy playing dress-up. The marshals had picked up their prisoner from the holding cell at San Simon to transfer him by rail to Reddington penitentiary.

Harold had been found sitting outside his cabin near Wheeler's Ridge on a Sunday morning, undershirt stained red, the butchered bodies of his wife and two children still lying in their beds. Frank had tried to picture it, wondering what expression the man had on his face as he sat there, what he must have been thinking if he'd been thinking at all.

Frank saw Harold frown as he muttered something to himself.

"You got something to say there, Harold?"

There was a pause as Harold continued to look out at the night sky. "It don't look right."

Frank exchanged a look with his deputy. "What doesn't look right, Harold?"

"The stars. One of 'em went out. Not for the first time either." Harold sunk back in his seat, shifted his bulk, which forced Ethan to adjust his arm. The young deputy scowled, but Harold paid him no attention.

Frank counted the hours until he'd be back home in Wilcox, food on the table, his wife asking how it had been, and Frank lying to her like he always did these days.

It was fine.

Nothing was fine, though. Frank could feel the world slowly decaying around him. He'd sit there on the porch after dark, staring out into an endless night, the desert wind curling across the town. There was some inexplicable fear that had started to grow inside him, like a distant bell ringing, warning of some terrible thing approaching, but one that was too far and indistinct to understand. Or maybe his wife was right. Perhaps he'd been in this job too long, sat across from too many men like Harold. Lately, there seemed to be more and more of them, symptoms of some unknown sickness.

"Why'd you do it, Harold?" said Ethan, eyes on the prisoner. Frank felt a twinge of irritation at the younger deputy engaging the man. Maybe it was a sense of protection, disguised as an annoyance. He could tell Ethan thought he was smarter than their prisoner, which was a danger in itself.

Harold shook his head. "Maybe I didn't do it. Maybe this is all a grave miscarriage of justice."

There was a smattering of other passengers in the carriage. Ethan had given them the once over, just in

167

case. Far as they knew Harold didn't have a gang or any associates, but it paid to stay vigilant. Frank saw a few of them shift in their seats, pretend they weren't eavesdropping.

"I suppose they're going to hang me," said Harold.

"You deserve worse," said Ethan, trying to sound tough.

"Maybe. How many lives you taken, deputy?"

Frank knew the answer. One. A case of public disorder that had gotten out of hand. Middle of the day, the perpetrator was nasty drunk, trying to pick fights. Ethan went to intercede, and the man pulled out a rusty Colt. Frank knew Ethan only meant to fire a warning shot, make him drop the firearm, but the angles were all wrong, a bullet through the gut, and the drunk was as good as dead before he'd hit the dirt.

"More than you'd think," said Ethan, and adjusted his hat, tugging at the brim.

"Uh-huh. Okay, then." Harold smiled, liked he had the measure of Ethan, which probably wasn't far from the truth.

Frank was about to tell the prisoner to pipe down when the train lurched forward, accompanied by the sharp metallic screech of breaks on steel. A suitcase fell from the rack, collapsing open, spilling its guts. The train shuddered to a halt.

Frank brushed his hand against the gun in his holster, to remind himself of the options. He leaned out, looked down the carriages, then nodded at Ethan.

"Uncuff him."

"Marshal — "

"Do it." Frank switched his attention to Harold. "Harold. The moment those cuffs are off, you put those hands on your head, just like you've been taught. They

168

go anywhere else, we've got a problem. Do you understand?"

Harold gave no indication either way. There was a wave of concerned chatter from the other passengers, craning necks to look out windows. All Frank saw was the desert and the dark horizon, his reflection peering at him from the glass like a ghost. Frank looked back across to where Ethan was removing the handcuffs. Harold locked eyes with Frank, then made a point of raising his hands, and placed them on his head.

"Go check the engineer's cab," said Frank. Ethan hesitated. Frank nodded down the aisle. "Go on. And be careful."

Ethan rose and moved down the aisle. He looked to the passengers as he went, told them to remain calm, that there was nothing to worry about. Touching the brim of that hat like it was a charm, rather than a nervous tic. Frank turned his attention back to the prisoner.

"I'm going to ask you to keep your hands on your head, Harold, and stay right where you are."

Harold complied. He still didn't take his eyes off Frank, or change his expression. "What do you think it is? Something on the line? Mechanical failure?"

"I think it's you shutting up and sitting there quiet."

"Just making conversation, marshal. All we know we could be here for a while." Harold gave a gap-toothed grin. "Might be nice to get to know each other."

Frank wondered if this is what Harold had been like, on that morning. Nice and calm. Friendly even. Turning to his wife as she slept. Standing over his children's beds. Frank kept his hand on his holster, told himself if the big man moved he'd have no issue putting a round in him.

169

Perhaps it'd be quicker and easier that way, for all concerned.

Ethan passed through the two carriages that led to the engineer's cab. He nodded to passengers as he went, letting them know that there was nothing to worry about. Ethan was glad to be away from the prisoner. It wasn't easy, sitting next to the man, knowing what he'd done, knowing he was going to hang for it.

Ethan's father was a preacher. Their God was one of fire and vengeance; the burning lake waiting for those who had sinned. Ethan often thought of how it would feel, to be on his knees, before the glory, judged for what he had done, taking a man's life, a Commandment broken beyond repair. Frank had said it wasn't the same thing, not when you had a badge, but Ethan didn't see what difference that made.

He reached the engineer's cabin, found the door bolted and locked. He could see the engineer through the window, their back turned. Waistcoat and hat, head tilted to the side. Ethan knocked on the glass, but the engineer didn't respond. He rapped harder, but there was still no reaction.

Ethan looked back down the carriage, considered going back to the marshal. What would he say though? "I knocked, but there was no reply." He could already see the smirk on the prisoner's face at that one. No. Ethan had been sent to deal with this, and that's what he meant to do.

He drew his .44, fished his handkerchief from his pocket. He placed the cloth against the glass, then struck it hard with the butt of the gun, the window breaking beneath it.

He'd have expected some response from the engineer after that, but the man just stood there, head to one side, still with his back to him. Ethan wrapped the handkerchief around his knuckles, used it to knock out the remaining shards. He reached in, unlocked the bolt from the other side.

Ethan stepped into the engine cabin, his boot crunching on broken glass. Still, the engineer hadn't turned.

"Excuse me, sir." Ethan cleared his throat as if he hadn't just smashed his way through the window. "You okay there?"

He reached out and put his hand on the engineer's shoulder, turned him around. The engineer's face was oddly calm and blank.

"I heard something," said the man.

"You heard something?" repeated Ethan.

The engineer nodded. "Out there. In the dark."

"You heard something, so you stopped the train… right here, middle of nowhere?"

The engineer seemed to consider that. "I wanted to listen to what it was saying. Would you like to listen too?"

"I'd like you to get this train moving again, sir." Ethan knew he was channeling Frank's voice, the way Frank spoke to people; polite but with that firm grip, so they knew that business was meant.

"I really think I should share it with you."

Ethan told the engineer that he had no interest in hearing anything, but the engineer had started speaking anyway. Within a few moments, Ethan had stopped arguing with the man. He just stood there, head tilted, listening to the words.

Harold's arms were starting to ache. He tried to figure out how long he'd have to hold this position. The train stopping was a bonus, the deputy being sent away even better. But he knew if he went for the lawman, with the distance between them, he'd come off second best.

Maybe it was worth a shot. Crack the man's head against the window, make sure he stayed down, then get moving. Down the steps, across the track. Start running. See how far he could get. But thirty years and it felt like every day had been a battle with himself, a war that could never be won. He wasn't sure he could find the energy to move now, even if he wanted.

"If you're thinking of trying something, I wouldn't," said Frank.

"Wasn't thinking anything," said Harold.

He could see the marshal shift his attention down the carriage. If there was ever a time, this was it. But the marshal's hand still rested on his gun, and Harold had never been that fast. The expression on the lawman's face though — it seemed to have shifted. The man almost seemed confused. Harold craned his head to look behind.

"No moving," said Frank.

Frank could see Ethan coming back this way, the engineer behind him, as they moved down the aisle. They were being followed by other passengers, some odd little procession. Ethan went slow, stopped at each person along the way, seemed to be telling them something. The engineer talking to those on the other side. Whatever they were saying, it seemed to be having some kind of effect. People stopped moving, listened intently. Their faces fell into repose. You might say they even looked at peace, but that wasn't quite right. More like a lack of expression.

At first, Frank thought they were evacuating the train. But he noticed how they all seemed to wear the same look, how their mouths all seemed to be moving in time, reminding him of a Sunday congregation.

Frank could feel that distant bell ringing, that warning he didn't understand.

They were one carriage away and getting closer.

"Ethan," said Frank, loud enough for his voice to carry. "Deputy."

Ethan didn't respond. Frank repeated his words, raising the volume, which caused passengers nearby to react.

No way Ethan couldn't have heard that. But he still didn't show any recognition. He was leaned over, talking to a woman in her sixties, face framed by a green-ribboned bonnet. She shook her head, confused. Seemed to be disagreeing with whatever Ethan was saying. He kept talking though, and her expression of annoyance smoothed itself out. She rose up, and Frank could see she was speaking alongside Ethan now. He could swear they were saying the same thing.

"Harold. On your feet."

"Marshal?"

Frank didn't know why, but he felt an urgency building, the closer Ethan and the others came. They were almost at the link between cabins.

"On your goddamn feet. Come on."

Harold rose up, turned. He saw the passengers coming their way. "What's going on?"

Frank dug out cuffs. "Put them on."

Harold watched the passengers as they moved closer. His first thought was that this was some form of prairie justice, a lynch mob who knew what he had done, but this didn't quite fit. You'd expect faces contorted in anger, a sense of furious justice. These people looked calm. He could hear them talking now, low voices filtering through. He couldn't make out the words, but their form seemed to swim towards him anyway, soft and quiet, drifting their way into his head, until Frank's voice cut in, hard and sharp.

"You put them on, or I put a bullet in you."

Harold fumbled the handcuffs, slipped them around his wrists, but made sure not to make them too tight. He saw Frank bring up his Colt.

"Hey now, wait a minute, marshal…"

Frank fired upwards, a warning shot. It was like a cannon going off inside the carriage. Harold instinctively flinched, as a sharp ringing knifed through his skull.

The oncoming crowd didn't even react. The passengers in the carriage did, rising to their feet, demanding to know what the hell the marshal was doing, discharging a firearm like that. Even as they remonstrated with him, Frank could see the ones furthest away turning and changing, shoulders slumping, mouths beginning to move in time with the rest of the herd. There was half a carriage between them and Frank now.

"Ethan. You will answer me right now." Frank only waited for a second, and then he gestured to Harold. "Let's move."

Harold stayed where he was, not understanding. "Move where, marshal?"

"We're getting off the train."

He shoved Harold along, down the aisle, away from the swarm of passengers. Their voices were starting to rise, and it felt like a wave trying to pull Frank back in its flow. He moved to the side door, yanked the handle, felt the cold night air sweeping in.

He thought about the other night on the porch, looking out at the desert, seeing the stars overhead, swearing that one had just gone dark. The wind across the plains, the way it seemed to murmur, indistinct, and that fear that gnawed at him, day by day.

He didn't know why, but he knew they had to get away.

The two men stumbled onto the track-side. Flat desert land spread out all around them, dotted with scrub, black mountains in the distance. Frank looked back, could see the passengers still moving along the carriage. Ethan and the engineer were at the front, leading this strange parade.

"Get walking." He pushed Harold forward, away from the train. Frank found it hard to gather his thoughts. They seemed fragile, disintegrating whenever he got close to them.

"You feel it too, right?" said Harold. "Them words."

"Keep moving."

"Getting into your head, like an idea that came from somewhere else."

"I'm warning you," said Frank. "Not another word." He gave Harold a shove for good measure. He looked back, saw Ethan at the train exterior door, silhouetted in the frame, a dark outline with the blazing light behind him. The image struck a strange, unknowable terror into him.

Frank called out for his deputy to stop, but he knew it'd make no difference. Ethan moved down onto the track, that gentle flood of passengers following him.

Frank and Harold kept moving. Harold with his cuffed hands in front of him, heavy steps across the ground. The two men, under the starry sky, nothing but rocks and dust around them. They were dwarfed by the landscape. Behind them, the crowd kept coming, moving at a measured pace, no rush, no hurry. The voices carried on the night air, talking as one. Even though the words were indistinct, it made the lawman and prisoner feel unsteady, every step unsure.

"Cover your ears," said Frank.

"You got me in cuffs, marshal."

Frank considered reaching for the key. He wasn't sure how long he and the prisoner could keep moving like this. No destination in mind, that crowd still coming. Even if he uncuffed Harold, that didn't solve the problem. They'd have a tough time over the terrain, especially if something were following them. They could gain ground, but sooner or later, fatigue would kick in. Even worse, when the sun came up. Desert heat. Dehydration. None of this was good.

Frank turned, steadied his arm. He pulled the trigger. The muzzle flashed in the night. The crowd didn't slow down. Stopping to take the shot meant that the voices were just that little more distinct. He fired again, the roar of the gun a welcome distraction from their insidious murmur.

Two warning shots, in full view. That was enough.

Frank lined up a shot on Ethan, closing one eye, centering his aim. It was like someone else had taken over the deputy's body. Ethan had always had an awkward gait, that self-conscious air. This Ethan moved like ripples across the water. His mouth opened and closed, in time with the others, speaking as one. The words seemed to reach across the landscape, so it was like their lips were right next to Frank's ear. Talking. Whispering. Screaming.

176

For a moment, Frank forgot where he was. He was only aware of the void beneath them all, waiting to pull them down, collapsing them into the space between words. That darkness that had always been there, hiding in plain sight, and now his eyes were open, and he could see its true face.

He managed to squeeze the trigger.

The shot hit Ethan right below the brim of the hat, and the deputy toppled backward as if jerked by an invisible rope. Frank saw Ethan's body twitch, and even in the night, he could see Ethan trying to rise up again, the mouth still moving.

The noise of the weapon had seemed to break whatever spell had been cast on him, and Frank managed to turn away, grabbing Harold by the arm, dragging him on.

"How many bullets you got left, marshal?"

"Not enough," said Frank. He hesitated, weighing up the odds. The words were forming again, closer and closer. Frank tried to focus on the prisoner as they staggered on. "This is what's going to happen. I'm going to take off your cuffs. We pick up the pace, put some distance between those people and us. I don't know what the hell this is — I just know it's nothing good."

"You trust me?"

Frank glanced back at the shapes behind them, the distant train a fading beacon in the night. He didn't have much choice. He could leave the man, but Frank had a sense of duty, unshakeable even here in the dark. "Raise your hands. Quickly now"

They had to slow down, as Frank took out the key, tried to slide it into the cuffs. Harold looked up. He couldn't remember seeing a night sky like this. He saw blazing stars emerging from the darkness where they had been concealed, reborn and renewed, glittering celestial patterns that melted and merged across the hemisphere.

It was beautiful. It was terrifying.

The cuffs came apart with a click.

"Move," said Frank, checking his weapon.

"Marshal?"

Frank gazed up at Harold, heard the dullness in his voice.

"I'll tell you why I did it. To my wife. To my children." Harold moved forward, and Frank reacted, raised a hand to block. But Harold grabbed him, turned him. Harold brought his free arm up around Frank's neck, forcing a choke-hold. There was no emotion to what Harold was doing. It was just the way things were.

"It wasn't no voices or no stars either."

Frank kicked and struggled. He snapped his head back, cracked it off Harold's nose, could feel that impact response of warm blood. It made no difference. Harold's grip was an unbreakable vice. Frank felt bones splinter. He couldn't breathe. The night closed in, thick and fast.

He heard Harold say, "I did it because I could."

Then Harold twisted hard and broke Frank's neck. Frank's body crumpled and fell. Harold picked up the scattered gun.

The voices were closer now. He could see the congregation of passengers, their placid faces in the moonlight. A choir coming to greet him.

Harold kept taking small steps backward, boots scuffing against the dirt. He checked the chamber. Two shots left. Could put one into the crowd, then one into himself. Or he could turn, start running. There was a weariness though, one that had seeped into his bones, made them heavy and dull.

He tried to keep walking, but it felt pointless. Look at these people behind him. None of them had cares. None of them seemed burnt up with anger, driven by waves of incoherent rage. They seemed to have found peace, whatever that meant.

Harold knew what kind of man he was, had known all his life, even if he'd tried to hide it.

Then one morning, something changed, and he let his true self shine, just for a moment, but that was enough. Sitting there on the steps, blood on his hands, the sun glinting through the trees.

Harold tossed the gun aside. He got down onto his knees and stared at the forms coming closer and closer. He let their words swell up around him. Whatever they were saying, maybe it was worth hearing. Perhaps it wouldn't be so bad after all.

He felt the world break open beneath him, the silent maw at the end of it all.

They kept moving, across those Great Plains. The moon fell, the sun rose.

A town emerged on the horizon. Closer and closer with every step.

The voices carried on the breeze. They were looking forward to sharing the word, with all the good people that lived there.

The deputy walked alongside the prisoner, their mouths moving in unison, the words flowing from a distant place, far inside. They felt nothing now, beyond the shapes of the sound. There was only the void, and it was everything they could have hoped it would be.

CHRISTINE MORGAN

THE CROSSING AT BONY FORD
by Christine Morgan

"It ain't the drop but the stop," Momma always liked to say.

That was, whenever Corey would make that quote about how a body could get used to anything, even hangin', if he did it long enough.

I loved them both, and it pained me awful when they died. Funny how those same sayings came back to me now without being much of a comfort.

Not the drop but the stop.

Get used to anything, even hangin'.

I heard their words in my head over and over as I sat on a thin bunk with a thinner blanket all that was between my rump and its flat mattress. Where who knew how many others sat before me, iron bars between them and the rest of the world, the wide free world with all its promises. How many names had been scratched on the brick wall in the back, with its one tiny window? That window, also iron-barred, was so high up I needed to stand on the bunk and still strain myself up on my tiptoes to peer out. Peering out only showed me what I most did not want to see.

The jail here in Joshua Flats was built at the end of what passed for a town, just at the edge of where the land stopped, or started, being flat ... depending on what way a person was headed.

180

To one way, there lay a stretch of sand and scrub dotted with tumbleweeds and the weird, many-armed, shaggy, spike-bristling trees that gave the town its name, the desert rolling away under the heat shimmer toward the golden grasslands of Antelope Valley. I'd heard how, in the spring, wild poppies would just fair to cover the ground, a bright orange forever of them rippling in the breeze.

To the other way there rose up the Tehachapis, so named for the hard climb they were said to be. The Army used to have a fort up in the mountains, abandoned now. There were mines as well, though not so much for gold and silver. Mostly for something called borax, cottontail or cottonball or such the like.

The view from this one tiny window, though, showed me nothing but the way I'd be going, and it was neither toward the grasslands or the mountains. It was toward a low hill topped with a wind-gnarled oak.

Another of Momma and Corey's exchanges came to mind at the sight of it.

"All's any town needs," Momma would say, "is a church for the saints and a saloon for the sinners."

"And a gallows tree t' keep them all honest," Corey inevitably added.

A gallows tree, that's what it was. On a scraggly hilltop where crosses and headstones leaned every which way, making a rough graveyard ringed by a crooked picket fence.

That's where I was headed. Travis Baines, not even twenty years old, bound for the noose.

Why, they'd even built up a plank platform and scaffold by that there tree, under the stoutest branch. That's where they would rig the rope. I could see from here how previous ones had rubbed a pale rut in the

181

bark.

I let go of the bars and sat myself back down, wishing I hadn't taken that further look. Made my neck hurt just to contemplate … the coarse choking burn, the snap if I was lucky and the slow strangling kick-dance if I wasn't.

Did I deserve to die that way?

I didn't reckon so, but, here I was.

I'd been drunk, I'd been stupid, and I'd killed a man.

I was sober now, but the rest hadn't much changed. Sober, but still stupid, and a man was dead because of it; there'd be no arguing on that point. They'd gone and buried him up on that very hill; I'd watched them do it. And they'd dug another hole in the dirt at the same time, a hole they'd fill once I'd finished twitching.

And that would be the end of me.

Come high noon tomorrow.

Or, rather, high noon today, because somehow I had gone and whiled away the whole night. Couldn't recall sleeping, but at some point I must've because I woke with a miserable crick in my spine. Just what I needed for my last day on earth.

The patch of sky through the tiny window had a peculiar tinge to it, a hazy sort of rusty green. Twister weather, the homesteaders might've said. Or maybe smoke from a brushfire, or blowing dust … mattered none to me. Soon enough now, a deputy'd bring me a tin plate with whatever it was they fed the condemned for their final breakfast. Eggs and bacon? Biscuits and gravy? Cornbread and beans? Vile black coffee strong enough to knock the shoes off a horse?

I found the prospect of breakfast mattered none to me either. Had no appetite to speak of. I turned myself this way and that, hoping to work the crick from my spine, and then my jaw about hit my boot tops when I realized the cell door's lock was askew. Not busted, but askew, enough so that it hadn't caught properly. A little jiggle there and it might well pop loose.

What was in my head? Jailbreak? Escape? Run like a coward yellow-bellied dog?

"Beats hangin'," I heard Corey say.

Not in my mind, that was. I heard him clear as anything, my brother's whiskey voice, like he was standing right behind me.

When I looked, though, of course the cell was empty but for me.

Whether I'd really heard him or not, the advice was as good.

"Better a live dog than a dead wolf," Momma said, for once in full agreement with Corey.

Unless it was a trick of some kind. A trap. They'd fixed the lock that way on purpose to test if I'd face my fate like a man or not. If I tried sneaking out, they could be waiting there to catch me, and then ...

Well, and then what? What would they do? Shoot me?

I went to the cell door. I gave it a jiggle. It made a pained squeal and I held my breath, sure that a deputy would poke his face in and demand to know what I was up to. But none did. I jiggled the latch again and it did pop loose. The hinges creaked slow as I eased the door open, holding it careful so it didn't swing back and slam with a clang.

The jail house was silent. I crept out like the lightest-footed mouse there ever was, expecting harsh shouts with each step. But nobody stopped me. Nobody snoozed at the desk. I got clear across and out, into that hazy rust-green morning light, to find Joshua Flats as quiet and peaceful as could be.

Now I was out and not sure what to do next. I'd had a horse, Corey's horse, a dun-brown beast he'd named Muddy, but Muddy was stabled in the livery and I knew I was pushing what luck I had far enough already. I'd do better to get myself out of town on foot.

That was my plan, right enough, but something - morbid curiosity, I suppose they'd call it - drew me on up the hill at the edge of town first. Why I felt compelled to go any closer to that gallows tree, I had no idea. Or maybe it was the hole I wanted to look at, the hole that would've been my grave. What I might do, I had no idea there either. Dance on it and laugh? Piss into it?

Nothing stirred in the town, not so much as a cat or a cock. I clambered over the picket fence into the graveyard. Only then did I figure out it wasn't the hole meant for me that had drawn me here, it was the hole meant for the man I'd killed. I didn't even know his name. I had put a bullet in him, the blood had poured out like someone sprung the bung out of a barrel, and he had died gasping on the boardwalk out in front of the Joshua Flats general store.

All because I had been drunk and stupid, and he'd had the bad luck to come out of the store right then with his parcels, bump me, and send me staggering into the street, where I stepped square in a fresh cow pat. He'd been about to speak when I plugged him. Maybe about to apologize, for all I knew, and offer to buy me a drink to make amends.

I hesitated at the end of the dirt mound. They'd stuck a wooden cross there, but no name was on it. Another traveler like me? Passing through? A miner, a ranch-hand?

Seemed I'd never know after all.

184

My gaze drifted as if on its own to the tree, bare branches hooked and bent, clawing at the hazy sky. I rubbed my throat. I swallowed. I swiveled my head side to side and felt that crick in my spine give an awful twang.

"You best get on your way, son."

The voice was not Corey's, not Momma's, and not in my head. I spun around to see a man not half a dozen paces from me. My hand slapped leather, or would have if they hadn't relieved me of my gunbelt and holsters.

The man smiled. It was a thin smile but not unkindly. He was tall and lean, and he wore what I was surprised to recognize as a uniform from the war, *the* war, the War Between the States as they called it. That had been back years ago; Momma's eldest brother fought and died in it, but Momma's eldest brother had worn the Union Blue, and this tall stranger here was dressed head to foot in Confederate Gray. He was old, too, with a full silver beard, and long silver hair spilling from under his hat.

"Best get on your way," he repeated. "They'll be after you soon. Coming for you. Hot on your trail."

He was surely right about that, I knew. Once they discovered the empty cell, there'd be a posse of men riding out from Joshua Flats to hunt down the murderer who had himself a date with the ropemaker's daughter.

But I didn't move. "Who are you?" I asked. My mouth was powerful dry, and the words came out in a croak.

The old soldier's eyes were brown behind round spectacles. Like his smile, his eyes were not unkindly, but there was a coolness in them. "Time's a-wasting, son. Get you going, now."

"Where?" I asked, not knowing why.

He pointed off across the desert. "Make for Bony

Ford. They can't chase you past that. And if you're there before nightfall, you might catch the next stagecoach."

"Stagecoach?" I felt for my pockets, but I had about as much money as I had guns … which was to say, none at all.

From the other side of the hilltop there arose a sound, an eerie sound not quite a hiss, not quite a rattle, not quite a clicking.

"Hurry along." The soldier dug into his own pocket and flipped a coin at me.

I caught it and saw it was a silver dollar. "Mister --"

The eerie sound arose again, nearer now, and something about it brought all the fine hairs on my arms and the nape of my neck to quivering straight up. I tried to see what was making such a noise, and when I looked back, the old soldier in Confederate Gray was gone like he'd never been there at all.

But he had been, because I held his silver dollar clenched in my fist. I could see plain as day the scuff marks where he'd been standing. What I could not see was any tracks leading from there, or anyplace a man that tall could have got to and hid.

The sound again, and it seemed to be from several places at once. I thought of snakes: sidewinders, rattlers, big diamondbacks; I thought of scurrying lizards and strutting scorpions.

Then I thought I best do what the soldier had said and get out of there, get on my way. The direction he'd pointed was as good as any. Better than most, because when the posse went looking for me, it was about the last way they'd expect a fugitive from justice to hightail it.

So, hightail it in that direction is what I did. I was some glad to have Joshua Flats fall away behind me.

Never mind that I had no horse, no provisions, no canteen, nothing but the clothes I stood up in and this one silver dollar.

The sky kept on with its hazy rust-green, like copper that's begun to go bad. There was no wind to speak of. Despite that, the Joshua trees as I passed gave these stealthy rustles, almost as if they moved to watch me go by. The air had a flat quality, a funny taste, that too like copper. I started in to wonder if a lightning storm was brewing, or if there'd be a downpour, sudden floods, and I'd drown in some arroyo instead of swinging at the end of a rope.

I kept an ear perked for pursuit, but all I could hear was the rustling Joshua trees and, occasionally, sometimes near and sometimes far, more of the hiss-rattle-clicking that set my hairs on end.

Until, that was, I heard the screaming.

Screaming, and crying, and carrying on something terrible.

I broke into a run, struggled up a rise, fought through a stand of scrub at the top, and saw two children up on a boulder in a dry wash gully below.

The one screaming and carrying on was a little girl, in a check-gingham dress and bonnet, only she screamed more with anger than anything else. The boy, even littler, sobbed as he clung onto her apron. This hindered her some in what she was doing, which involved swatting with a stick at the ...

My eyes saw the things, and my gut believed them, but the rest of me was dumbstruck all the way down to my toes.

I had never, in all my born days, seen or imagined the like. Drunk or sober, waking or dreaming.

They were like snakes, but they weren't. They had

187

the long, sinuous bodies of snakes, but they ran on lizard-legs and scrabbled with wicked claws at the side of the boulder; their tails, which sported rattles, also sported the venom-dripping stingers of scorpions. Hard scaled plates covered their heads and ran the lengths of their backs, and sprouting out to either side of their necks were jointed limbs ending in serrated pinchers.

They moved fast. They made that sound I'd been hearing.

They were also, each, about the size of a man's leg.

I stared.

And here was this child, trying to fend them off with a stick. This girl who couldn't have been no more than eight or nine years old, trapped with her kid brother on this boulder in the middle of a dry wash.

I thought of myself and Corey when we were small, how I had looked up to him in every sense of the word. Corey would have protected me until his last breath.

Before I knew I was going to, I'd snatched up a rock off the ground and hucked it at the nearest snake-beast. It whipped around and suddenly half of them were streaking at me, rattles shaking for all they were worth, that clicking, chittering hiss louder than ever and hatefully evil.

Yelling, hollering fit to split, I grabbed for a stick of my own and set to laying about in a full-on fury. I felt a couple pinchers snag at my pants, I felt a stinger jab at my boot but not go through the good leather. A nasty brownish liquid spurted out whenever I struck one of the things, bitter-smelling and looking like tobacco juice.

I beat three of them into the dirt and then the rest skedaddled. I saw another two by the boulder, one back-broke so that its front end tried to drag the crippled hind end along, the other walloped so bad there was barely

188

anything left but limp scraps.

"You both all right?" I asked, in a coughing wheeze because my dry throat was sore and felt swollen from all the hollering, as well as having nothing to drink all day.

The children looked at me as if they had never seen another person in their lives. I went up to the boulder, brought my bootheel down on the crippled snake-beast's skull – it crunched like a boiled egg, very satisfying – and tried again.

"You all right?"

The girl nodded. The boy, his face red and blotched and snot-streaked, only snuffled.

"What're you doing way out here? Where's your folks?"

"They went on ahead," the girl said. She had braids the color of molasses and freckles sprinkled across her snub nose. "Momma, she got a job school-teachin' down San Diego way. Daddy, he's takin' us to meet her there."

"And where's your daddy at?"

She shrugged, and I saw despair flit through her big brown eyes. "Daddy, he said stay right there, wait by the wagon. But Amos --" Here, she jerked her chin to indicate the boy. "Amos wandered off and I went to fetch him and then we couldn't find our way again."

"I want Daddy!" Amos wailed.

"Can you help us, mister?" asked the girl.

"I want *Daddy*!"

"Hush him up before those ... whatever they were ... before they come back," I said, and cast a nervous look around. "Let's get a move on. What's your name?"

"Cora," she said.

I felt like someone had just walked over my grave. Which, given how I'd begun this day, wasn't anything I wanted to think about.

189

"What's yours, mister?" she went on.

I almost told her, but reckoned how it might not be so smart, what with me being a hunted man and all. "Corey," I said.

She beamed brighter than a little ray of sunshine. "That's like my name!"

I heard that hiss-click-rattling again and knew the pleasantries had to wait. "Come on. There's supposed to be a stagecoach stop ahead here somewhere, maybe a town. That's as good a place as any to start looking for your daddy."

They'd been walking quite a while by then, and with Amos all tuckered out it fell to me to hoist him up and carry him along. He was a hefty sack of potatoes. A real misery to my cricked spine and stiff neck. I found it none the easier because I was also reluctant to leave behind the stick I'd used against the snake-beasts. Hadn't been the best weapon, but it was still a sight better than nothing at all.

Cora kept her stick, too. And, soon enough in that way children had, she'd gone over right cheerful. Skipping, chattering, fair to peppering me with questions – why was the sky that strange color, did I think it was going to storm on us, was there a wildfire someplace, what were those funny trees, and those snakes, what in the world had those been, was all California like this with funny trees and strange sky and snake-things?

I answered as best I could, only resorting to lies when her questions took a turn for the personal. Amos had dropped off to sleep with his head on my shoulder.

We walked and walked for what seemed like a hundred years. Sunset approached, not in a blaze of red and gold like there often was when the air rode heavy with smoke, just a dull, leaden, burnt-looking sort of sunset. It'd be on toward dark soon, and I had yet to see anything resembling a town, a stagecoach stop, a ford, a river, or the like.

Had that old soldier pointed me wrong? Sent me to wander aimless until I simply dropped from thirst, heat-stroke and starvation?

Amos woke, lifted his head from my shoulder, looked behind me, and shrieked in my ear so loud I thought my head would crack open.

I spun. So did Cora.

After all that previous clicking, hissing and rattling, they'd come after us in total silence. Gathering their numbers. Gaining ground. Closing in. Now a great swarm of them were there. Some had crawled their way up the Joshua trees or perched atop rocks. That dull, sullen, leaden-orange sunset painted over them, making their stingers gleam with the wet drips of venom.

"Run!" I shouted to Cora.

At that, the swarm let loose with a terrible ruckus. They rushed at us. I could smell them, the stink of them, a nose-wrinkling mix of tobacco juice and rancid bacon, curdled milk and sour beer. It washed over us like a bad wind.

I let the stick fall and ran for blue blazes. For a moment I thought how if I wasn't weighed down by Amos … but I couldn't bring myself to cast the kid aside. Shoot a man while drunk, that I had done, and that did make me a killer, even a murderer. Leaving little Amos to be torn apart by those monsters while I saved my own skin? That would make me the lowest of the low.

So, I ran. I would have shoved Cora along, would have picked her up too if I'd've had to. The girl, though, was fast on her feet with her braids flying straight out from her head. She paused once to glance back and I shouted again for her to run, run, keep going, not to wait on me but *run,* goldurn it!

The goldurn it, that part slipped out, I hadn't meant to swear at a child.

"I see somethin'!" Cora cried.

I didn't see a thing, and then I did. A wide, glassy ribbon curved through the desert, a river, slow and sluggish, catching the burnt color of the sky like a mirror so smooth, except for one stretch where it shallowed out over a lumpy bed of stones ... the ford! And, on the river bank, the stark outline of what appeared to be a wooden shed or shelter of some kind ... the stagecoach stop!

Amos had half to throttled me by then, his chubby arms cinched tighter around my neck than a dance hall girl's corset. "There, make for it, make for it!" I choked.

We ran. Cora's bonnet whisked off and I trampled it into the dust. Shadows lengthened around us, Joshua tree shadows reaching with their bristly arms.

"Horses! Look, Corey, look, horses! Horses and a stagecoach!"

I wanted to call for them to hold up, wait up, wait for us, but Amos had me in that death grip. My boots pounded from loose sandy soil onto pale, pebbly rocks that gritted and grated underfoot.

Horses, yes indeed, horses, a team of six, tossing their heads and stamping their forehooves amid the cast-up driftwood on the riverbank, snorting, eager to be on their way. The stagecoach was a far sight bigger and finer than it had a right to be in these desolate parts. All I could make out of the driver was a man-shape in a duster and a hat, sitting up high, holding the reins.

The shotgun rider swung down from his seat with a lantern, which he raised as he opened the door to let the waiting folks start getting in. The light that lantern shed was a whitish-green that made me think of marsh fire. It shone pale and strange on the faces, which themselves had a pale and strange look about them. I saw the glint of money as they handed over their fares and climbed aboard.

None of them paid us any mind at first, as we raced toward them with that skittering, slithering swarm of death on our heels. Then, as Cora screamed again, begging them to wait, someone at the back of the line looked around.

"Cora?" he asked, in a voice that sounded like a man just waking up.

"Daddy!" The little girl spurred on so quick that pebbles and chunks of crushed stone spattered at me.

In my arms, Amos commenced shrieking again, eager this time, and he let go of my neck to wave his arms at the man.

I near collapsed onto the boards at his feet. The swarm of snake-beasts veered off, raising one final, furious, cheated hiss.

I lay there gasping, gulping, feeling like someone had stuffed my throat with barbed wire. There was a commotion above me as Cora, Amos, and their daddy embraced, all talking at once. When I heard my name – or my brother's, that was – I lifted my head on my sore, aching neck.

"This is Corey, he saved us!" Cora said.

I looked up.

The man looked at me.

"Daddy ..." the little girl went on, frowning, "why's there so much blood on you, Daddy?"

Because it had poured from him like someone sprung the bung on a barrel, that was why. It had poured like

193

that after I shot him in front of the general store in Joshua Flats.

"Stage is leaving, folks," the shotgun rider said. "We got a schedule to keep to. Don't be holding up the show, now."

Without a word, Cora and Amos' daddy scooped up his children, one in the crook of each arm. He ducked as he entered into the stagecoach with them. They all three vanished from my sight as if a black curtain had fallen into place behind them.

I pushed myself to my hands and knees. Had to steady my own head as I did it, since it seemed my neck wasn't fit for the task any more.

The riverbank along the ford was, I saw, littered with skeletons, not driftwood … bleached skeletons picked clean. The pale pebbles grating beneath my boots hadn't been pebbles at all. They were bone-shards, the ivory slivers of ribs, the knob-ends of joints.

The stones poking up from the ford itself weren't stones. They were skulls. Cattle skulls, those long-horn skulls unmistakable, coyote skulls, their naked teeth sharp and feral, human skulls, rounded with empty eye sockets staring. The dark water slipped around them slick and oily-like - poison, it must be, some powerful poison.

The far side of the river was lost in gloom. I couldn't make out hide nor hair of what might be over there.

"You coming or not?" asked the shotgun rider. He held out a leather-gloved hand. "Last chance."

The driver shifted in his seat to grin at me from beneath the brim of his hat. In fact, grinning was all he could do, what with his bare jawbones leering fleshless white.

I understood then. I touched my throat, feeling at the

194

swollen welt where the rope had dug into my flesh.

I grasped the rider's hand and let him help me to my feet. His hand then turned over, cupped and waiting. I fished the silver dollar from my pocket and dropped it into his palm. His fingers closed over it.

What was it Corey liked to say? A body could get used to anything.

I climbed into the stagecoach, knowing that whatever else might happen, it would be nice to see him and Momma again, on the other side of the river, past the crossing here at Bony Ford.

JACOB FLOYD

RISE, VEGA
by Jacob Floyd

"Rise, Vega."

The world was dark and blurry – a silence full of humming. Vega heard the voice from far away. The whisper, he knew it well - a whisper that spoke of seduction, treason, destruction. It was the whisper of a mentor and a nemesis. It was *her* voice.

Vega tried to move his mouth but it was made of sand, the jaw locked in place by some foul liquid. He struggled to move his limbs, but they felt compounded by a thick mass. He was stuck between walls of some kind – not steel or wood, but something moveable, though packed in all around him, rendering him immobile.

Mania. I hear you. What have you done to me, now?

The sinister chuckle floated along the darkness, surrounding Vega. Invisible though it was, its ring was deafening and its hold one of iron. Mania had him again.

You did this to yourself, Vega. As you most often do.

Bullshit, Mania. You always have a role to play in my misfortunes.

Accept blame. Your actions are your own.

Yeah, but you don't make it any easier for me, do you?

Perhaps you'll learn something one day.

196

Ever the mentor, you are. How can I ever repay you?
By shutting your mouth.
You know that won't happen, not as long as I have my tongue.

Vega could feel her smile.

I think I can remedy that.

Well, shit, he said.

And that was the last thing he said as Mania removed his tongue.

That ought to do it. Now, if you're a good boy, perhaps I'll return you to the Overworld that you love so much. Then you can have your tongue back.

Vega felt a rush of cold air engulf him, and the walls around him began to loosen. That's when he realized he was in the grave…again.

Damn Mania and her ghostly bullshit, he thought. The sound of his internal voice was distant and weak. No doubt she'd done that to keep it away from her mind. *When will this damn woman ever leave me alone?*

Never – that was the deal long ago. Vega ate a bullet and wasn't ready to go. He had some other shit to get done. Then along came Mania, who didn't look so deceptive, and she made a promise to him in exchange for a service, one that never ended, it would seem. Now, here he was, all these years later.

How long had it been? Hell, he couldn't even guess anymore. All he knew was ever since he finished his "service", it'd been *Do this; Do that.* He couldn't even ask her for a favor without some insane task to do in return. Mania's wants and visions were endless, and so Vega's work was never done.

The dirt around him crumbled away into the void, and his soul sank with it. This wasn't an ordinary grave. This was a grave in the Underworld, where Mania reigned supreme. Her powers were almost limitless aboveground, but down here, they were without restriction. Death and darkness were her domain, and where the spirits of the dead walked, she ruled. As it would seem right now, Vega was among the dearly departed.

But hell, this wasn't the first time.

And I'm sure it won't be the last.

I can still hear your thoughts," said Mania.

Vega shrugged, thinking weakly, *When have you not been able to?*

This time, you are incorrect. You are running out of resurrections. A man can only die so many times before his soul is broken.

So Vega then knew he had to find a way to keep bullets and blades out of his hide, just one more thing to worry about in the dirty prairies of the Wicked West. It wasn't like all the strange monsters and venomous creatures weren't enough already: the sandcrawlers and shade roamers; the dead drifters, the hell horses, the one-eyed woods-worms; and worst of all, the Shadow Walkers. The thought of those damnable things made even his soul shiver. Vega wasn't afraid of much, but the damn Shadow Walkers were enough to make him turn the other way.

The Wicked West was full of nightmares and dark forces. That's why he needed Mania. Vega had magical abilities, which is why he could be resurrected, but he needed someone to help him use them properly. Mania had magic mastered better than most supernatural entities in the entire Life and Death Spectrum. He was lucky that she had been the one to claim his soul – well, mostly lucky, anyway.

Vega fell rapidly through the darkness of the Underworld. Down, down, down – such a long trip to the bottom. He still hadn't gotten used to it. Before long, he could feel the cool begin to warm, and the darkness start to glow. This was the hardest part for him every time – the passing through.

Like the roar of ten-thousand trains, the rumble of the Earth's core turning burst through the humming silence. Vega's soul went rigid from the pain. As he fell, the orange inferno within the world rose up from the pit and swallowed him. That's when his spirit began to scream.

The burning of skin is one thing. But the burning of the soul is a whole different monster. That's the very essence of living. The body is just a shell. It hurts when it's burned, but the agony of your existence roasting in open flames hot enough to keep a planet turning had no words.

Deeper the soul of Vega was plunged into the fire, past the yellow and orange flames, into the darker shades of red. Soon, he was moving through a white hot world where the heat was so severe one didn't even have the mind to wish it away. All they could do was burn and scream until the blazing white dissipated, fading into darker shades: white into gray, gray into blue, blue into brown, and brown into black. The fire became cold. It was a freeze you could not imagine. As Vega fell, the freeze ripped away his spirit and bent it, broke it, twisted it into odd shapes. The Black Void that was the source of the flames and the darkest magic in the universe came into sight. This was no longer Earth. Vega had passed that long ago. This was the portal into another plane – the plane of the Beyond, where Mania awaited his arrival.

The Black Void opened up and the Eye of Existence came into view – the Unblinking Eye; the Eye with No Lid. It never stopped staring. It only shifted its gaze. It turned in the socket of the Black Void, the eye of some unimaginable cosmic terror lurking in the far reaches of the vastness of space.

Vega fell into the eye and was soon wrapped in a yellow hell. This was the last hallway, the last tunnel, the final descent into the Dead Lands. One last explosion of conflagration and Vega tumbled through the lower end of the furnace. His eyes closed and he slipped away, going into the slumber of actual death.

When he opened his eyes again, the world was hazy, and blurrier than the grave. The burning was gone. The freeze had lifted. Removed from the compacted plot, Vega could experience mobility once again. He lifted his arms and was shocked at what he saw. His hand was pale, skinny, and skinless -- the hand of a skeleton. He rolled up the sleeve of his black duster and saw his arm matched. Feeling frantic, he reached inside his shirt and felt the bones of his chest and ribcage. He lifted his right leg and removed his boot, and just as he feared, he was looking at the foot of a wraith.

What was this? This had never happened before.

I told you, you have died too many times. You come ever closer to the end. Many more times, and you will be in the Underworld for eternity. I can restore your flesh, but know that the next time you come here there could be damage I cannot repair. I can control the Underworld, but not what happens at the Gate of Anubis. That is His realm.

That name made Vega shudder every time. Why'd she have to bring Him up? No doubt Anubis would take a little piece of Vega at every opportunity. Vega was an

Underworld newbie when he double-crossed the God of Mummification – which, aboveground, people associate that simply with wrapping ancient Egyptian royalty in gauze, but in the grander scheme of things, it also entails pulling a soul from the shell, and it gave Vega the heebie-jeebies each time he thought about his corpse and spirit being in the hands of a deity that can't seem to stop being pissed off at him. If it weren't for the ancient Overlord of the Afterlife's noble sense of duty, Vega was sure he would have found himself missing pieces of his soul, or parts of his body, or wandering one of the many pits and mazes of the Dark World – none of which were pleasant. Begrudgingly, it was yet another instance where Vega owed a debt of gratitude to Mania.

"Stand up and shut up, Vega," Mania said as she approached the writhing skeleton there on the Underworld floor.

Slowly, Vega's body returned to normal. His viscera reformed in their cavities, his eyes came back into being. The dermis began to wrap itself around him as the veins appeared, sucking in the blood. Muscle, tissue, ligaments, tendons, arteries, and all other manner of the internal human highway formed inside the belligerent bones of the wild outlaw. Once his face was whole, he reached into his mouth, searching for his tongue. It wasn't there.

Mania smiled and held it up in her hands. "Looking for this?"

He looked up at her. She stood above him in her red and black cloak, billowing in the cold Underworld air sweeping through the tunnels. Where this wind came from, Vega could never figure out. The imposing figure of his magical mistress loomed above him, tall and broad. She beckoned to him with a long, slender finger, and he was pulled to his feet. Mania stood about a foot taller than Vega, who was no short man. He leaned back to look into the swirling pools of her magenta and blue-speckled eyes. Her fiery red hair and tawny complexion cast a spell of their own. The colors of her essence arrested those who gazed upon her; the contrasting rays of her appearance created to project her supernatural powers – arcane and otherworldly. Despite Vega's lack of enthusiasm for her visits, she was never any less awe-inspiring each time he stood before her.

"I'll give it back to you if you complete my task."

What else could Vega do? He shrugged and nodded.

"There's a bar on the outskirts of the prairie." She paused, allowing him a moment to consider his surroundings.

At first, Vega waited patiently for her to continue. The prevailing silence was awkward for a few seconds, and he became impatient. How the hell was he supposed to know what to do if she didn't tell him the mission?

Mania crossed her arms in frustration, tucking Vega's tongue under her right elbow. His eyes flickered down to it momentarily before he realized he was supposed to do, know, or say something…well, maybe not say. Though he had no doubt it would have amused her to watch him try.

"There are only a thousand or so prairies in the Underworld, Vega. Would you not like to know which one you now stand upon?"

At that moment, Vega was glad she had removed his tongue, because his frustration reached a boiling point. *I just died and I'm running out of resurrections; I showed up here as an eviscerated skeleton; you have my tongue; I'm sorry if knowing my surroundings wasn't a top priority, especially when I'm standing here with the ruler of the Underworld who is both omnipotent and omniscient down here.* The words screamed through his mind like a bitter wind from a mountaintop. Mania wouldn't have liked it very much. Hopefully, she wasn't reading his mind.

Despite the anger, Vega looked around to take in the terrain…and the core of his soul (his heart of hearts) nearly stopped. The dark black sky and the icy blue land, eternally frozen; beyond that, jagged hills and a red light burning in the sky beyond them. Vega knew what was on the other side – a land of saber-sharp grass, several feet high, rain that fell from an atomic sky capable of searing your flesh; if you made it to the river, you would have to endure the indescribable stench of a millennium of festering souls, punished for their unabashed evil. One slip there and you're done, for if you so much as dip a toe into the water, you will be infected with their fermenting evil and endless agony; infested with the foul funk of their endless sentence, the rot of their spiritual disease abscessing in their core, putrid and rank, more vile and disgusting than any abominations of the Earth. Make it past the river and the land only gets worse – monstrous mountains with mouths that eat spirits, spiked canyons that impale people and slowly tear their bodies apart, quicksand that constantly heals anyone that sinks into them, keeping them alive but trapped in an eternity of smothering. It's called Hell's Prairie and the horrors are endless.

He looked at Mania. His eyes said enough so she could understand.

You're punishing me for something. What is it?

Mania smirked. "Got your attention now, do I?"

Vega held out his arms and shrugged.

203

"I'm so glad you asked. You see, I need your skills to cross the prairie to the west. Now don't worry, that's the shortest trek through the land, and you won't have to cross the river, just the Frozen Wasteland, the Plains of Pain, the City of Temples, and the Cactus Field."

Vega flashed Mania a smart-aleck look with a thumbs up.

"Yeah, I know. Once you reach the crest in the dunes – don't worry, these are not the same as the Highway of Dunes or the Dunes of the Dead. These are just a simple scattering of average-sized dunes approaching the end of Hell's Prairie. Once you have crested them, you will see A Town in Shadow – that's its actual name – and in that town will be the bar. The bartender has something that belongs to me and I need you to get it back. Once you bring that to me, I'll return your tongue and send you back to the Overworld."

Vega shrugged again and brought his hands up in a sign of confusion. He then pointed to Mania and then in the direction she had indicated he would need to travel.

"I assume you're asking why I can't do it, since I rule this world and wield such power over it."

Vega nodded.

"Well, A Town in Shadow isn't actually the Underworld. It's in the Gray Area, just barely out of my jurisdiction. That's the little section of the Beyond that is sort of its own entity. You know what I mean?"

Vega rolled his eyes.

"We have rules you know."

Vega felt around for his belt, hoping his pistols hadn't been taken. To his relief, they were still there: two long-nosed, twelve-shot, 1930 Eastwood Pale Riders, the best handguns that existed before the Turning of the World. They were his pride and joy ever since he took them off a bounty hunter he was hired to hunt down. The bounty he'd collected was hefty, as the man was one of the most dangerous hunters in the land. But the Eastwoods were worth more. You could set them to fire anywhere from one to twelve bullets at once, and the velocity in them was so powerful they could send a shell twice as far and three times as fast as even the J. Wayne Cannon Blaster made at the turn of Century 7A. Those beauties went unmatched for a long time, until Century 7V when the Eastwoods were made.

7V, Vega thought. *God have mercy. I should have been dead before 7W. Like real dead. Now, here it is, what? What century was it when the world turned? I think it was...*

"Vega, you better get going if you want to make it back to the world of the living. Your Eastwoods are loaded. You have more ammo in your pouch."

His trusty pouch still hung at his hip. It was a tough pouch, Bulltaur hide tied together with the shed skin of a Rock Snake. It was a weapon in itself, but it held everything he needed: his Cup of Life, his Dragurian dagger, his Plague razor, his bottle of Blood Kiss, a South Cemetery reflector to ward off the creepy creatures of the Vampyrian Valley...and the Amulet – the one to call on Mania.

She gave that to him so long ago. He remembered the day well. They had just finished a raid on the Dragon Spine Mountains where she absorbed the fire of a Black Sire, the daddy of all dragons, to save his life. They stood atop the mountain, with the smoke rising up from the opening in the mountaintop. The white mist danced around her face as he looked up at her. The wind from the east blew in, making her look like a radiant fire prepared to consume the world. The sun was setting, shining upon her, enriching her skin. Maybe it was her skin enriching the light of the sun. She smiled, handed him the Amulet, and said, "When you need me, hold it in your palm, and whisper my name."

So long ago – things had changed. Now, he was a miserable immortal and she was, well, the same. Only she had to protect his immortality from the number of supernatural forces that wanted him dead for good.

"Off you go, Vega. Time's wasting."

Mania waved him off. Vega shook his head and started walking.

Watching him walk into one of the most dangerous parts of the Beyond, Mania had to smile. If there was a human man capable of completing this quest, it was Vega. He might have a mouth on him, and a pretty lousy attitude sometimes, but he had skills and powers beyond the reckoning of mortals, and that's why she could never let him go.

Vega pulled his heavy black duster around him to keep off the cold. He was almost to the edge of the Frozen Wasteland. Luckily, he had managed to pass through unseen by any Ice Giants or Snow Gnomes.

Ice Giants were big lumbering oafs who lacked coordination and grace. They were hard to vanquish, but Vega knew he could get by them without much problem. But those goddamn Snow Gnomes were peskier than a fly stuck to an ear drum. They were only about three feet tall, but they were strong as hell and could run fast and jump high, and they could throw snowballs through an igloo. And they often did. The most annoying among them would gather together and throw snowballs at igloos scattered throughout the Frozen Wasteland until they collapsed. It was asinine behavior, but that was the point of existence for those frozen dingleberries.

After passing through the Frozen Wasteland, Vega came out onto the Sunlit Road, which was constantly lit by the Great Ball of Fire beyond the hills. It might sound good, but it isn't. The Sunlit Road cut right through the Plains of Pain, which are just as pleasant as they sound. This meant that the constant light revealed any traveler to the various beasts and torturers that lived in the land.

On his way through, a few people and creatures eyeballed him from the shadows, but none approached. The air was thick with the smell of blood and decay, and the sounds of screaming, wailing, and crying in pain. The Plains of Pain were notorious to those who have traveled the Beyond as a place to avoid at all costs, because any souls pulled from the road would live in unimaginable torment for as long as they were there. It's been said that even the Fallen One stays away from there. But Vega found that hard to believe. The Fallen One ruled over Hell and Vega had glimpsed that place before and it was like the Plains of Pain times ten. He imagined some bigshot in the Plains invented that rumor to sound important.

Vega continued along the Sunlit Road for many miles, seeing creatures and hearing wails, but never having to defend against attacks. Sometimes Vega forgot how imposing he was, especially after standing in Mania's massive shadow. He was bigger than other men. Some folks used to mistake him for a Wood Beast or a Forest Walker – primitive ape-like creatures man spent centuries searching for but failed; finally, at the Turning of the World, they emerged from hiding to reclaim their lands. They were ultimately peaceful, but they did not like to be bothered. They didn't appreciate gawkers and trespassers. Vega, with his beard, bushy hair, and immense size, did actually resemble one of them at a distance. Many creatures would just as soon dodge Vega's path than cross it. No denizens of the Plains were huge monsters, just mutated creatures and foul, human ogres nobody wanted. It was not likely Vega had a match in the Plains, but any man would go down to the right numbers.

In the distance, Vega spied the edge of the "sunlight," and knew he was on the verge of crossing into the City of Temples – not a wretched place, but not inviting. One might be surprised at how unpleasant many souls were in the Beyond.

Many of the temples harbored tribes content just to exist and carry out their daily routines. Though time did not flow in the Beyond the same way it did aboveground, there was no rising and falling of the sun, just places where the light from the Great Balls of Fire reached and where they did not. As long as he avoided the Outcasts and the Fire Chasers, he should be fine. The Outcasts were cannibals and the Fire Chasers were pyromaniacs who loved to burn people alive in the name of some weird god Vega had never heard of before learning about them.

With a hand on one of his Eastwoods and his eyes to the distant temples, Vega stepped off the Sunlit Road and entered the darkness that preceded the city. He estimated an hour's walk before he arrived. The good thing about being dead is your body has more endurance. You still have a body, and though it's identical in every aspect, it's different than the flesh of the Earth. Vega wasn't sure what exactly the spiritual body was comprised of, but he knew it was tougher than the living. You still felt pain and other sensations but you could move longer, spend more energy. You didn't need to rest as much. Sustenance was still necessary, only not as often, though many ate and drank regularly for enjoyment, and also for the nostaligia of it. An hour's walk would be easy.

And it was. He soon crossed the shadows into the dimly lit City of Temples. Around most temples were large bowls glowing with fire; strung along the sides of most temples were bright red lanterns. This was all the light the city ever had, making it susceptible to unsavory souls, which is why many inhabitants kept to themselves. Most of the bad folk here were drifters, not citizens, other than the aforementioned tribes to watch out for.

Strange noises pervaded the shadowy corners of the city. Vega saw shapes moving in the dim glows of the nearby fire bowls. Many of them were moving beyond the reach of the light. He put both hands on his Eastwoods, ready to draw and fire. Eyes watched him from the dark crannies as he passed by. Soft swishes in the chubby grass put his senses on high alert. He wouldn't turn, however. That was often a trick. You turn to see what's creeping up on you and you get blindsided by the coward at your side.

Vega's keen eyes allowed him to spot a small gathering a few yards ahead of him. They had not been there a few seconds before. He was walking into an ambush. Without a second of hesitation he ducked into the shade and made for the nearest temple. Once he disappeared behind it, he backtracked to a temple he'd already passed, circled around it, and looked out to where the group of shadows had been. They were not there, but no doubt someone was still watching.

Vega went to the other side of the temple wall where he currently stood and peeked around to see if he saw any of the sneaks coming through the darkness. None. They were hiding too. Vega then cut directly across the open passage between the temples and stopped behind the next one and waited. Minutes of silence passed, stretching across the City of Temples. The pathways were empty, the temples were silent. This must have been the time most people stayed indoors or slept. Many people slept and rested because they wanted to, same as eating. The routine brought them comfort.

Soon the silence was broken by the soft rub of feet on dirt and grass, and the faint hissing of quiet breathing. Whoever was after him, they were near, and they were on the side of the temple to his right. He slid around to the left, walked the wall, and peeked around again. No one. So, he took off across the grass. There was no passage here, and so he made soft leaps as he ran, to minimize the swish of the grass.

Just as he found refuge behind another temple, something struck the rock beside him, causing a spark and metallic twang.

Spark Darts.

Nasty things, those were. You had to have precise aim and hit someone in a vital area, but if you did, the dart would light a fire inside their body. He had seen someone hit with one once. They screamed so hard that he thought their voice box would shatter. He watched the fire crack the skin, turn internal organs to jelly to fall from the man's orifices, and then come roaring through his eyes and mouth before finally erupting from his entire body. Not pretty, and not quick. You had to be a rather sick individual to use that sort of ammo – which meant he was likely dealing with Fire Chasers.

Vega's senses were keen when fight mode took control. He could now smell someone coming around the corner before him as he ran. His Eastwoods were out, aimed, and ready to let loose. When the shadow stepped into view, he plugged one shot from each gun into it – in the chest and the forehead. No matter what manner of creature this was, bullets puncturing those spots would take them down.

The shadow fell and as Vega passed, he looked down and saw it was, just as he suspected, a Fire Chaser.

Two shadows moving to his left as he ran out from behind the temple caught his attention. He turned the Eastwood in his left hand and fired twice, gunning both Chasers down. More were coming, but they were far away and he didn't want to risk wasting ammo. He had plenty, but when dealing with Fire Chasers, the seconds it took to reload an Eastwood could be the last seconds a man's heart was beating, and dying down below was some damn bad news.

Shooting while running would do no good in this fight. Vega took a short jump forward and rolled across the ground twice, then sprung into the air once he rose to his feet. As he drifted across the air, he turned to the left, took aim, and shot down the oncoming shadows.

When he hit the ground, he kept running. To his right he saw three more Chasers. They were silly looking fellows, with their long gangly frames, wild orange hair, and stupid grass pants. It was his opinion they should consider shaving their heads because that bright hair made them an easy target when they were in light. And he proved this theory after leaping on a temple wall and using his left foot to ricochet himself away from a spark dart. After pivoting, he turned and fired at the bouncy tangle of orange coming his way, and shattered the skull

211

beneath it. He fired at another before hitting the ground and chuckled as it flipped backwards into the air.

He ran a little further, then hearing someone coming up behind him, he turned quickly and fired, blowing the Chaser's left arm to pieces. As soon as he turned, he saw another come around the corner of the temple and almost met him face to face. But Vega quickly rolled to dodge the Chaser's swinging arm. When Vega was back on his feet, he shot the enemy square in the face.

Before he knew it, two more Chasers were upon him on each side. They were too close to shoot, so he quickly went into defense mode. He swung to the right, swung to the left – connected both shots and sent the men backwards. That wasn't enough to stop them, and he knew it wouldn't be. He twirled his guns back into position and shot them both – one in the eye and the other in the asshole as he was bent over, struggling to his feet. Vega smirked when he saw the explosion at the top of the Chaser's head. These Eastwoods sure could punch.

There was just one more remaining, and he was out in the open, not far away. Instead of using anymore bullets, Vega put the guns away and ran as hard as he could straight towards the Chaser. Before the Chaser could raise his blowgun, Vega ran right over him, knocking him to the ground and trampling him with his boots. As he passed over the Chaser, he heard and felt the bones in his neck and face snap and break.

Vega then ran on through the City of Temples.

Vega stood before the Cactus Field looking at the tall prickly plants pressed so close together. These cacti had spines like spears. Vega knew there was an open path leading through this maze – a path to keep you from getting impaled. But he had to work out in his mind which way to go.

He walked along the edge of the vast field back and forth three times and saw six openings. He eliminated the two closest to each side because he knew those would be too easy and would likely cut off just before leaving the field. He stood gazing ahead, creating mazes in his mind. Eventually, he eliminated one of two openings that were very close together. He could tell by following the cactus tops that the two paths entwined a little ways in. He deduced that there's no way one of them was the correct path, because if one was the way out that would mean two openings led out, and there's no way the devious architect behind this field would allow that. That left three possibilities.

He decided to examine each entrance. The first one, furthest to the left of the remaining three, was a dark tangle of very old cacti. They had grown oddly, much different than Overworld cacti. The tunnel looked to stretch on forever into the mouth of darkness. The air was stale and there was no sound of anything living – which he knew there were certain assortments of peculiar beasts that lived among the cacti. He decided this was a dead path and moved on.

The next entrance was the centermost of all the entrances. It lay dead smack in the middle of the field. From his first glance, Vega thought this was the most likely because many would believe it to be the least likely for being too obvious. He saw droppings and smelled life in this tunnel, and felt a bit of a breeze blowing from within. He quickly ran to the next entrance to see how it looked – very much the same. Now, he was down to two and he couldn't decide which.

There's always the Amulet, a sly voice said inside his head.

The Amulet – yeah, no doubt *she* would love it if he had to call on *her* for help.

No, I can figure this out on my own.

But if you choose the wrong path…

Yeah, I know. Leave me alone, voice messenger. If I could just get higher.

Vega turned to survey the scene around him. The only things resembling trees were the damn cacti, and he sure as hell wasn't about to climb one of those. The closest temple was too far away, and he didn't want to deal with anymore Fire Chasers.

Vega searched the area for anything that might give him a higher perspective. There was nothing – no trees, no rocks, nothing.

Well, shit, he thought. *Guess there ain't but one thing I can try.*

Vega jogged to the far end of the field, back the way he had first come. He took a deep breath and did a few small jumps, lifted one leg at a time to stretch them, then readied himself.

She ain't got no say over my leaping abilities.

Vega broke into a hard run, heading straight for the field. When he was about twenty feet from the center, he ducked into a roll, then just like his maneuver against the Fire Chasers, he tumbled several times, then sprung up on his feet and blasted himself into the air. He gave the jump about thirty-percent and rose about sixty to seventy feet. This was not the course he wanted to take for a few reasons. One was it took a lot out of him to jump so high, and another was the exposure.

But the move was worth it. When his jump hit its apex, he looked out to the field and could see the exiting path. It was, as he suspected, the path cutting right through the heart of the field. The designer had done an excellent job hiding it. If not for his extraordinary vision, he would have missed it. But he got a good eyeful as he drifted through the air. Once he began to descend, he grabbed hold of his wide-brimmed, dusty dark-brown Stetson and prepared himself for the fall.

The ground came up to meet him like an anvil. Vega crumpled beneath the impact. This was the other—and main—reason he didn't want to jump. No matter how many jumps he made, the landing always left him feeling flat and shattered.

He rose and stood before the correct entrance. Nothing dangerous other than the cacti was known to roam out here in the field (and rumor did have it that some of the cacti roamed). But things changed down here all the time. So Vega pulled his Eastwoods and stepped inside.

It was dark and stuffy in the field. The path before him stretched out of sight. Not much light revealed the way. The cacti here were so tall and broad and dopey that they towered and leaned to the point where the sky above the field was almost entirely blotted out. And it wasn't like the light in the sky was very bright to begin with. This field was just low enough to catch light from the Great Ball of Fire hanging beyond the hills and mountains.

Vega walked on silently, hands still full of Eastwoods. Several quiet minutes passed and he began to relax. So far, the trek had been relatively uneventful. Even the skirmish with the Fire Chasers wasn't much. The path through the field hadn't even narrowed. For as tall and wide as he was, Vega didn't come close to touching any cacti.

This might not be as hard as I feared, he thought.

He came upon mighty spider web clinging from one side of the field to the next, connected by cacti, blocking the path. Vega stopped a few feet from it. He wasn't scared of spiders. He actually kept a few giant ones he killed as decorations near his cabin back home on the prairie. But this web was too obvious, too big, and too out of place. The spider to weave it would have had to be rather large, and there wasn't much down this path for a regular spider to live on, much less a large one. He hadn't heard, seen, nor felt one insect the whole walk. This smelled very much of a trap, but what kind? If he moved it, would the spines from the surrounding cacti shoot out and gouge him? Would some of the hanging cacti arms fall down upon him? There was only one way to find out.

Vega wrapped his duster around him and lifted the collar until it covered his entire head. The coat was durable and thick enough for his lifestyle of danger and death around every corner. He lifted the Eastwood in his left hand and shot the left side of the web, top and bottom. That side fell. He waited. Nothing happened. He then repeated the process with the other Eastwood for the right side. The web fell to the ground and still nothing happened.

Standing-stock-still he awaited his punishment for dropping the trap web. But still, nothing happened. He turned to one side and looked, then turned to the other and looked. Finally, he turned around and looked behind him, then looked up. There was nothing but cacti. He turned back, took a tentative step forward, then another. After several steps, he decided it might have just been an oddly placed web. A couple of steps later, he found out he was wrong.

A ripping and crunching sound echoed behind him. The dimness of the path got darker. He turned to see the cacti blocking the entrance, and then saw more cacti move from their spots. These cacti took to the path and began moving forward.

Oh, bullshit," Vega thought and fired at the cacti.

The bullets were good enough to obliterate half a cactus, but the half that remained would keep coming. The bottom half would walk and the top half would crawl – and he just didn't have enough bullets to shoot them all, or the time to reload the Eastwoods, because these plants were moving fast.

Vega turned and fled down the path, which was a straight run most of the way. He was able to put some distance between him and the cacti, but a moment's hesitation and they could be on his heels, not only because they had speed, but also because they were everywhere and they followed him as soon as he passed them.

Well, at least the maniac who made this fucking maze gave me a chance.

Soon, Vega came to a bend in the path. From what he had seen while in the air, this turn should lead out in about a quarter mile. After completing the turn, he put on more steam, huffing and puffing as he ran. Something started hitting him in the back. The cacti were now shooting their spines. His duster, specially made by the Black Mage of the Dizzy Desert back on Earth, could fend off most things.

He hoofed it a little harder and began to see light down the path. The exit was near. He didn't know if the cacti could follow him out or not, but he'd worry about that when the time came.

Vega suddenly slammed his heels into the ground, crushing dirt beneath his feet. When he skidded to a stop, he was wobbling on the edge of a giant hole in the ground; and, by giant, it stretched ahead for about three-hundred feet.

The cacti around him, that he had just passed, jumped from their spots and came at him. The Eastwoods blazed like lightning, firing shot after shot until all cacti around him were down, and he was out of bullets.

All possibilities raced quickly through Vega's mind. Should he reload? No – there was no point. He didn't have enough bullets to take them all out, especially since it took two per cactus. He could muster the speed to jump the hole, but he would have to turn way back, and there wasn't enough space between him and the cacti anymore, and even if there was, he might jump too high and hit the cacti arms above him. He had only one real option, other than dying, and it wasn't a good one.

Vega looked behind him to see the cacti were nearly upon him. Several began shooting their massive spines. Several spears came at him at once. Vega twirled and dropped into the chasm.

He plunged quickly into darkness. He couldn't see how far down the hole went. For his purposes, the deeper it went the better. But, in case this hole was shallower than it seemed to be, he had best do what he planned to do quickly.

The cacti stopped at the edge above him. He was now off their grounds and out of range of their senses, so they returned to their stations. Vega allowed himself to fall just a bit more, then shifted his weight towards the wall. He had to time this just right, if he didn't, he could snap off his leg.

The wall drew nearer, he bent his knee. It was only a few feet away. Closer. Closer. Now within a few inches, he struck out with his feet, aiming his heels at the wall. Just a split second was all he needed; he hit the mark and flew upward. The wall on the other side was now drawing near. He leaned back, stretched out his legs, and when the wall was within reach, he bent his knees, and struck out at a slightly tilted angle and sped towards the other wall, moving slightly upward. The other wall raced towards him, and he repeated the last action, and flung himself toward the opening on the other side.

The opening was coming on quicker than he expected. Now he feared he had pushed too hard and would end up skewered by a long cactus spine hanging over the field. His coat was tough, but the velocity at which he was traveling might render that protection ineffective. He had to slow his momentum.

As he soared towards the edge of the opening, he reached up a hand. He wasn't sure what result this action might produce, but it had to be better than impalement.

Vega came to the opening, reached out and grabbed for the edge, dug his fingers deep into the soil, and was able to shift his body so that he flew sideways as opposed to upward. The end result was still unpleasant as he slammed into the ground, bounced several times, rolled, kicked up dirt around him, and came out on the other side of the Cactus Field.

He lay there for several seconds, breathing in the dank air of the Beyond.

When he moved to stand up, he was sore, aching, and pissed off, but he was in one piece and all those pieces were in place. He had lost his hat, though.

He looked around for his hat. He wasn't going to leave without it. It was only a few feet away from him, lying on the ground. Vega picked it up, adjusted it, and pulled it tight, then continued on his way.

Finally, A Town in Shadow.

Pale yellow lights shone like monster eyes from the shadows ahead. This town really was in shadow. A large plateau rose up to the town's east, blocking all light that shone from the Great Ball of Fire. This left the town perpetually dark. As Vega approached, he wondered why they didn't just build the town on the plateau. Then he thought maybe they liked the dark, and that wasn't very comforting. He'd never heard of the town before Mania mentioned it so he didn't know what kind of cliental the establishment he was looking for catered to. Considering the surroundings, he doubted it was a classy joint.

As he walked, he saw the Monster Mountains had ended in the east, and now they were falling behind him. This really was beyond the Underworld; those mountains were said to span the entire length of Mania's domain. This was brand new territory for Vega.

Vega stepped into A Town in Shadow and immediately spotted the bar. It was among the first cluster of buildings to his right. It was relatively quiet, but it didn't look classy. It was long and squat, tattered with some boarded up windows. The parking lot was gravel, so it must have been somewhere on the outskirts of Hell. Not many people were out on the streets, but this town definitely stank of shadiness. Vega didn't pull his Eastwoods yet. That would be inviting a fight. But he was sure glad he had reloaded them before he arrived.

He stepped through the swinging doors entering the bar and looked around. There were a few patrons inside

– one man tucked away in the farthest corner of the place, another man asleep at a booth, and a couple of guys at the far end of the bar. Behind the bar was a tall, slender woman with dark hair. She was tall enough to look Vega in the eye, and she did as he stood in front of her.

"Can I help you?"

Vega was about to answer when he remembered he didn't have his tongue. Boy, he was sure Mania was getting a real delight out of this. She must have been incredibly pleased with herself.

With a sigh, Vega grabbed the bartender's notepad and pen off the counter. In it he wrote *Mania sent me. She said you have something for me.*

Vega slid the note to the bartender. After reading it, she didn't have the most pleasant look on her face.

"Mania? What the hell does she want?"

Vega wrote again. *Just the item you have for me. She said it belongs to her.*

"I don't even know who you are."

Vega started to get the feeling Mania might have pulled a real good prank on him.

Vega was still holding the pen, and he felt it start to vibrate. The tip was glowing. He put it to the notepad and the pen started writing on its own.

You weren't supposed to tell her I sent you, idiot.

Vega wrote back – *Oh. How was I supposed to know?*

Just ask her for the Knot.

The words vanished, except for 'the Knot.'

Though he had no clue what it meant, he handed the note to the bartender. That's when she became furious. She slammed her hand down on the countertop, causing

221

glasses to rattle and fall off, and exclaimed, "Who are you to ask for the Knot?"

Dumbfounded as to why he had offended this woman so deeply, Vega just stared at her. She pointed to an item sitting on a shelf behind the bar. It was very similar to an Ankh with its arms facing down.

"That item is sacred!"

Of course it is. That's why Mania sent me to retrieve it. If it was a normal mission she would have called someone else.

It was abundantly clear that the bartender had no intention of giving him this sacred Knot. It was also clear to him that he had no intention of bargaining with her, and he was damn sick of waiting, walking, fighting, jumping, and this entire quest altogether. He leaped over the bar, grabbed the Knot, and leaped again and made for the exit. The bartender screamed behind him. He heard the explosion of her kicking through the bar. Strange blobby blue shapes emerged from a backroom and gave chase with the bartender leading the charge.

Vega burst through the doors and ran. The bartender and the blue blobs were not far behind him. The blobs were fast and noisy, chirping and beeping some odd sounds. The bartender sounded more like a hurricane raging in off the sea. Mania had really shoved him into the toilet bowl with this one.

"I'm gonna kill you, you son of a bitch!" the bartender yelled.

"Beep meep seep tyweep keep deep heep!" said one of the blobs.

"Chipita-tu-lu-huhuhu-do-kwe-kwe-kweeeeeeee," another one chirped.

In a few seconds, all the blobs started squawking, squeaking, beeping, and cooing until it sounded like a thousand alarm clocks all with different ringers and buzzers going off in succession before blending together.

This is the most ridiculous job I've ever had, Vega thought as the thunder of the bartender's voice rumbled in some garbled roar of noise his ears couldn't possibly decipher.

Why does she care so much about this damn thing?

The blue blobs, who didn't run so much as hop at an ungodly fast speed, were gaining ground. The bartender was pounding dirt too. Vega was finally starting to wear down. But in the distance he saw a hill. He didn't know how well these blobs could jump, but he was willing to bet not as well as he could. The bartender he wasn't sure about. She seemed capable of a lot of physical feats. If she couldn't jump the hill, Vega imagined she would just punch her way through it and meet him on the other side.

Okay blobs, let's see what you got.

Vega breathed deep and started running as hard as he could. He could hear the sounds of his pursuers beginning to fade behind him. The odd ensemble of sounds from the blue amorphous masses picked up urgency – almost a panic. The bartender was growling for Vega to give back the Knot. Something about this item really meant a lot to her. What about it could make Mania desire it so much?

Probably because it means so much to them and she likes ruining people's lives... and their deaths.

Vega was rapidly closing the distance between him and the hill. He looked behind him and saw the blobs had fallen back, but the bartender was in hot pursuit. She wasn't too far behind.

Facing back to the hill, Vega readied himself for the jump. He was going to have to give this one a little more effort than the previous two. He ducked his head, ran a few meters, and then jumped. He rose about two-hundred feet into the air, sailing quickly towards the hill. As he was coming down, he estimated that his leap would bring him just past the edge of the hilltop. He was right on target. He landed just past the cliff, rolled, and started running.

The blobs had stopped, but the bartender made a jump for it. She sailed about a hundred-and-fifty feet into the air, but she didn't have the range. She smacked into the hillside and rolled to the ground. The blobs started *yak-yak-yaking* and *chit-chit-chittering*. She stood up, turned to them and yelled, "Shut up!" and they went silent.

She then called as loud as she could to Vega. "You will not escape the wrath of the Goddess. The Knot of Isis is sacred. That one was made with her blessing, and she will *not* be happy you have stolen it. You can run as fast as you want, jump as high as you can, but she will catch you. She will hunt you down and destroy you, outlaw!"

When the bartender said "Knot of Isis", Vega skidded to a halt. With his eyes wide, he looked at the Knot and thought, *Isis? Oh hell, Mania. What have you done?*

"Do you hear me, bandit?" she yelled. "You tell Mania she will have to answer to the Great Goddess for this. She can't hide from Her in the Underworld. You will both pay dearly!"

When Vega did not answer, the bartender turned and whistled. The shrill sound rang through the air and traveled for miles. In the distance, an animal noise, like a vicious pack of wolves, could be heard. Coming from A Town in Shadow was a streak of churned up dust making clouds in the air. The growling and barking continued.

Oh, what now?

Whatever it was, it was fast – a lot faster than Vega. It was already more than halfway to the hill. The bartender looked up, unable to see Vega, but smiled because she knew he would not get away now. She would reclaim the Knot and let Isis know, and she would be rewarded for a job well done.

The streak was now approaching the blobs. The bartender yelled, "Jump, Booboo!"

The creature kicking up dust leaped into the air, catching more air than even Vega could. It must have been a good five-hundred feet in the air, easily, and it fell to Earth like a tiny comet.

And tiny was the word for it. When the dust cleared and the creature hit the hilltop, Vega almost laughed as he stared at a white toy poodle that couldn't have been anymore than ten pounds. It began to growl. Vega held up a hand.

Nice poochie. Please don't hurt me. But the smirk on Vega's face was quickly wiped away when the dog barked so loud and hard that it blasted Vega backwards about forty feet. And before he could even rise, the poodle was on him – kicking, pawing, jumping, twisting, and biting. Vega couldn't keep up. The dog was much too fast for him. It looked like nothing more than a white growling blur pummeling him with a mallet. Vega kept falling back, to his knees, back on his elbows, on all fours, on his back. This Booboo creature was too much. Vega rose to run away, but Booboo snatched the cuff of his pants between her teeth and yanked him back and up into the air. She swung him in a circle and tossed him towards the western edge of the hill.

Vega hit the dirt and slid to a stop. He looked at the oncoming train that was Booboo. She was trotting, bopping along like the harmless lap-pet of an elderly socialite. Her ears flopped, her tongue lolled from her mouth, and her dark brown eyes looked like she was about to lick Vega to death. But he knew better. He did not want to fight anymore. This snack-size hellion was whipping him all over the hilltop. He knew when he'd been beaten.

God, I hate myself for having to do this.

Vega reached into his pocket and grabbed the Amulet, held it up, and thought, *Mania, bring me back.*

The Amulet began to glow with alternating colors, spanning the spectrum. Light then shot out in all directions and began to dance around the air. The glowing force rose high above Vega, expanded, and then sailed down towards him. Booboo leaped for her target and landed on his chest, knocking the air out of him, just as the light came down around them.

They were swallowed and taken back to the Underworld in a polychromatic, kaleidoscopic tunnel that hurled them through time and space. Booboo was still punching at Vega, despite the velocity at which they travelled. She was knocking him around in circles and he wished to God or anyone that this beating would end. This was the most embarrassing whipping he'd ever taken.

Come on! My boots are bigger than you! his mind screamed.

Soon, the tunnel opened up ahead of them, and they were unceremoniously dumped out right at Mania's feet.

"Booboo!" she exclaimed when she saw the toy poodle. Booboo looked up and barked, wiggling her butt and wagging her tail before rising up on her back legs and waving her front paws around for Mania to pick her up.

When Mania obliged, Booboo began licking her face.

"Oh, I missed you Booboo."

Once the reunion was complete, she set Booboo down and looked at Vega. "You got the Knot, I see."

He nodded.

"Okay, here's your tongue." She tossed it at him and he reached for it. As soon as it landed in his hand, it went right back into his mouth.

He coughed and then said, "You sent me to get a dog *and* to steal from Isis?"

"No, I sent you to get the Knot, knowing that you'd bring back Booboo. Isis stole her from me a long time ago and I've been waiting for the opportunity to retrieve her."

"So this item really does belong to Isis?"

Mania nodded her head.

"*The* Isis? The Almighty Goddess of the Universe, Goddess of the sky and magic and life and death, Isis?"

"There's only one Isis, Vega."

"Are you out of your mind?"

Reaching down to pet Booboo, she smiled and said, "My name *is* Mania."

"You know, you've helped me make a lot of enemies during our time together, Mania, but this has to be the worst thing you've ever done to me."

She finished petting the dog and stood up. "Oh, stop complaining. The Knot of Isis will protect you from death, and we both know you can't afford to die many more times."

Vega raised the Knot and looked at it. "You mean I'm invincible?"

"Not invincible, but pretty close. You'll be really hard to kill. And the bonus about that is if you do die, you'll be able to bypass the Gates of Anubis because you're carrying a divine artifact of life and death. Also, if you go to any burial grounds, you'll be able to open a portal to my realm, and I know how much you love to visit me."

"But won't Isis come after me? I can't fight Isis, Mania. You know that."

"Relax. You know how many of those things exist? *She* probably doesn't even know how many there are. She won't even notice it's gone."

"I don't know. That bartender I took it from seemed pretty mad."

"Oh, they're all like that. All of her guards think their jobs are so much more than what they are. They think guarding a Knot or some other Isis item is a big deal. Isis doesn't even appoint them. She doesn't even know who that bartender is, probably. She probably won't even notice Booboo is gone. Stop worrying." Mania then flashed a sly smile and said, "Besides, now you need me more than ever."

Vega wrinkled his brow. "What do you mean?"

Mania shrugged, shifted her weight to one side, and put a hand on her right hip and said, "If Isis *does* find out you took the Knot, she *will* be pissed, and she *will* come looking for you, and *you* can't fight her. You just admitted to that. So you'll need me."

Vega became angry. "Why, you sneaky, dirty, underhanded, conniving little…"

With a smile on her face, Mania flipped her hand at Vega and said, "Be gone."

Vega was thrust backwards into the passage between the worlds, past all the stars, the prisms, the various shining lights, the Unblinking Eye, Earth's core, and dropped into complete darkness.

He lay there, smelling wet sand and burned wood. The smell of alcohol got into his nose too, but he couldn't hear or open his eyes, so he lay there in blind silence.

A few seconds later, a voice whispered...

"Rise, Vega."

THE MAN FROM TURKEY CREEK CANYON
by Lee Clark Zumpe

The Bowery, New York City – 1880

Two grim gentlemen lingered like impregnable shadows in a secluded alcove within the Tub of Blood saloon on 45th Street. A cloudy gray haze hung over the table, its borders expanding, fed by a steady stream of smoke from a slow-burning Turkish tobacco cigarette nestled between one of the men's fingers. Its misty swirls and nebulous folds conjured up the ghosts of dead galaxies.

"I counted 24 souls." The two prospectors scratched marks upon tablets, recording their return on this lucrative concern.

"A profitable return, then. You should be pleased."

Outside, as the first light of dawn grudgingly infiltrated the street of forgotten men, Skinner Meehan, Dutch Hen, Jack Cody and Sweeney the Boy examined the last victim of the night's massacre. The gruesome death of Hop-along Peter brought to mind the discovery of Brian Boru's corpse years earlier, his body half-devoured by dock rats where he fell outside the tavern in a drunken daze. In the Bowery, of course, death had become a pastime, a spectator sport. Should authorities bother to investigate, they would surmise the carnage had stemmed from some gang-related dispute.

"I believe it is your turn."

Long Home, Arizona Territory – 1884

"What brings you to Long Home, my lad?" A burly Irishman, Wasatch Wickham stood behind the bar scanning the Golgotha Saloon for troublemakers and outlaws. Aside from some rowdy cattlemen congregating around the faro table, the evening seemed to be mercifully calm and quiet.

"Passing through is all." Johnny dithered over his fourth mug of lukewarm coffee, teasing images from the shadows swirling through is aching head. A year of perpetual intoxication had disengaged him from all recent memory. He knew a string of countless sins and degenerate indiscretions lay smothered by his callous conscience. He knew his indulgences had earned him implacable enemies and malevolent allies. He could not say with any certainty, however, what road led him to this particular scab of a town. "Just passing through."

"Ay, no one ever stays 'ere long, o'course." Wickham leaned forward, rested his elbow on the mahogany. "Say, lad – seems the fella in the carner knows yeer face. Might oughta go have a weerd w'him, ay?"

The tall, scruffy veteran of the Mason County War looked over his shoulder. A lone figure sat at a table in the far corner of the saloon, smoke and darkness conspiring to cloak his face. Only his eyes pierced the hazy gloom, reflecting the dull red glow of his cigar.

Johnny expelled a long-drawn-out sigh, as if his lungs alone could exorcise all the demons that dwelled in his otherwise vacant and soulless shell. Evil tainted a man, made him conspicuous in a crowded room. Like an ebon beacon it stressed every iniquitous fiber, emphasized every delinquent trait. A lifetime of wantonness had left him branded so that no matter how obscure and remote the venue, someone always recognized him.

No matter where he stopped for a moment's peace, someone always lurked in the shadows, gunning for him.

Aggravated by the disturbance, Johnny gulped down the last of his coffee, paid off his tab and shambled across the floor of the saloon toward the solitary gentleman waiting patiently at the secluded table. Drawing closer, he watched for the glint of a pistol ably extricated from its holster, watched for the telltale twitch of a muscle or tremor in the man's placid expression.

"Welcome to Long Home," he said, warily tipping the brow of his black bowler cap. His demeanor and manner of dress distinguished him as one not long removed from more lush and lavish surroundings. "Take a seat. If my intentions were hostile, your brains would be scattered all over the saloon by now." Johnny, disarmed by his confidence, slid into a chair facing the man. Dark-complexioned, willowy and shamelessly wicked, he spoke with an unidentifiable accent that suggested close ties to the Old World. "Pleasure to meet you, sir. I've been admiring your work for several years."

"And you are…"

"The exchange of monikers upon such a fortuitous encounter seems appropriate, doesn't it?" He crushed the remnants of his cigar on the tabletop leaving a streak of ashes quivering in the draught. "Call me Ebenholz."

"I'm Johnny. Johnny, uh," Johnny rubbed his eyes as he struggled to penetrate the miasma blurring his mind, to relocate the scattered pieces of his miserable existence blotted out by self-abuse in bars and brothels and opium dens throughout the territory.

"Don't trouble yourself, Johnny. It's your skills that I wish to employ, not your memory." Ebenholz flashed a sinister smile so beguiling Johnny shrugged off all of his apprehension and frustration. Staring into his eyes was like looking into a mirror. Johnny recognized in Ebenholz the same seething misanthropy and universal disgust that had raged within him since birth. "I presume at this stage of your career you would not take offense to being considered as a hired gun, Johnny."

"No sir."

"Excellent. I have a proposition for you then." At that moment, a sizeable group of cowboys wandered off the dusty streets of Long Home, channeled like livestock through the swinging double doors. Dazed and bloodied from a skirmish that had clearly not turned in their favor, they shuffled toward the bar where Wasatch Wickham welcomed them with whisky and an animated Irish salutation. Ebenholz evaluated the newcomers curiously, weighing their potential worth against the promise of his present company. Still seemingly satisfied with his choice, he plucked a scroll from his vest pocket, pushed it across the table toward Johnny. "Are you familiar with the stage stop at Dos Cabezas?"

"Yes sir."

"In two days time, a wagon train will pass through there. Their destination is of no importance." Ebenholz cradled a wine glass in his palm. He sipped some

unnamed liqueur, some dark and syrupy fount of spirits
that hemmed in a multitude of minuscule flecks
gleaming like the shimmering stars of twilight. "Led by
a man named Bowen, the caravan seeks to settle in these
parts, to establish a utopian commune where they may
worship as they please. I need you to make certain that
their journey continues uninterrupted."

"They need a gunslinger, someone to keep the
outlaws from attacking them and the Indians from
raiding the wagon train."

"Yes, but," Ebenholz said cautiously, concerned that
revealing too much information might make Johnny
suspicious. "More specifically, I am quite convinced a
small band of Chiricahuas will attempt to slaughter the
settlers shortly after they leave Dos Cabezas. I need you
to arrive at their encampment and see to it that the
massacre I have foreseen does not take place. You'll find
a map on that scroll that will take you to them."

"You want me to take on a Chiricahua war party
alone?" Johnny leaned back in his chair, the corner of his
lip curling in a scornful smirk. "I'm flattered you hold
my abilities in such high esteem, Mr. Eben...whatever
you said your name was...but it sounds to me like you
need the services of the United States Cavalry."

"You discredit yourself. I have faith in your skill and
in your will." Ebenholz's eyes narrowed, his head tilted
as he leaned forward. "You neither surrender to shame
nor wallow in remorse. You are devoid of guilt, beyond
self-reproach. Moreover," he smiled, leaning back in his
chair, "you have been reinforced by circumstances
beyond your reckoning – conditions which have
bestowed upon you a degree of imperviousness."

"I don't follow..."

"You should open your eyes, Johnny." Ebenholz chuckled, pushed himself away from the table and stood. He tossed a few dozen bullets on the table, each one forged from silver and branded with unrecognizable symbols that held no meaning for the outlaw. The clatter turned a few heads, drawing attention Johnny despised. Even Wasatch Wickham glanced, stopped dead in the middle of spinning a yarn for his newest patrons, and raised a thick, bushy eyebrow at the transaction taking place. "Use these. Walk like a shadow amongst them in the moments before sunrise – they will not see you. Kill them all."

"And then? What about my money?"

"You'll be amply rewarded after you complete the job." Ebenholz patted a breast pocket so that the clang of gold coins chimed like an unspoken source of inspiration. "Meet me in Turkey Creek Canyon in four nights." He started to walk away, sidestepping the beaten and bloodied cowboys. More than a few looked like they were ready for the grave. "You do remember Turkey Creek Canyon, don't you?"

Johnny knew the place well enough, though he could not recall what incident inexorably tied him to it.

Sulphur Springs Valley, Arizona Territory – 1884

Not even the long ride to Dos Cabezas could clear the cobwebs from Johnny's mind. He remembered only faint fragments from his life prior to arriving in Long Home, glimpses of gunfights and brawls and a series of pointless scuffles and scraps culminating in a handful of more recent skirmishes tied to some bitter vendetta.

While the faces of those lives he had snuffed out glared at him from the pit of his emasculated conscience, the particulars of life continued to elude him. Nevertheless, he doubted neither his proficiency with a pistol nor his capacity to kill without clemency – the blood in his veins ran like spring-thawed ice.

Along the way, he had watered his horse in Tombstone early in the morning where he helped himself to a shot of whisky at the Oriental Saloon when the acting barkeep failed to acknowledge his requests. Before leaving, he had paused along the mining town's main thoroughfare as a procession of local ranchers solemnly paraded toward the graveyard with some slain soul whose speed apparently did not match his boasts.

Johnny had similarly obliged more than a few such individuals in his day.

"Takes more than speed," a bystander whispered, as if reading Johnny's thoughts. The man's pallid face rippled with twitching muscles as if something swarmed beneath his ashen flesh. "Guts. A belly full of hate. That's what you need."

"Billy?" For a moment, Johnny thought the man standing next to him looked like Billy Clanton. "That you Billy," he asked, stumbling over the words even as he recalled the day he watched Billy and two McLaury brothers laid to rest after a fierce shootout.

The stranger turned and shambled down the street, silently following the mourners toward the all-too-familiar burial ground.

In Dos Cabezas, Johnny watched as the wagon train Ebenholz spoke of arrived. The declaration "devoted parishioners of the Starry Wisdom Church" had been painted in bold black letters on the side of the leading prairie schooner. The group's leader approached a town official, negotiated for various supplies and comfortable lodging for the evening for his womenfolk and declined invitations of liquor and gambling for the gentlemen in his congregation.

"We seek only shelter and food," the preacher said, his tone somber and stern. "We will continue on in the morning." His flock seemed a peculiar sort, not fit for the hardships of life in the Arizona territory. Dismal and tightlipped, they filed into a nearby inn without speaking a word, without lifting their gaze from the ground beneath their feet and without reacting to the vulgar comments of a few inebriated cowboys.

Johnny pilfered a bottle of gin from a negligent bartender and spent the day expunging his recent attempt at sobriety. If abstinence could offer no reprieve from his lapse of memory, alcohol could at least temper his frustration. Hours crept by as barroom conversations blossomed and withered all around him. In the evening, a few games of chance ended in heated contention, resolved by the smoking double barrels of some shootist's shotgun or the bloodied dagger of a devious delinquent.

The wounded slithered off to find medical assistance or to cower behind some apathetic officer of justice. The dead found themselves hastily divested of all worldly possessions by pitiless scavengers while waiting for their bodies to be hauled away by indifferent custodians assigned to aid the resident undertaker. Their souls, however, recoiled into adjacent shadows, confused but compelled to linger just beyond the border where ghosts dwell in residual nightmares.

Johnny saw them, skirting the edges of the establishment, numbering in the hundreds. He stood on the periphery, residing in neither world but still a part of both. He understood, finally, what Ebenholz meant about walking like a shadow. He had opened his eyes.

When the lights finally dimmed, Johnny headed out of town. Above Sulphur Springs Valley, the stars stretched from one horizon to the other like shimmering maggot holes in the dusky hide of night. The corpse of the universe rotted in its cosmic tomb as carrion feeders digested the putrefying residue of extinct civilizations.

The Chiricahua encampment sat along the edge of a creek the wagon train would ford in the morning on its westward trek. Johnny approached the tee-pee closest to the brook instinctively, using the sound of flowing water to mask his approach. An Apache knelt beneath the moonlight, washing his face and hands. Watching him, Johnny wondered how many of his friends and family had been slaughtered by nefarious frontiersmen, driven from the lands of their ancestors or afflicted with diseases introduced by settlers and traders.

Their refusal to capitulate when faced with overwhelming defeat made them admirable in Johnny's eyes. Had he been a sympathetic man, he might have forgotten about the task at hand. Compassion, though, had never eclipsed the dark engines that drove him to kill.

The Chiricahua suddenly turned, looked straight at Johnny and tensed. Johnny froze. Though the fading night revealed nothing, the Apache could not ignore his instincts.

Before he could issue a warning, Johnny silenced him with a single shot from his Colt Peacemaker. The blast echoed across the valley as the first streaks of dawn illuminated the eastern sky. Johnny wheeled about, a sudden wave of invincibility imparting a spitefulness and thirst for blood more consuming than anything he had previously experienced. Prepared to gun down the rest of the war party, Johnny faced an unbearable revelation. Waiting for the action, he heard only the startled screams of women and children woken by the shooting.

Slowly, cautiously, they scrambled out into the subtle radiance of dawn, anxiously scanning the landscape. Finding no trace of the killer, they fell to the ground near the dead man's side, tears streaming. Their screams grated Johnny's conscience, evoking the screams of widows he had mocked. Their tears drowned out his determination, washing away the barriers stifling his memory. Their grief inspired in him an unfamiliar sense of responsibility, filling him with insufferable shame.

Ebenholz lied. These Chiricahua had no intention of raiding the wagon train.

Johnny holstered his six-gun, refusing to complete the job.

Before the sun emerged from its hibernation, Johnny slipped into the shadows.

Turkey Creek Canyon, Arizona Territory – 1884

Ebenholz shook his head in disgust. His brother, Teufel, would surely ridicule him over this defeat. Johnny's poorly-timed epiphany had left him shy of his quota.

"A pity." Always arriving at the most inopportune moments, Teufel emerged from the compounding dusk, flicking stray stardust off of his cloak. The two men faced each other towering over the stone-covered grave of Johnny Ringo. "Occasionally, even the wickedest soul can turn on you."

"These things happen." Ebenholz frowned. "Redemption is a pesky bane to our stake, is it not?"

"Quite." Surprisingly, Teufel did not dwell on the unfortunate turn of events. "I'm sure your next choice will be better suited. Perhaps one of your parishioners would make a viable contender; unless you're enjoying all that devotion and ritual worship."

"No. Not yet. I'll nurture those seeds for a future harvest."

"Have it your way," Teufel said, kicking Johnny's tombstone. "Just remember: I'm currently ahead by 23 corpses. Choose your next player wisely."

Whitechapel, London – 1888

Ebenholz watched as the man inspected the surgical instruments with an intuitive veneration that bordered on obsession. Already, dark designs had begun taking shape in his mind – horrible, wicked and merciless undertakings that would leave scars in history. With the stealth of a shadow he could go about his work, a master of his craft commissioned into service by a kindred spirit.

"Kill them all," Ebenholz whispered.

ONE WAY OUT
by Bryan Dyke

A drip sounded under the washed-out tone of music. A fly buzzed nearby. A nearly naked man, gagged and blood-soaked, clad in only his boots and tattered jeans, groaned as he listened to the slow patter of slimy water upon the filthy floor, followed by a softer tap of his own blood.

The man known as the Ranger stirred and saw the first gloomy light of the cursed world once more.

He squirmed in the chair as the fog of reality clarified; he was within a room, deep underground. He shifted his body and felt the pain all over. One of his eyes cracked open a little further to see more of the hypnotic light. Then the fuzzy sound of music gained volume.

He tasted the salt and brine of his own blood. He heard his heart pumping that blood. He heard too, the crackly pops of his lungs as they struggled to breathe in and out; the Ranger gave a muffled half-cough through the gag and dry heaved at the end. His abdomen spasmed in a million sobering nerve ends.

The pain brought him from the stupor quick enough. He had napped during the break in the torture session, but now he knew his captors were ready to further plague him. He had lulled into some paltry state of sleep, though not dreaming...no never dreaming...for his

241

dreams were long gone, taken from him, like everything else. Now, only the nightmares of the real world remained. That was enough. Despite the dire nature of his current predicament, with the remainder of his life in question, he still had a mission to complete.

The reconnaissance of the Cult of the Sleeper's enclave-citadel had been a failure; the Ranger had a spotty memory of his capture and the battle in the boggy trenches around the facility. He remembered too, that several of his comrades were already dead. Yet how he had been taken alive, or who was even still alive, was beyond his ability to recount.

Pain and raw anguish swelled and burned once more in his head and bones. It reminded him of the most important part of his plight; the murderous Cult of the Sleeper had finally caught him. Now he was a dead man sitting in a torture chair pending the settlement of old accounts.

But he was not dead yet.

The Ranger choked again on the gag. As anthem to the madness, the washed-out music fully formed in his ear; it was a long, meandering riff of an old Allman Brother's song. For a moment, he gave a mad grin. Even in hell, it was nice to be reminded of the old world.

It didn't take him long to feel his hands tied to his back with barbed wire, routed through the metal lattice of the seat back, but his feet, there was a give to the knots he had rubbed, this too made him smile.

The room was nearly bare; stained everywhere with blood and brown streaks, the walls lined with metal hooks sharpened down to horrific bent blades. God only knew what had gone on in here over the years, but the Ranger figured that it was probably a lot like what was unfolding now.

His body was split open in a half dozen open wounds, most of which were minor, but painful, festering, and messy. Fresh cigarette burns dotted his chest and stomach. Three of his ribs were broken and he felt a stiletto stab into him with each choppy breath. Another of his eyes was nearly swollen shut and his nose was broken...again. But there were many other scars as well, old wounds and gouges all across the exposed flesh.

On a small table at the back of the room he saw the silvery finish of his revolver, likewise his long-bow and quiver with a half dozen arrows. His dirty black balaclava, blood-stained was there, along with his hatchet and clothes. All of it was far enough to be hopelessly out of reach. Still, the man in the torture seat never placed any faith in a feeble thing like hope. He had seen his own blood before, for the age-old scars over his muscled body were not earned waiting for alms. To range and come back again, this was his way...and, as it was, he had left blood on the trail.

There were other items on the table as well: a rusty sledge, a pair of pliers, a ball-peen hammer, knives, picks, razors, and piles of gory rags. The tile floor was painted into a ritual set; a pentagram and other angular shapes that the Ranger knew were magical binding glyphs, the sick and misguided ruminations of his lunatic captors.

If it were not for the deep pain all over his body, he would have laughed at the sloppy attempt at magic and sorcery; as if he, of all people, was some summoned demon caught in a rite of black magic. *They are going to take your soul*...he told himself, now even with the pain he managed a chuckle that became a hacking choke.

A torrid scream sounded over the music in the next room, a horrible death shriek, followed by a quivering gurgle. The Ranger figured it was Holcomb, one of his partners in the ill-met reconnoiter. Time was running out, for murder was an obsession of the accursed cult of maniacs who held them.

Only a few candles and a flickering wall-mounted light illuminated the chamber. The back wall, near the lone door, was painted with the same litany of characters, pictograms, and hieroglyphs. Most were written in blood, or a brown substance he assumed was human excrement.

The music carried on with Greg Allman's voice, and the Ranger could not tell if it was a sobering sane chord, or yet another tune struck in the key of madness and idiocy. There were other, arguing voices beyond the door, the hissing curses of his captors as they fought among themselves.

The Ranger took a moment to listen to the song, for it was the closest thing he could do to dream. Then he listened even closer to the men he knew were outside the room. He focused on the voices. Evidently, someone or something the men expected was late.

On the floor in the epicenter of the room was the most horrifying detail; there was a shallow pit where the tile broke apart, pipes were torn upward like the rib-bones from a messy exit wound. Below the hole was an oily surface, only partially like water that somehow lapped and tossed. The sink hole was ten feet across at best, and only god knew how deep. He could smell the scummy brine above the filth of his own body, and guessed the chutes led out to the nearby lake men once called the Salton Sea.

The Ranger had thought the Cult of the Sleeper were a pack of delusional, glue-sniffing, loons, just another nut job clan of tattooed, cannibal assholes, and freaks that idolized the slimy creatures that owned the seas and the bloody oceans. He'd seen them pray to the bastard demigods called the Deep Ones at night, to name themselves after their careless god in tribute, to dance about fires and act out brutal human sacrifice, *to ritually consume human flesh*. There were many unhealthy new religions across the murky wastelands in this new Dark Age, but the abominable Cult's brand of idolatry for the vile was perhaps the worst.

No, he had thought the Cult were just groupies for those dark, gibbering, things that ate men alive and gnawed on their bones. Those Deep Ones of the oceans had come like lice with the calamity of the apocalypse, too – come with the dark clouds of turmoil and inexplicable pandemics. Now the Deep Ones and their sleeping god were just another set of unrelenting pricks who wanted power, not so different than this Cult of glorified assholes who adored them.

Still, it was tough to think of anything over the pain in his body and the sound of Gregg Allman's voice.

Suddenly, the door swung open and the song thundered. The drums sent his bones tickling with agony and irritation. It was a good song, however, and if he was to die, there had been worse elegies.

The thin cultist in the doorway was shirtless; his malnourished build littered with mucky marks and tattoos of scales and strange characters. He wore round dark tinted goggles over his bald, scarred head. An undead grin smeared on his face, beaming with awful sharpened teeth that were filed down to needles. The man's own neck was lined with welted, poorly healed scars where he had evidently tried to give himself gills.

Aptly, the freak's name was Ghoul, and he and the Ranger had already been acquainted.

"Time for more fun!" Ghoul announced over the roar of music. He leaned on the door jamb and rocked his hips like he was fucking the air, rhythmic with the wild music to his back. Likewise, he stuck his tongue out like some cold-blooded Yuha lizard as he moved for the table.

Behind him a shorter man filed in, a clone of the skinny cultist, except potbellied with a sweat-stained wife beater on. Ghoul had called him Mr. Meepers.

"I don't want to skin this one, no," Mr. Meepers said. "They die so quick when you skin them first."

Ghoul stared at him now with slavering pride. "How many times I got to say it, Meepers? Not this one. Not this sonofabitch...no; this one's tha' mutherfuckin' Ranger double fuckin' danger...best scout in all the land, scourge of the whole damn Californias, he is. He's our big celebrity guest tonight."

"Never met nobody famous," Mr. Meepers agreed.

Ghoul flicked the Ranger's bloody ear with his finger. "Look at that face, Meepers. Handsome ain't he? Got you' at last, we did it," Ghoul said. "Tell Ghoul, Ranger, how's it fucking feel now?"

He ran his knuckles over the Ranger's broken ribs and pressed hard. In his life, the captive man had experienced more physical trauma than anyone should, but even he could not resist groaning in pain.

"Ticky...tic... tickles...." Ghoul giggled to himself as he kept tickling the Ranger's chin and knuckling his ribs.

"He's handsome alright, Ghoul. Get 'em talkin, Warfar said. Didn't he?" Mr. Meepers spoke. "But watch 'em good, cause he's trixsy and full of them sneaky ways."

Ghoul laughed and perused the tools on the table. "Yeah, I know what goddamn Warfar told me, Mr. Meepers," he replied as he brought up the ball-peen hammer. "But our celebrity guest's in luck; turns out the Deep Ones want to meet 'em too."

"Sorry boss, I didn't realize we was havin' more company," Meepers answered as he glanced down to the churning pit of water below. "Guess, that's why Warfar doesn't want 'em dead just yet."

"No, I guess not. Warfar can go fuck hisself, mate. We can still have fun, anyways Mr. Meepers." Ghoul answered.

"Toes...they like toes you know," Meepers mumbled. His own teeth chattered, and the Ranger could smell his pungent breath from two yards away.

"Ah...yes toes," Ghoul answered. "I think you're dead right. He won't need them anymore, I reckon'."

The Ranger shifted in the chair. He stared at the lapping black water as it churned. Still, he was far from the actual irradiated cesspool known as the Pacific. How had the Deep Ones burrowed this far inland?

"But now them Deep Ones are late, you know," Ghoul said.

"That sure is a far swim, I figure, under mountains and in those Dhole chutes they showed us," Meepers answered. "Heard Warfar say they don't like coming this far with all the thick salt and bad water."

Ghoul slapped Meepers on the back of the head.

"Ouch!" the stunted cultist cried.

"Don't go talkin' none about Dhole tubes and what we found down below, that's none of his concern," he growled. "Warfar would feed you to them if he knew you was tellin' our secrets."

"Sorry, Ghoul...Meepers is awful sorry."

Ghoul turned his attention back to the Ranger.

"Nope, Warfar said he wants to talk to you first, that *They* want to meet ya…got something special in store for you. Imagine that, the Deep Ones noticed *you*."

The Ranger knew the one named Warfar they spoke about was the head of the murderous cult, a real asshole butcher, and a man Chief Comstock and the California Militias had been fighting with for ten hard years.

"I was hoping that after all, they'd let us have ya' for meat, we're awful hungry in here," Ghoul said. "Sick of stringy mountain goat and lowly desert pilgrims."

"Yes, always hungry," Meepers said. "He's awful meaty and the boy's always hungry."

Ghoul nodded. "But those Deep Ones are hungry too, and they like good eats, same as the next one. Maybe they'll toss us some good bits when they've finished with you."

The cultist tapped his watch, the glass cloudy and the hands broken. Meaningless. "Time's a tickin'." He laughed again and danced around the room.

"Look there!" Ghoul's face went red as he pointed to the Ranger's feet. "All hell, sweet Mr. Meepers you damned idiot, you forgot the shoes."

The two looked down at the boots on the Ranger's lower extremity.

"Oh, right boss, there they are," Meepers mumbled. "I'm sorry. I hadn't gotten to them yet, and just forgot."

"Sonofabitch, Meepers, we can't leave them boots, you know, not for them below, or for Warfar comin'," Ghoul said, "-especially if you want them toes *before hands*."

"I'm sorry Ghoul, Meepers is very sorry, please don't hurt me this time," Again, the man was bawling.

Ghoul paused, staring at the shorter man. After a tense moment passed, he flashed a smile of rotten teeth as wide as the dead Salton Sea.

"Get...it, Mr. Meepers? Toes... *before*...*hands*...beforehand," he said. "You missed my goddamn funny joke, you dumb son of a bitch."

Again, Meeper's bawl broke into a matching wide smile.

"Yes, very funny, Ghoul...you're such a funny one," he answered, laughing.

"I didn't say stop crying, yet," Ghoul shouted, his teeth flared.

Meepers began to cry and whimper.

The moment dragged out as the Ranger struggled for breath through the soaked gag. The music still swirled endlessly, a song without end.

"There, there, Meepers, get it all together and quit clowning around. For the love of hell, take off those boots, will you."

Meepers began cursing wildly, swearing in some language the Ranger did not know.

"See that, Ranger? You got Mr. Meepers all upset," Ghoul spoke. "Well damn fool, untie 'em then and toss 'em here. We'll stack 'em nice and neat next to his other goodies. I'm gonna be nice too and let you have the first of them toes."

"But Ghoul, I don't know how to tie 'em or untie," Meepers cried.

"Well, cut 'em then, you have a knife."

"Oh yeah, I have one of 'em." On cue, he extended a long Buck Knife from his belt, shiny silver. His stunted face still twisted in his own wide demonic style with tiny malformed chickpea teeth set in a pool of red gums.

Suddenly, the music scratched off. There was a strange, guttural moaning and shouting immediately audible from deeper within the facility.

"Jesus will they never end with that racket?" Ghoul spoke." No music, and I ain't workin' over that racket without no goddamn tunes."

He stormed out back into the hallway, leaving the chittering Meepers alone with the bound Ranger.

Now Meepers turned to the Ranger, practically licking the blood off his face, breathing heavy as a dog.

"Warfar said talk you up, get 'em to talk about Comstock and those boys outside the wire," Meepers grumbled. "Truth is I don't think it matters none. Deep Ones gonna' kill you all, anyhow. Fry your brains and show you the Sleeping God under the Sea, yep."

The Ranger bit hard on the gag. Meepers awkwardly still hung near his face, as if he was going to take a bite. This close, the toad of a man smelled like spoiled vinegar and bad body odor.

"Now for this damn boot." Meepers went to his knee with his blade ready.

In that moment, time was both a spark and sludgy drip; the Ranger's eyes turned to slits of honed balefire. Meepers bent down and cupped the captive's foot with one hand and lowered his silvery blade just under the bottom lace. In the same sliver of space and time, the concealed boot blade in the toe popped open, and sharpened steel glimmered in the weak light. Time oozed to a sludgy flow. On cue, the music kicked back on at the start of the same song.

"Christ, what's that?" Meepers grumbled as he stared at the boot blade. Then time unfroze, and swift action followed; the Ranger's foot, now impossibly free came upward to the cultist's head in a violent blur, both knocking the knife from Meepers' hand, and ruthlessly plotting the business end of the boot-knife directly in the bare throat of the lunatic. The Ranger torqued the edge and nearly broke it off in the short man's trachea. Fresh blood sprayed. Meepers choked and wrapped his hands around the spitting wound. Gregg Allman rasped onward as the guitars moved on to a frenzied solo, now joined by the gargling and gurgling of the cultist's last seconds of life.

The Ranger moved like a whirl, his hands flailed to free himself from the wire bonds and he kicked out again, rocking himself loose and to budge his body.

A pool of blood formed by Mr. Meepers, chumming the dark water below in a pit of dusky churn. The Ranger knew he had only seconds to free himself before the door swung open or something worse emerged from the cold depths of that horrible pit below.

At last, he freed his bloody hands from the last of the garrote wire as Meepers twitched to his death on the ground. Both of his feet were out a moment later, and he had completely wriggled from the chair. Now he stood, and whatever happened next, he would die on his feet.

Gregg Almann's voice washed out within with the hypnotic guitar as the door swung open. The piercing screams and strange low moans were amplified as the door split and the tall form of Ghoul stood in the gap.

"Music's back!" Ghoul declared, arrogantly insane. Without looking at the details of the room, he had already gone into his dance routine when he looked up to find the Ranger's hatchet coming down into his melon. He cried as he gripped the axe and the Ranger pulled it backward and kicked the cultist in his knees. Ghoul fell to the floor quivering, dead a moment later.

The Ranger pulled him back into the room and laid his corpse next to Meepers. Then he felt a sharp pierce to his temple, a ringing in his ears, a warning sign from the lapping pool that the Deep Ones were coming, for they always made men's mind hurt and human heads burn.

In his travels, he had met the creatures known as the Deep Ones; he had felt the burn of their effect on the brain. They were a miscreant void-race, spawned of the past tumult of churning Armageddon. Whether it was a sonic ability or some strange pheromone, the effect was a hyper-advanced biological defense; a mild hypnosis, coupled with migraines and burning prefrontal pain. If they were coming now, it was time to leave.

Complete darkness eluded the room as a morbid light flickered below. In the deep passage within the lapping waves, rays glowed off the ebony surface, and under. Now the same light caught the silvery finish of the pistol as the Ranger lifted the weapon and spun the cylinder. After he had checked the bullets he tucked it into his waistband. He gathered the rest of his gear, the bow and arrows, and at last he put on his filthy mask, the black balaclava.

Just like that he was free in a house of horrors with a gun in his waistband, a bow on his back, and a scoured axe in his hand. No man could ask for anything more.

Even better, it was time to work again.

The hall was dingy and slime-coated. Trash and sludgy dirt was everywhere. Broken florescent lights pulsed and sizzled, rats, bugs, and crawling insects chittered. The air was almost cold down here, and the Yuha heat was almost pleasantly cut by the depths and distance underground.

How far under the desert was he? Even the Ranger had no clue.

He had not liked the mention of Dhole tubes, and wondered if the rumor that there were burrowed holes that zig-zagged deep under the cult's citadel were true. It was said those monstrous Dholes, the mindless burrowing titan-worms built like semi-trucks, had dug through the entire earth, spreading radiation and filthy creatures in their ruined wake. It was not far of a stretch to think those tubes could have filled with water over the years, or worse, spread all over the Yuha and let the cult come and go as they pleased.

In the hall, now there was a strange absence of the horrible screams that the Ranger had previously heard. Now there was only the animal-like grunting, panting and the shaking of metal. He followed the noise, duck-walking and staying in the shadow. Pain flooded his every nerve, but he was a man used to working in the worst conditions, and he was nowhere near giving in to the agony of broken bones. For now, the path was empty, and it twisted beyond his sight.

He crept within the next room, through a wide open door, keeping ever low and out of sight. He heard the racket louder before he wedged open the door; hard, painful moans from inside, an angry coitus of two of the cultists locked and writhing as one animalistic mass, engaged in a familiar deed in the middle of this surreal nightmare. As the weak lights flickered, a cultist woman was on top of her man, neither were clothed, but their bodies were so marked with piercings, tattoos, and alterations it was difficult to discern any details. Her barbed-wire hair slammed against her back as they both cursed at each other and contorted. The act was violent, devoid of any love, or humanity as the woman growled and hissed, the bed rocking and cranking as she swore and hissed some more. The door was ajar and the pair had no concern if anyone else heard.

"Give these lovebirds some privacy," the Ranger said to himself as he slowly backed out.

The next room had what was left of his comrades.

Chalmers and Ace Holcombe were just as dead as Ghoul and Meepers. The naked men were both heaved into a depression and shower-like area with a pool of blood all around them, the bodies mangled and mutilated. They had clearly been tortured before they died. Now both their throats had been slit from ear to ear, and there was no need to take a pulse. Their eyes were both open and agape, staring at nothing but the scummy ceiling.

It would have been nice to bury them, he thought. But he knew he too would be dead if he paused to perform such an act. The solace of ritual and ceremony meant little in this day, and any death in this broken world was respite enough from the pain of reality.

Chalmers had done time in the Moto-gangs of the High Plains to the east, and was no saint himself. Holcombe was a happy-go-lucky gunslinger from way up of Aguas Calientes. Now that man's eyes were like pasty chalk and his skin white as ivory, dead at the bottom of the shower.

For a moment, the Ranger lost himself in the milky eyes; men were not unlike this cursed Earth they were all damned to now walk, inexplicably twined in the same mortal yarn. Both were doomed, and it mattered little whether whatever was left was cosmic dust, floating in the cold of space, or a grease spot on the bottom of an old shower.

The Ranger whispered a few words under his breath, collected himself, and made back out for the hall.

The hiss of the arrow sliced the air like a soaring shrike.

He pinned a beefy cultist with a bolt as he sat at a small card table square in the throat. Another cultist lay dead on the ground, bleeding in a pool with an arrow half-buried in his temple. The Ranger noticed that the choking one wore strange rubber gloves and a rubber apron. A third arrow put the last man out of his misery. There were no more guards in this portion of the room, but much of this chamber was obscured.

The Ranger's heart raced at what he saw next.

This room held what the men had been sent in to find: a large metal array with twisting gears and cogs. There was a work bench where another mirror device sat. *Two of them, not just one like Chief Comstock had thought.* Comstock had called it "Hephaestus' Forge", but the Ranger had considered that line just more bullshit out of the mouth of the wily old Kumeyaay warrior-chief.

The machines in question were two ammunition presses, bullet packers, makers, with matching gunpowder drums stacked along the walls. Loose brass casings and finished rounds were sprawled in wide whiskey barrels and old shipping boxes all over the room. There were other crates of gunpowder and other finished ammo boxes stacked up to the tall ceiling and beyond. Piles more were simply strewn across the room in baleful heaps, like a twisted treasure room stuffed with gold coins in a mountain of power. Brass casings as far as a lowly scout could see, just like a dragon's hoard.

"Hot damn," the Ranger could not help but say aloud.

Despite the pain all over his body, he took it all in as he dripped his own blood and hobbled within the great room. *Pay dirt.* This was the cache that Ole' Comstock was after. It had only taken seven good men's lives to scope it out. But sure as hell, it would shift the balance of power in the Yuha in the crazy cult's favor. That was bad.

Sadly, the rounds were too big for the Ranger's old Colt pistol, and most were military grade 5.56 millimeter or .308 caliber, long rifle rounds, not fit for the ancient six-shooter.

Still, the Ranger moved deeper into the room. There were no sentries posted this far within their lair, and none of them would have had the caution to expect a black-hooded fiend and abattoir like the Ranger so far within their midst.

The room stepped down as the heat grew, past the ammo press and sprawled hoard of rounds, a nearby tinkering sounded, pounding metal.

Shadows took over the path, dancing with fresh flames and burning ovens. None of it seemed to vent properly. Only the dimwit cult would put forges so close to such a stockade of gunpowder and ammo.

The nearby ovens roared with a heat greater than the Yuha. *I could blow this place sky high,* the Ranger considered. He could picture Comstock and his boys, somehow not so far off watching as the whole place popped in a swollen mushroom cloud. But then he'd be dead too, and as much as the Yuha wouldn't care to see another grease-spot, that wasn't the bargain he had made. Nope. He wasn't one for suicide runs, and damned all hell, he was walking out of here one way or another.

Sparks and metal heaved as the heat from the ovens billowed, nearly catching some of the loose powder.

Heck, it wouldn't take long for these assholes to blow themselves sky high, he considered.

The clinkering neared; a firm, rhythmic tapping. Behind the forges were multiple rows of blades, homemade spears, knives, and axes. Then he caught his first glimpse of the pounding stone and anvil, and it was not unattended. Two cultists were here spitting and cursing, covered in sweat and filth as they spoke with one another. They wore thick mittens and old asbestos aprons. The bigger of the two was swinging a blacksmith's hammer on a wad of metal.

He was almost at them before the other looked up.

"Who the hell?" An arrow caught the observant smithy directly under the neck and he spilled instantly. His comrade was slow to react, and before he could cock the bludgeon in his gloved hands the Ranger had cleft him across the temple with his hatchet and kicked at his legs. He went down hard, and the hatchet was there to see him stay down.

Just like that, both were dead; the Ranger stood over them and recovered his arrow, and wiped the beading sweat and blood from his eyes. The balaclava on his head was already soaked, but he liked it that way, and liked too the idea that those he would kill would not even see his face. In that way he had much in common with the murderous cult, for within his evil soul, the man they called the Ranger liked killing and hunting men as well.

As it stood, the mission was only half *done*.

"Time to get the hell out of here," he said under his breath.

The Ranger slunk down the halls, stalking with his bow ready. He sent two more cultists to their wayward gods in a blur of sailed shafts. He moved like a wraith, recovering the arrows and tucking them away. One of the men he had downed still twitched and he cut his throat with a forceful swipe.

The rooms past these two were even stranger, a lab of sorts, empty and filled with flickering florescent lights. There were bodies in tanks here, human bodies...a dead woman. Her black hair spiraled outward like a wild tree in the green fluid. Next to the tanks, there was a greasy metal table, complete with straps and restraints, tables of stainless steel cutting tools. Beside that was another torture chair, much like that to which he had been previously strapped.

What the fuck were they doing down here? he asked himself. But it was an idle thought in a moment of madness, for truthfully, he didn't care. He knew not to get wrapped up in senseless questions many years ago. The Cult of the Sleeper were servants of a vile god and the slaves of the insane. There was little logic to the hellish winds of their madness.

Still, there was no apparent way out; as he moved down the hall now it dropped again, deeper down, as the mold-stained lights pulsed.

He ducked his head around a large arch, and there was a mess of sleeping bodies within. These were soldiers, slumbering in their leathers, clutching weapons, axes, and blades. It was a barracks of sorts, though the men and women within were piled like cows and

258

livestock in the room. The air smelled ripe and flies swirled, but there were no extra guards, and most in the room appeared to be asleep. Thankfully, the cult kept no dogs as guards, and if they did, the smell may have been better.

This was not the goddamn way out, he cursed to himself. Carefully, he backed out as they snored and other lost voices whispered.

He slid down the halls again like an eel, taking to the shadow as the palisade widened, now a wide arch opened into yet another room. Unfortunately, it too dropped downward, deeper, as the sprawling apartment opened.

The space was clearly some sort of chapel or temple, it was marked all over with etchings and more of the mad clan's symbolism. The Ranger had never understood their weird adoration for the creatures from the sea, and that unnamable black god who once more slept eternal.

Now the Ranger saw one of their equally perplexing holy men; a dark priest in the midst of another vile black rite. The man raised his arms in the air, clutching a curved ritual blade in one hand, his nails long and menacing.

"Gaa...daar, Din, Habin-Sir Ushanti... Dagon.....they will quake when those of the Deep inherit the Earth," the bald mage whispered. He moved now to grab the dagger with both hands, and cock it back, high and ready to downward thrust on some faint, floundering mass at a meager alter.

On instinct, the Ranger let an arrow fly and re-nocked his bow. The arrow planted directly in the mage's back. He knew the move had been stupid, and regretted giving away his position.

Don't be a goddamn hero, he swore to himself.

The vengeful cultist hissed like a gassy orb as the arrow sunk into the devil. He buckled over his would-be victim, revealing he was not alone; a woman was here, under his gasping body chained in the corner cowering, her clothes tattered rags.

She was badly cut and beaten and her white dress was stained and streaked with scarlet and muck. There was an awkward pause now and the Ranger was paralyzed with the implication of protecting innocence.

"I won't hurt you," he spoke low to the woman. She was silent for a moment. Calm, yet there was a strange glimmer in her eye, a look the Ranger knew all too well.

This complicates everything, he knew. *Damn all hell, don't be a hero,* he repeated. He didn't bargain on rescuing anyone, and he sure as hell didn't have time for a wounded girl who couldn't fight along his side.

He needed to be *shadow* and *fury* to escape this hell, and it would be worse still to crawl or sneak his way out of this mess with another. Still, he noticed something again in her stare as she whimpered.

His eyes fell on her, and for a brief moment she flashed him a pooled gaze of compassion, perhaps even thanks. A fleeting glimmer of lost humanity.

If it is that the eyes are portals to the souls, however, then here were gates to evil and treachery; for every soul in the catacomb of the Cult of the Sleeper was soured and lost, and the hapless woman at the Ranger's feet was no different; her attention fled off him only slightly, a twitch of the eye, a tell of betrayal. In the glassy reflection of those eyes the Ranger saw the two forms behind him. He smelled them next. The Ranger moved, whirling like a chthonic sirocco into action. Sure enough, two men emerged from the inky shadows within the room, drawn blades, and barred fangs. Now they came at him, but he was ready.

He shot an arrow point-blank into the first assailant. The shaft hit home and landed in the neck of his target, sending the cultist back to the shadow, choking; then he met the wrist of the next killer's downward slash with his hand. The blade hung in the air as both men strained to get the upper hand. The cultist went to brace his assault, but the Ranger moved smarter; he bashed the man over the head with his bow, sending him back, as he dropped the buck knife. The cultist was unfazed and quickly shook off the attack, renewing his charge with the dagger ready to slash.

The Ranger backed up to gain more space, just as the woman in the corner swept out his leg with her outstretched arms. She clawed and hissed, lunging at him like a wild cat.

"Bitch!" he cursed. He backhanded her soundly to send her off him as he focused on the charging devil.

He found himself on the slick tile floors, struggling for footing and did all he could to swing a leg upward and out to kick the approach of the crazed cultist. The move paid off; the maniac's shin cracked like a twig in the flickering light, and he screamed as he too went down to the bloody pooled tiles. The woman now raged anew at the Ranger and lashed out once more, scratching him across the shoulder, her nails like razors.

"I was to be his! My prince...life everlasting, the pools beyond the black shoal!" she screamed.

Now the Ranger did not hesitate; he brought out his hatchet and knocked her into next week with the flat end of his axe. There was a sound crack, and he held nothing back as she sailed off into the shadows and went still. Nor did he care if she was dead or alive.

Then he hobbled to his feet and ended the animal cries of the cultist with the broken leg.

Now a distant rattle shook the halls, a war clamor as the smell of smoke billowed. How a fire had started or an alarm was raised, he did not know, but either way, his time was up.

…and that was when all hell broke loose.

The smoke thickened as men shouted.

Figures came through the thick veil, then the whole camp hollered and rattled. The walls shook. For a moment, the Ranger wondered if Comstock had attacked early or come to save him.

No one will save you, he knew.

The Ranger took out his revolver and fired two quick shots down the halls without any care as to who the forms were. His comrades were all dead, and anyone and everyone was an enemy here. He hit one of the lead guards square in the face, crumpling him into a ball as a few more fell behind him. Now, the only path open was from where he had come. His feet ached as he flew now, back down the hall, past the gun press and the smoldering blacksmith's.

"Prisoner's escape!" someone shouted.

"Nah, they're all dead," another said. The errant pops of exploding gunshots could be heard as no doubt loose rounds in the forge cooked off in the fire.

"Look here, someone's killed off Axl and Calk!"

Smoke billowed and now he could hardly see in front of his face. He heard more swears, now muffled by the chaotic rumble of feet and metal.

The forms unloaded from the barracks hall, and further down the unexplored portions, they were pushing him back the way he had come, back to the smoking forge, and the torture chamber. There were too many, and without logic he moved back for cover, under the smoke, scurrying like a rat.

"Forge is on goddamn fire!" a frantic cultist cried out. "Get some buckets!"

He wondered if any second now the ammunition lode would catch fire and the whole dungeon would blow apart. Maybe it was for the best.

The cover of the smoke proved to be his only salvation; he ducked in the shadows and slit the throat of another confused cultist. Then he found himself back in the torture room. Meepers and Ghoul lay dead, his interrogation an afterthought.

Ironically, the familiar music pulsed on nearby, the skipping Allman Brothers song, the same song, caught in a repetitive rut with the old fashioned record player stashed somewhere.

In the room he stood over the water and looked down below to the churning depths of the pit. *Dhole tubes*...the thought echoed in his mind. If it was a worm tube, there was no telling where something horrible like this might lead.

Yet this pit to whatever other hell was the only way out. He coughed with the rising smoke as he hesitated.

"Down here!" he heard a distant voice scream. Footfall was closer now, armed men were coming.

Suddenly, however, the Ranger's head started to violently ring again. A high pitched squeal that put him to his knees, desperately trying to plug his ears but the sound was deeper in his brain – something far more acute than his own ears could handle.

Deep Ones...he had nearly forgotten. *They were expecting company.*

Then the pit rustled. He heard a churning above the shriek, and then a gurgling.

Horror incarnate; a wet hand flopped upward from the black, then another, covered with slimy, smooth skin, glistening flesh, web-lined fingers, tawny and horrible.

The Ranger thumbed the revolver at his waist. His head was on fire now, and the ringing in his ears turned the repeating music and panicky ruckus of voices behind him into a hazy wash of madness. Desperately, he tried to shake off the Deep One's innate paralytic aura. In fact, the sound of Greg Allman's voice was the only thing keeping his brain from turning to butter.

An inky form rose from below, a thick saurian head, foaming, frothing, The muscular legs heaved upon the tiles with webbed, wide feet as it preened, the frilly, terrible gills quivering and pulsing as the slouching jaw hung free, drooling and lined with needle-like teeth and larger, dagger-like incisors. The bi-pedal body dropped a pair of claw-lined paws with hooked talons for fingers.

The eyes were lost, but intelligent and deliberate. The monster chortled deep epiglottal clicks and slurps as it scanned the Ranger.

He knew he had only seconds to act, for these were the horrid benefactors of this cult, and however ugly and primal, they did have the power of black gods.

The Ranger's own sanity flickered. He had lost his mind long ago, and now what was left was a force of singular purpose to survive another day and beg, borrow, and bargain for life. But even he knew that now was not a time to run, but a time to fight, to stare into the madness and shoot back...and that is exactly what he did.

Complete the mission, he said to himself. The power of gods did not equal invincibility, nor were the horrible fish-men bullet proof.

The Ranger's head felt as if it would split out from his skull, and he hesitated for only a split second before he leveled the revolver and fired a shot at the dark shadow. The Ranger could see the teeth first, then saw the horrid oily blood spray with his well-placed shot. The monster screamed another awful shriek and cried aloud in agony.

For the Ranger, the vicious pain in his head culminated in terrible migraines, the throbbing voice haranguing and seething in what must have been curses and swears. The Ranger had seen them before and he knew of their evil, and this was not the first one he had laid low.

Then it spoke.

"I know you...." a horrible voice slurped. "You... who dream no longer....you who are not unlike us... a man who does not belong!"

The creature still stood, wavering, leaking a black, oily blood. Suddenly, it charged him, barreling like a blur. But the Ranger was fast as well; he leapt away watching the metal table behind him fold under the creature's awesome assault. Then it fell into a pile with the gnarled mess, floundering.

Besides the bullet wounds, the Ranger had split open the beast with his axe as well and now more of the terrible blood spilled. Again, the Ranger squeezed off a round into the dark form as it flailed its webbed feet in a grimy splash upon the deck and floor.

"You hear that?" he heard a voice call from the smoke.

265

The Ranger ignored the danger and shot again, then again. More of the black blood splattered. More smoke plumed now into the room.

"Death is a lie!" the creature gurgled to him, its horrible long mouth almost bent in a smile, its throat providing a sickening final laugh as it died.

There was a flop as the body of the Deep One slouched to the greasy tiles, flailed and contorted, not far from the husk of Mr. Meepers. Now a spill of black pus-filled fluid oozed onto the image of the pentagram, mixing with Meepers' blood.

The Ranger's head cleared and the ringing shrill died at once. The eyes of the beast went clouded and distant, stuck open staring at the high portions of the walls. Then it's terrible mouth regurgitated blood and bile, and he knew the monstrous demon was dead. The creature's horrible batrachian tongue flopped to the tiles, slimy and pink.

Yet there was no time to gloat over the kill; the cult was now nearly in the room. He could hear them *all*. He would have to fight them *all*.

Instead, he hung over the black water, horrific, still hesitating, the dull light deep and hypnotic, pulsing. It was suicide he thought, but there was that weak light under the dark splashes.

They had always taught him to know his way out, to never walk in a place that you did not expressly know how to walk out of. That paradigm had now gone to shit for the thousandth time. A sliver of hope was an infinitesimal speck of fleeting light. Yet what did any of it matter in a hopeless place within a hopeless world?

The water whispered of choking death. Old Greg Allman skipped one last goodbye. At worst, he would die, drown or be ripped to shreds by a waiting pack of sea-devils. For him, it was the only chance, and there was no inner battle as he slung his bow and jumped into the dark, oily void.

The Ranger swore as he leapt, for he knew that the Deep One, that damned fishy bastard had been right; death was nothing and there was now only one way out.

He nearly drowned in the first moment he was submerged.

The water was colder than he had realized. To jump in frigid water was always a shock far more sobering to act out than to realize. Muscles tense and shut down, the bodily urge to contort and paralyze itself is powerful and strong. Even now, the frigid Dhole tube squeezed him and cajoled him into taking a deep inhalation of the brackish fluid, but he did not, and his strokes reached out, for he had once been trained to swim in all sorts of foul conditions, and the turgid cold as well. There was nothing to grab him, save for the chill, and no waiting fangs or the open jaws of a coterie of the Deep Ones. Now he dived without regret or want, without thought. He was now a frantic, mindless thing acting out the only option left.

The light he saw grew. He swam on, stabbing pain all in his body, and already he felt drained.

His body spasmed and bled. Underwater, the shapes around him were a blur, yet his hands found slimy rock and winding roots, covered with clumpy reeds and dirty algae. He pushed on, swimming until he felt he had no more left. His own blood was thick in the water. In that cruel abyss, the Ranger was irresolute and unwavering, his strong strokes still reaching out, pushing him onward and out. Fear swirled in his head just the same, but he mastered it and swam on.

For a moment, he thought he felt firm hands wrap around him and he saw in his mind those curled claws of the Deep Ones as they lunged outward, with needle-like teeth and brindled bodies, swirling in the dark. But there was nothing except for a blur of dark green and brown, tangled milfoil, a shifty oblivion of incomplete shapes and throbbing weak light.

The water bubbled and for a moment he thought he heard a deep guttural curse, an enraged, verbose, swear carried under those murky fathoms in whatever abyss he had avoided. Who knows where else those dank tubes beneath his torture chamber had led? For now he only followed the hint of light, the blurry smudge in a drowned hallucination. Lungs bursting, he swam, if he was to die, he would die defiant, trying to live just a moment longer.

The once-meager light rushed now, blinding and strong. The shapes around him gained a new blurry wonder. His lungs felt like they would explode, like his body had pushed itself further than it had ever gone. He swam into a glaze of warmer water that grew hotter, loaded with green algae and scum. Upward he reached, then burst through the membrane of the water back into the fouler air of the California Coast, brine choked and brackish. Nevertheless, he gulped huge breathes of foul air as he waded for the shore amid the warm soup.

The Calipatrian wastes were before him; towering walls of mud, dirt, and stone leering down. He couldn't help but spit up whatever water he had swallowed. It was a cruel irony to escape the forges of hell only to be born back into the sweltering oven of the high Yuha – the only place that was hotter.

Right away, the light of the relentless sun punished him, but so too in that brilliance the voids and many-angles of the fortress to his back carved darker shadows, for the great walls of the Cult of the Sleeper stronghold scaled high into the dull grey of day. He kept to the shade, preferring still the solace of secrecy, yet no sea of arrows or gunfire erupted around him on the base of the moat. The cult facility was nebulous, laden with tangled concertina wire, and whoever guarded the place had no eyes on him now.

The water around the wall was a cesspool of churning moat, rotten, streaked with rainbow-oil surfaces and smelling of pungent offal and stagnation. There was stalked sedge-grass nearby, cattails and over-grown reeds that were brown and unhealthy. The Ranger made for their unwholesome cover as he waded further in the muck and mud, hatchet in hand. Biting things nibbled at him, and other suckers latched onto his bleeding skin, but he brushed most of them off and toughed onward.

He crawled as far as he could before he hit a mud rift, a deep canyon-cut where he could keep himself obscured from the tall walls of the Sleeper's fortress.

Eventually, the scrub weeds moved to thicker cover. He took again a moment to gaze back at the citadel. Smoke streamed from behind those walls, and the guards were fewer. He paused for a moment and saw tiny forms atop the battlements. The despot named Warfar's riff-raff were either unaware of his escape, or did not care, for both of the hapless guards wobbled on, droning and slouching with ancient rifles.

Then he heard shouts, not for him, but for the growing plumes of deep black smoke. The cult, those bastards, had bigger problems to attend.

The Ranger resumed his escape; the muddy canyon split further, and he flattened his body on the hard packed gravel and gypsum-laced mud as he crawled. The heat swelled over, and the bite of the desert was already attacking his nearly broken body in waves.

After a while, he relaxed, convinced he was not followed or chased. He was two miles or more away, following a small inland stream when the cooler air of the shade took him, and despite his better judgment, he passed into his own oblivion of sleep. The water nearby churned; he saw a vision of that green Deep One as it slobbered a smoky last breath. The last thing he thought of was Greg Allman's voice as he fell asleep into his usual dreamless nothing.

Upon the dry hillside, the sullen Chief Comstock sat atop his horse with a pair of riders next to him. The Kumeyaay Shaman Brilliant Moon flanked him on his own horse like a feathered spirit-lord of the dream lands. This god, however, had a sawed-off shotgun leveled at the Ranger while the beaten man crawled from a narrow crevice in a nearby mud fissure. Next to Brilliant Moon was Major Moses Creel of the California Regulars, a rugged black man cradling a dusty Thompson lever action.

The land here was bleached and salted, and already the dead Yuha lowlands looked much the same as it had when men had reigned. Mirages sizzled in the distance, and nearby the alkaline-laced top of the soil dappled the surface of hard-packed sand, giving the deceptive appearance of a fresh snowfall. This far in, even the desert was something false and deceptive.

"Just what in the hell you been through?" Moses Creel asked, eyeing the nearly dead man.

Brilliant Moon lowered the shotgun. "Where are the others?"

"Dead," the Ranger growled matter-of-fact. He coughed up blood on the desert floor and now took his feet. "They have the press," the Ranger said. "In fact, there are two."

He held up the .308 round and handed it to Comstock. The chief's eyes pooled with both fear and wonder.

"Did you see any long arms? Any black rifles or older stuff?" Major Creel asked.

"No," he answered. "But there's something else, somehow they're aligned with the Deep Ones. I saw one of them down below, stinking and fishy. They've got tunnels all under there. At least four hundred bodies billeted within, maybe another fifty more on the perimeter. They were heavily armed, but I started a bit of a fire. They're light with men inside and on their wire. My guess is the main group is off somewhere. It might be a good time to hit 'em."

The Chief considered the words. His eyes met Creel's in a wordless exchange.

"Fish Heads in the Salt Sea? Impossible." Brilliant Moon asked.

"I saw 'em with my own eyes," the Ranger replied. "Sent him back to their goddamn god, too. There was talk of Dhole tubes under the old fort. I took one out, I think. No tellin' where else they run."

Comstock gave him a stern look, his sunburned face nearly scarlet, and the war-paint in his gaunt features making him look carved from ancient wood. "Dhole tubes?" he mumbled to himself.

"It changes nothing," Creel injected.

The feathers of Comstock's headdress were tossed by the steady eastern winds. The whole goddamn Kumeyaay Nation was to his back, a war-party, loaded with men and women atop rough ponies, armed for bear with spears and rifles. Moses' men were there too, a mixed batch of topside settlers and a remnant of the so-called California Regular Militia decked in camouflage fatigues.

"Goddamn…you *are* on the War Path ain't you?" the Ranger asked.

"You've done well, Ranger," the man answered grimly. He snapped his fingers backward as he holstered his ancient rifle.

Another dusty camouflaged man came up, leading a fresh horse with loaded packs.

"Payment, like we said… plus two day's ration for the ride north," Comstock snapped. "A horse to get you back to wherever the hell you want to go."

"Much obliged," the Ranger replied.

"We been fighting' hard for this patch of land. My crew's united all the old clans, tribes, and two-bit towners for a hundred miles. We got this asshole Warfar pent up and beat, and we're fixin' to raid 'em if you haven't figured. You could join up with my group, go back down to the Salt Citadel and hit those bastards. Trust you me, we're gonna wipe them and any fish heads off the face of the Yuha, the sonsofbitches. I know you got more than a score to settle with the both of 'em."

The unrelenting wind howled across the desert flats and the Ranger mounted his horse. He wavered for a moment, woozy, then took the reins. He didn't even consider the offer.

"Thanks, but no thanks, chief," the Ranger replied. "We had a deal, and I'm done here."

The Ranger knew more words would be unnecessary; he thumbed the pistol at his waist as the moment hung, the desert and high Yuha may have been the biggest liar in the world, false as a flickering mirage, but Chief Comstock was an honorable man, one of the last, and a deal was a deal.

"It ain't done, sir, not by any long shot," Comstock replied. "But I guess you figure you seen enough to take the one way out you can, and I can't say I blame you."

The Ranger nodded as his hand eased off his revolver.

"God damn, Ranger, relax." Comstock added. "You know one of these days you're going to have to stand up for something more. You can't play this game forever."

Upon the horse, the wounded Ranger already felt as if he would wobble off back to the Yuha, but he held firm.

"None of us can, chief," the Ranger replied as he gave a quick version of a salute. Comstock nodded again, spit a dark wad of filthy saliva, and chewed on his plug of tobacco as the Ranger turned his horse north, for the mountains. Soon the winds took him in, and he hardly felt the numb pain all over his body as he dozed on the horse and trod north.

In the end, the man called the Ranger knew Chief Comstock was dead right; humanity was circling the drain after all, and it was only a matter of time before everyone got flushed.

That was it.

This was the world after the fall, into a dark frontier, burning with white light. No refrain. No answers.

It would be easy to say that the Ranger never knew what became of Comstock or his raid on that horror-show citadel of the Cult of the Sleeper. It would be easy to say, that by dawn he was a hundred miles away, back in Julian, safe, and never to see the good-for-nothing shores of the Salton Sea again.

But that, like the goddamn Yuha Desert itself, would be a lie.

IT'S NOT ONLY OUTSIDE
by Micah Castle

"How many people do you think's left, Cassidy?" Clayton asked from across the room, sitting on a chair at a crooked table in the corner of the bar.

Cassidy glanced at the doorway off to the side, at the dust-covered bar counter, the mirror opaque with grime. "Not a lot, I'd guess. Probably a dozen, or two. God only knows where they're hiding, though." He licked his dry lips and adjusted his jeans. *Probably in the jailhouses and prisons. Poor bastards weren't smart enough to get out when it started, like me.* The stolen, sheathed knife hidden under his shirt was uncomfortable against his skin.

Endless droning and wailing whispered through the shuddering rickety, wooden walls of the bar. Humidity-heavy wind whipped through the flapping doors, carrying the scent of death and decay, of the numberless corpses enclosing around them. Sand and dust and ash drifted through the open doorway, piling before it.

"God," Clayton said, running his dirtied, long fingers through his unwashed blonde hair, "that moanin'. I can't stand it." He put his face in his hands, shaking his head. "It's just so damn awful. All those people consumed by that black wall."

275

Cassidy quickly moved from his chair to another. "We all have to go sometime, Clayton. Be it the black wall, disease, a bullet to the head, or something else."

Clayton sat up, ran his hand down his face. *Is he closer? No... Just my mind playin' tricks.* He leaned to the side and peered past the dusty, empty tables and chairs, out the doorway. Beyond the desert littered with corpses and bones, abandoned wagons and decomposing horses, the black wall still moved towards them. It blocked out the horizon, the periphery of the world, except for a sliver of the blue sky above. It was as though a giant cliffside made from a starless, night sky tightened around them.

Although it was some odd miles away, Clayton could make out the small sinewy, black tarred arms clawing frantically towards them, the tiny gleaming heads covered in muck and oil rising out from the amorphous, bubbling mass. If he strained his eyes, he could distinguish one out of the thousands it consumed, but it only made his head hurt worse. Their moans carried on the wind, sending a shiver down his spine.

Cassidy moved to another chair. He untucked his shirt and undid the flap of the knife's leather sheath.

Clayton looked away and found Cassidy sitting closer than he was before, or was he? Clayton rubbed his eyes, shaking his head. His temples throbbed. He couldn't remember where Cassidy was sitting originally, that part of his mind lost in a haze. *Hadn't had a drink in years, but I still feel drunk from all this runnin' and hidin'. What I'd do for a drink now.* He chuckled a little. *At the end of the world and I'm trapped in a bone-dry bar. Funny how life works...*

"What do you do for work?" he asked.

Cassidy shrugged. "Not much. More of a drifter than anything. Do what I could to get by. What about yourself, Clayton?"

"Deputy, if you could believe it."

He laughed, grinned. "Now how'd a deputy end up in a place like this?"

Clayton tried to remember, but only vague images of the black wall, of the townspeople crying, of the skeletal arms from the wall tearing people from streets and homes into itself flashed through his mind. It was before him, looming, reaching, then he couldn't recall anything more.

He shook his head, wiped his eyes. "Can't remember, and you?"

Cassidy shook his head, too. "Same. Just a blank spot between when it started and here." *Except for the jail door finally swinging open after picking it; the sound of the chair crashing and breaking over the sheriff's back; the wall standing over the town, reaching for me and everyone else; the taste of sweat, copper, and something bitter in my mouth, hightailing it—*

"Have a wife or any kids," Clayton abruptly said. "Cassidy?"

He stretched his neck shoulder-to-shoulder. "No lady to speak of and no children that I know of, at least. Planted my seed in many brothels, but never stayed long enough to see if a child came of any. How about yourself?"

Clayton smiled. His lips cracked and bled. "Had a wife, and a child on the way, if I remember right. Cindy was her name. Long chestnut hair, big doughy eyes, legs that were longer than the train tracks. Even with her big belly, she was still as beautiful as the day I met her at the market…" His voice broke. He closed his eyes, inhaled a shuddering breath.

Cassidy silently removed the knife from its sheath, holding it to his side, and moved to another chair. He was now only two tables away from Clayton. Something jittery moved in his empty stomach and sweat formed under his arms. *Haven't felt this way in years, before that big fool who wouldn't stop breathing, shouting, and got me put in a cell.* He stopped himself from grinning.

"But, she's gone now, the child, too." Clayton continued. "Taken by that thing out there." He pointed blindly. "Some people from a town I passed through — can't recall the name — running for my life, said it was a curse on the world, because of all the sinnin' we do… I tried to believe that, but now, I don't think that's the truth."

"Oh?" Cassidy asked. "What do you think it is, then?"

Clayton rested the back of his head on the top of the chair. His hair parted from his forehead. Tears swelled and spilled down his stubbled cheeks. He kept his eyes closed, preferring the darkness within than the one outside. He took a deep breath again. "I think it's just somethin' else out there — high above the clouds or deep in the oceans — decided to show us its hand. It's been waiting for years and years for the perfect cards, and now it can throw them down on the table and collect its winnins'."

Another chair, another table. One table away now. A pounding started in the back of Cassidy's head, and he couldn't help but shake his leg. *So close.* His grip tightened on the deerskin handle of his knife. *So goddamn close I can smell the blood.* "Are you saying that it's something like God out there, doing those

278

things? And we're just the chips on the table, ready to be scooped up, whether we like it or not?"

Clayton opened his eyes, and idly stared at the creaking rafters. "No, nothin' like God... Somethin' older, much older... A god before God. Somethin' that doesn't care about us or this place." He heard something faintly scratch on the floor and he straightened in his chair. Cassidy sat across from him, a grin across his dust-caked, patchy-bearded face. His red-rimmed eyes were wide, wild.

"You know what I think it is, Clayton?" he asked, tapping on the table, keeping the other hand beneath it, gripping the knife held to his thigh.

A cold finger ran down Clayton's back, and his groaning stomach knotted. He knew those eyes — seen them many times out on duty before the end. Cassidy's eyes weren't normal; he had killers' eyes. He swallowed the speck of saliva collecting in his mouth. "What's that, Cassidy?"

He leaned forward. "I think that the black wall isn't important. It's like everything else in this godforsaken world. It takes what it likes and leaves nothing behind but sand and dust. Its purpose, its reasoning, doesn't make a lick of difference."

Clayton's mind hitched. He didn't know what to say. He dumbly nodded. His sweaty palms instinctively wanted to reach for his holster, but he knew it was empty, lost the revolver while running, so he kept them flat on his lap.

"There has and always will be things in this world taking what's not theirs. And, do you want to know something else?"

Sweat beaded Clayton's forehead, forming small streaks of mud above his brow.

279

"The black wall isn't only enclosing around us. It's within us, growing, gnawing, and everyone who's left will be a part of it one way or another."

"Wha— what are you sayin' Cassidy?" His lips quivered.

Cassidy leapt to his feet, his chair crashed onto the floor, and leapt across the table, tackling Clayton to the ground. Before Clayton even realized he had fallen onto his back, Cassidy knelt on him, over him.

Cassidy held the knife to Clayton's neck, piercing the outer layer of sand coating his flesh. His eyes filled with tar, oil, gloom. *"It's already inside me,"* he said, grinning, revealing black tinged teeth and gums, and pressed the blade deeper into Clayton's flesh. Black blood cascaded over Cassidy's hand, pooling and soaking into the backside of Clayton's hair. *And, it was already inside you, too.*

In Loving Memory of Snow White, known most
affectionately as BooBoo

2010-2020

AFTERWORD

Thank you for reading. We hope you enjoyed the anthology. We thought of *The Dark Frontier* after putting out a submission call for weird west and western novels and novellas, but didn't receive anything we thought was right for the company. We thought putting out an anthology of weird west might be a good jolt for Wild West Press. Weird west, while definitely having a fan base, is a genre that's mostly carved just a little corner for itself in the realm of speculative fiction. In the grand scheme of the literary world, there's not that much out there, and most of what's out there tends to be a one-off written by an author who writes primarily in another genre – usually the genre which she/he has blended with the western; and while we are open to submissions for traditional westerns, the indie scene isn't exactly overflowing with that genre, at least not in our corner.

The concept of weird west fascinated me as soon as I heard of it. When we decided to open the anthology call, I wanted to think of something themed but not requiring stories to follow one linear narrative. So I thought what about a western set in a world that's on the edge of disaster – not quite in ruin, but damn near there. That's how I created *The Dark Frontier*.

Initially, the idea was to blend sci-fi, fantasy, and horror into the western world. But, it seems us already having a foothold in the ever-interesting horror community produced mostly horror submissions. When we put out the call, with the brief back-story included, the Wild West Press inbox was flooded with western horror and that's the direction the anthology went. To be fair, the title *The Dark Frontier* doesn't exactly conjure images of fairies and unicorns, or spaceships and androids, galloping and flying across colorful fantasy landscapes.

While going through the submissions, I saw a theme begin to develop. We received many stories with similar concepts but very different plots and narratives. Two stories I even thought almost served as Point A and Point B for the book, and those were "On the Road to Madness" and "It's Not Only Outside" – with the former introducing the void creeping over the world, and the latter showing the last stand. I also felt that the latter was a perfect ending for the book, not only due to the dark wall creeping up on the final two men, but also for the question it posed.

"Cargo Mountain" was placed before "On the Road to Madness" because it introduces you to the mountain and the sinister voice. "One Way Out" preceded "It's Not Only Outside" because "One Way Out" carried a sense of finality to the struggle presented throughout the book, while "It's Not Only Outside" served as some sort of epilogue that presented the moral of the story. Between those were other stories that showed dark forces falling upon the world, and civilizations ruined by cataclysm and the struggle those living in those civilizations faced. The antagonists ranged from lone demon-like creatures to abominable monsters to just really wicked human beings. These stories blended together perfectly.

I also like that "The Crossing at Bony Ford" introduced the reader to the afterlife and then "Rise, Vega" took the reader deeper into the Beyond. This entire anthology came together like pieces of a puzzle falling into place.

One other thing I want to mention before I end my blathering. We were both really thrilled with the presence of the strong female character in *The Dark Frontier*. I know some people get bored with the identity politics in the literary world, and we understand because we don't really get into it, either. However, I enjoy strong female characters and well-written female protagonists and antagonists, and we are both glad that we have quite a few in this book.

In the end, we are both really proud of this anthology. There is nothing but great stories by great authors in this book and we are glad they decided to trust us with their works; and, we are especially glad you, dear reader, trusted the work by taking the time to read it. We certainly hope the anthology gets some love because it was more than a year in the making, and these authors waited for a long time to hear back from us (we were so swamped with other things – sorry you all), and then they waited even longer for publication. We hope their wait was worth it and that they are as proud to be a part of this as we were to produce it and bring their excellent stories to the book so that everyone could enjoy their paths through *The Dark Frontier*.

Thank you for reading,
Jacob Floyd

ABOUT THE AUTHORS

CHARLES R. BERNARD is a writer who lives in Salt Lake City, Utah. He lives next to the largest city-operated cemetery in the United States; a necropolis that sprawls out over a square kilometer.

Charles is lively company, though.

ARMAND ROSAMILIA is a New Jersey boy currently living in sunny Florida, where he writes when he's not sleeping. He's happily married to a woman who helps his career and is supportive, which is all he ever wanted in life.

He's written over 150 stories that are currently available, including horror, zombies, contemporary fiction, thrillers and more. His goal is to write a good story and not worry about genre labels.

He not only runs two successful podcasts - Arm Cast: Dead Sexy Horror Podcast - interviewing fellow authors as well as filmmakers, musicians, etc., The Mando Method Podcast with co-host Chuck Buda, talking about writing and publishing – but he owns the network they're on, too: Project Entertainment Network.

He also loves to talk in third person because he's really that cool.

You can find him at http://armandrosamilia.com for not only his latest releases but interviews and guest posts with other authors he likes! E-mail him to talk about zombies, baseball and Metal: armandrosamilia@gmail.com.

STUART CONOVER is a father, husband, rescue dog owner, horror author, blogger, journalist, horror enthusiast, comic book geek, science fiction junkie, and IT professional. With all of that to cram in on a daily basis, it is highly debatable that he ever is able to sleep and rumors have him attached to an IV drip of caffeine to get through most days.

A resident in the suburbs of Chicago (and once upon a time in the city) most of Stuart's fiction takes place in the Midwest if not the Windy City itself. From downtown to the suburbs to the cornfields - the area is ripe for urban horror of all facets.

You can find more of his work and follow him at:

https://www.stuartconover.com/
https://twitter.com/stuartconover
https://www.facebook.com/StuartConoverAuthor/

LEE CLARK ZUMPE has been writing fiction and poetry for more than 20 years. His work has appeared in *Weird Tales*, *Space and Time*, *Horrors Beyond*, *Corpse Blossoms* and *Space Horrors*. He has earned several honorable mentions in *The Year's Best Fantasy and Horror.* By day, he works for Tampa Bay Newspapers as a staff writer and entertainment columnist.

AUBREY CAMPBELL writes short stories across a wide range of genres, from science fiction gunslingers to gothic mansions riddled with magic in the mountains. Outside of writing, she collects cats and works as a librarian's assistant. Find more of her work at aubreycampbellauthor.weebly.com

JOANNA PARYPINSKI is an author of more than twenty short stories and two novels, a member of the Horror Writers Association, and an English instructor. Her fiction has appeared in *Nightmare Magazine*, *Black Static*, *Vastarien*, *Nightscript*, and *Haunted Nights* (ed. Ellen Datlow & Lisa Morton). One of her stories was listed as a notable selection in *The Best American Science Fiction & Fantasy 2018*. She lives with her husband in Los Angeles.

CASSIDY FROST is predominantly a horror writer, but also meddles in other genres. Her tone is a mix between innocent and ghastly, and by switching between the two she creates a unique experience for the reader. She lives in New Brunswick Canada.

If you'd like to get in touch with her for writing and art related inquires, you can email her at cassidykfrost@gmail.com.

She also has a blog at https://cassidy-frost.com.

DOUGLAS SMITH is a multi-award-winning Canadian author described by *Library Journal* as "one of Canada's most original writers of speculative fiction." His fiction has been published in twenty-six languages and thirty-four countries, including *Amazing Stories, InterZone, Weird Tales, Baen's Universe, On Spec,* and *Cicada.* His books include the novel *The Wolf at the End of the World,* the collections *Chimerascope* and *Impossibilia,* and the writer's guide *Playing the Short Game: How to Market & Sell Short Fiction.*

Doug is a three-time winner of Canada's Aurora Award and has been a finalist for the John W. Campbell Award, CBC's Bookies Award, Canada's juried Sunburst Award, and France's juried Prix Masterton and Prix Bob Morane.

His website is www.smithwriter.com and he tweets at twitter.com/smithwritr

A little about **HAWK & YOUNG**:

Elsha Hawk won writing competitions in 2009 and 2010. She is a teacher for special needs middle schoolers, and the 'girl in the chair' for *HawkandYoung.com* from Indiana.

Eddie-Joe Young was a freelance writer for the *Cajun Press* in Avoyelles Parish and went to college on a writing scholarship long before he met Hawk. He currently works on a tugboat on the Mississippi and the Gulf of Mexico.

Hawk and Young are best friends, but have never met in person. They started writing stories together in 2008. It wasn't until 2017 that they decided to create Hawk and Young and build an 'Empire' from a distant galaxy that keeps interfering with ours. In addition, they have a couple epic fantasy tales involving a dragon and her rider, a boy and his teddy bear, magic, pirates, and ninjas in the works.

Hawk and Young have been published in *Antimatter Magazine* and *Martian Magazine*. They have a new serial story on a new website called *Lords of Magazine Street*.

Facebook: https://facebook.com/HawkandYoung
Website: http://hawkandyoung.com
Blog: http://hawkandyoung.wordpress.com
Serial story: https://lordsofmagazinestreet.home.blog/
Twitter: @HawkandYoung

JACK LOTHIAN is a screenwriter for film and television and currently works as the showrunner on the HBO / Cinemax series *Strike Back*.

His short fiction has appeared in a number of publications, including *Weirdbook*, *Hinnom Magazine*, the *Necronomicon Memorial Book*, *The New Flesh: A Literary Tribute to David Cronenberg*, and *The Best Horror of the Year Volume 12*. His graphic novel *Tomorrow*, illustrated by Garry Mac, was nominated for a 2018 British Fantasy Award.

CHRISTINE MORGAN divides her writing time among many genres, from horror to historical, from superheroes to smut, anything in between and combinations thereof. She's a future crazy-cat-lady and a longtime gamer, who enjoys British television, cheesy action/disaster movies, cooking and crafts. Which latter two led a recent podcast to refer to her as "The Martha Stewart of extreme horror," so, make of that what you will!

Her short stories have appeared in dozens of anthologies, as well as the collections *The Raven's Table* (Viking-themed horror, with a companion volume due out in late 2020 or early 2021) and *Dawn of the Living-Impaired And Other Messed Up Zombie Stories* (zombies, obviously).

Her novels include the historical pioneer blizzard snow monstery *White Death*, the Edward Lee sequel *Lakehouse Infernal*, the totally trashy *Spermjackers From Hell*, the soon-to-be-rereleased *Murder Girls*, and others.

She also takes on editing and proofreading gigs, is a regular contributor to *The Horror Fiction Review*, has twice earned an Honorable Mention from Ellen Datlow in the *Year's Best* series, and been nominated in various categories of the Splatterpunk Awards.

Christine currently lives in Portland, Oregon, where she works the overnight shift in a residential psychiatric facility. She is always glad to hear from readers, as well as other authors (and hey, agents, publishers, movie people, it's all good!)

JACOB FLOYD is the author of *Night of the Possums* and *Chainsaw Sisters,* and a book of poetry called *Man in the Shadow Land.* He and his wife Jenny are known as The Frightening Floyds. Together they have authored several nonfiction paranormal books including *Haunts of Hollywood Stars and Starlets, Aliens Over Kentucky, Be Our Ghost,* and *Strange and Unusual Mysteries.*

The Frightening Floyds own Anubis Press (nonfiction paranormal), Nightmare Press (horror), Wild West Press (weird west and western), and Poet Tree Grove (poetry). They are also former paranormal investigators and tour operators.

They live in a small town just south of Louisville, KY with their four cats (Baloo, Narnia, Pandora Opossum – also known as Pandy Possum, Pandy, and Big Mama P – and Maleficent, who also goes by Baby Bat and Bat-Bat) and their two dogs (Tarzan and Pegasus). They recently lost their beloved toy poodle Snow White, who they called BooBoo. She was very much loved and will be forever missed. She found her way into "Rise, Vega" and rested on the couch and her little bed beside Jacob as he wrote her into that story. Her remains and bed are still beside him as he writes, and they will always be.

BRYAN DYKE is flying blind on a rocket cycle in the clouds above Vermont, USA. He also lives there with his wife, Corinne, two children, Mayve and Owen, and a naughty dog named Lucy. He is a U.S. Army veteran and graduate of the University of Florida. An avid fan of the works of H.P. Lovecraft, Robert E. Howard, and Jack Kirby, he has several published short stories in various anthologies.

MICAH CASTLE is a weird fiction and horror writer. His stories have appeared in various magazines, websites, and anthologies, and he has three collections currently out.

While away from the keyboard, he enjoys spending time with his wife, aimlessly spending hours hiking through the woods, playing with his animals, and can typically be found reading a book somewhere in his Pennsylvania home.

ALSO AVAILABLE
FROM
FRIGHTENING FLOYDS
PUBLISHING

ANOTHER WEIRD WEST
ADVENTURE FROM
WILD WEST PRESS

BELLA

In an alternate 1800's America, where magic is real and dragons soar through the skies of the American frontier -
Topher had a good life, mostly. It wasn't great, but what can a young African girl expect living on the Edge of the World! She had a shack that she shared with her Ma, she knew what vendors she could pocket an apple from, and was better than anyone with a spitshot. What more could a girl in the slums expect?

Then that chucklehead Wasco rolled out of the mountains like a toppled boulder. Topher had figured he might be good for a penny or two if she showed him around. Before she knew it he had her trompin' around the Blacklands, getting shot at, almost eaten and damn near gutted by some bull-headed dandy!

Jacob, who was about the handsomest gunfighter a body could imagine, might be some kind of monster. Old Ying turned out to be one of them wizards from the storybooks and Li had a magic sword!

All because someone went and took Bella and Wasco aimed to get her back, and Topher had been too stubborn not to follow him. Yeah, it had been a good enough life. She just wasn't sure she was going to make it back to it, or if she even wanted to.

IF YOU LIKE THE PARANORMAL
TRY THESE
MYSTERIOUS TALES
FROM
ANUBIS PRESS

STRANGE AND UNUSUAL MYSTERIES

What you are about to read is not a news report; it is neither a bulletin nor an alert. Rather, it is a collection of accounts of strange and unusual occurrences – some solved, some unsolved, but all mysterious. These reports have circulated for decades; some so much that they have become the sources of legends and rumors, even theories involving deep conspiracies. Despite many investigations and countless hours of research, there remain many questions unanswered. However, for every mystery there is someone out there who knows the truth, who possesses the evidence to solve the riddle. Maybe that someone will open this book and find their report. That someone could even be you.

Ahead you will find tales of ghosts, missing persons, ancient legends, and extraterrestrial visitors. What are their stories, or, more importantly, where did their stories come from? Read the enclosed accounts and decide for yourself.

Please, join us – maybe you can help the Frightening Floyds solve a mystery.

AMERICAN CRYPTIC

AMERICAN CRYPTIC is an open-minded cynic's take on the uncanny and sometimes frightening things which border our accepted reality. Through thirteen stories and essays, author and filmmaker Jim Towns examines several legends native to his own roots in Western Pennsylvania, and recalls some of his own unexplainable experiences as well. From legends of Native American giants buried under great earth mounds, to a haunted asylum, to a phantom trolley passenger, this work seeks not only to present the reader with new and fascinating supernatural tales, but also to deconstruct why our culture is so fascinated by their telling and re-telling.

HAUNTED SURRY TO SUFFOLK:
SPOOKY LOCATIONS ALONG ROUTES 10 AND 460

Take a journey along Virginia's scenic Routes 10 and 460 eastbound to enjoy the lovely countryside and metropolises that spread around these two roads. Most of all, discover that some historical houses, plantations, battlefields, parks, and even the modern cities, have more than touristy knickknacks, ham, and peanuts to offer. Many have ghosts!

Bacon's Castle has spirits haunting it since the 1600s. Stay in a cabin overnight at Chippokes Plantation State Park and you might find you have a spectral bedfellow. The city of Smithfield has more to offer than the world's oldest ham; it also has some very old phantoms still stalking its buildings. Take a ghost tour of Suffolk and see why the biggest little city is also one of the spookiest. Discover the myths and legends of the Great Dismal Swamp and see what phantoms are still haunting the wildlife refuge. And if that's not enough, Bigfoot and UFOs are part of the paranormal scenery. These and other areas of southeastern Virginia are teeming with ghosts, Sasquatch, UFOs, and monsters. See what awaits you along 460 south and 10. No matter which road you take, the phantoms can't wait to SCARE you a good time.

HANDBOOK FOR THE DEAD

DON'T FORGET YOUR HANDBOOK...

Welcome all spirits! The Frightening Floyds present to you, *Handbook for the Dead* – a guide to help all new manifestations realize their functional perimeters.

Within this anthology, you'll read paranormal accounts from individuals who have experienced phantoms and disturbances that have not only chilled them, but also left them with some new insight into the supernatural. Now, they want to share their stories and wisdom with you. That way, if you're feeling a little flat, or even if you're a lost soul, you won't have to draw a door and knock.

Handbook for the Dead is sure to please the strange and unusual in everyone, and we promise it doesn't read like stereo instructions.

ALIENS OVER KENTUCKY

From the Frightening Floyds, the pair of paranormal enthusiasts who brought you *Be Our Ghost* and *Haunts of Hollywood Stars and Starlets* comes a new adventure into the realm of the unknown – *Aliens over Kentucky*.

This collection includes the most noted extraterrestrial encounters from the Bluegrass State, such as the Kelly Creatures Incident of 1955, the Stanford Abductions, the Dogfight above General Electric, and the tale of Capt. Thomas Mantell chasing a UFO through Kentucky skies. But that's not all. There are lesser known, but equally intriguing, reports herein, such as the train collision with the UFO, stories of unexplained crop circles and cattle mutilations, Spring-heeled Jack, the Meat Shower of 1876, and many eyewitness reports of various unidentified crafts. You'll also read a couple of personal experiences from the authors, and even Muhammad Ali gets involved in the alien action.

Join Jacob and Jenny Floyd as they dig into the mysterious cases and theories regarding Kentucky's "X-Files". Just be sure to keep one eye on the book and the other on the sky…

BE OUR GHOST

The Frightening Floyds invite you to be our ghost as we take you on a tour of the happiest haunted place on Earth! In this book, you will read about much of the alleged paranormal activity as well as urban legends spanning the various Disney theme parks around the world. From the haunted dolls of It's a Small World to the real ghosts of the Haunted Mansion, there are many spirits here to greet you. And make sure to say "Good morning" to George at Pirates of the Caribbean.

Enjoy the spooky and fascinating tales in *Be Our Ghost*! And don't worry, there are no hitchhiking ghosts ahead…or are there?

PARANORMAL ENCOUNTERS

The Frightening Floyds present *Paranormal Encounters*: a collection of 14 tales of true ghostly experiences. From a malevolent spirit remaining in an apartment, to a loving phone call from a lost relative; from a house with a sliding chair and slamming doors, to a snow globe moving across a bedroom; from a possible past-life experience to a ghostly stranger in a radio station, this anthology contains several strange and unusual stories that are sure to entertain fans of the paranormal.

HAUNTS OF HOLLYWOOD STARS AND STARLETS

Explore the dark side of Tinseltown in this collection of paranormal stories, conspiracy theories, curses, and legends about some of Hollywood's most iconic names: Marilyn Monroe, Rudolph Valentino, Charlie Chaplin, James Dean, Jean Harlow, Clark and Carole, Lucille Ball, Michael Jackson, Bela Lugosi, Lon Cheney, John Belushi, and the King himself—Elvis Presley—and many more. Join the Frightening Floyds as they take you on a terrifying journey through the city of glamour and glitz!

IF YOU LIKE HORROR,
STEP INTO THESE
TALES OF TERROR FROM
NIGHTMARE PRESS

THE GRAY MAN OF SMOKE AND SHADOWS

As a child, Hyeri's uncle tortured her. Years after escaping his brutal touch, she discovers a secret organization of vampires and joins the ranks of the undead. Gaining supernatural strength and speed, she seeks one thing: revenge.

When Hyeri unleashes her decades-old hatred upon her uncle, she's interrupted by a vampire enforcer who seeks to apprehend her for breaking company protocol and revealing her vampiric nature to mortals.

Hyeri fends off the assassin, but an errant attack wounds her uncle, and the vampires glimpse an evil that has taken refuge inside of him. The darkness desires to remain unknown and plots to silence them both.

Forced to combine their abilities, the vampire duo sharpen their swords and gorge on blood to increase their strength. Can they withstand the onslaught of Hyeri's uncle, *The Gray Man of Smoke and Shadows*?

Before they can find out, someone else stumbles onto their path. Someone with abilities they have never seen. This strange being, full of rage and vengeance, is hell-bent on destruction. But who will be his target?

Find out in Volume II of the Vampire Series of Extreme Horror based in South Korea.

BUTCHERS

Kidnapped, turned, and locked away in a concrete basement, high school student Sey-Mi is taught the ways of the damned. Her captors, beautiful and malignant, cruel and insane, torture her until she pledges allegiance to the *Gwanlyo*, a secret organization of vampires now obsessed with bringing her into their ranks.

Enter Cheol Yu and Hyeri, rogue members who want to liberate vampires and set them upon humankind like a plague. Their first act of rebellion is to persuade Sey-Mi to join them in their twisted objective of unraveling this draconian society of the dead. Before they can do that, they will have to dodge the Natural Police, an order within the *Gwanlyo* whose objective is to hunt down and butcher any vampires that break the organization's strict rules, and who are currently tracking Cheol Yu for murdering one of their own. Hyeri, who is no stranger to the organization's wicked methods of agonizing punishment, is hell-bent on bringing them down, and is prepared to lead Cheol Yu through the dark, abandoned streets of the *Gwanlyo*'s compound where Sey-Mi is being held captive. She doesn't intend to go in unarmed, however. Hyeri has a plan – one that might just burn the *Gwanlyo* to the ground.

Will Sey-Mi place her loyalties in the *Gwanlyo* that rules through terror? Will she side with rebellious conspirators who strive to bring hell to the world? Or will she carve out her own path through the flesh and bone of anyone who stands in her way?

Find out in *Butchers*, a novella of extreme horror.

CHAINSAW SISTERS

When Sis wakes up in her father's backyard, staring at a rickety old shed, she can't remember how she got there or even who she is. But she remembers Amy, the sister that disappeared long ago, the same sister that she now hears calling to her from the shed.

When Sis enters the shed she discovers that Amy is only there in spirit, and she is speaking to her through a new body, and that body just happens to be a chainsaw.

Amy reveals to Sis that she was murdered by a local crime ring and she needs Sis to seek revenge for her. Sis agrees to the task and as Amy guides her to the home of each man responsible, Sis uses Amy's new body to hack them to pieces.

But the situation isn't as straightforward as it seems. As Sis comes face to face with each man, she finds herself in the middle of unfamiliar flashbacks that put her at the scene of a heinous crime of which she has no recollection. In time, she begins to believe that these are not her memories and Amy isn't telling her everything she needs to know.

What lies ahead beyond the coming bloodbath is something darker and more disturbing than Sis could have imagined. Who is Amy? Who is Sis? And what connection do they both have to the men she's about to murder?

And why is her sister now a telepathic chainsaw?

ANIMAL UPRISING!

A lion, a hybrid, a bear – oh no! A goat, a gull, and a big black dog! Can't forget the roaches, the deer flies, and the tarantula hawk, or the abominable insect that rises from the earth! We got creepy crawlers and killer critters for everyone. Oh, you want mythical creatures? How about a malevolent spirit posed as a fox, a rambunctious jackalope, or a herd of unicorn-gazelles on a distant planet? Let's not forget the supernatural silver stag with the power to raise the dead. Oh, did I mention the giant mantis shrimp? Yeah – we got a giant mantis shrimp. Humankind really has their work cut out for them in this collection of terrifying tales of beastly butchery. Need to know more? Check out *Animal Uprising!* for all of the mayhem.

NIGHT OF THE POSSUMS

JACOB FLOYD

The night of the possums began on a chilly autumn morning around 2am in late October.

On a dark country road, a young man is torn to shreds by wild animals. The news of his grisly death rocks the town. When a similar death occurs later that day, the town is in the grips of fear.

In rural Bardstown, Kentucky, opossums have risen up against the populace. People are being maimed and devoured throughout the city. These are not your ordinary opossums, either: they are smarter, stronger, faster, and far more vicious—some larger than any opossum anyone has ever seen, growing as long as four feet and as heavy as fifty pounds, with teeth capable of cleaving bone.

As the flesh-eating scourge quickly spreads from one end of Bardstown to the other, a few of those who survived the attacks band together in an attempt to eradicate the maniac marsupials. But, the number of the beasts grows by the hour and the force becomes too insurmountable and the survivors soon realize escape is their only option.

But, beyond the berserk behavior of the carnivorous creatures is a darker secret—something ancient and unnatural that threatens all those who are bitten. Before anyone can find out what is driving these opossums to kill, the survivors must battle their way through the merciless onslaught of claws and teeth and leave the threat of Bardstown behind them.

POETRY FANS,
CHECK OUT
POET TREE GROVE

MAN IN THE SHADOW LAND

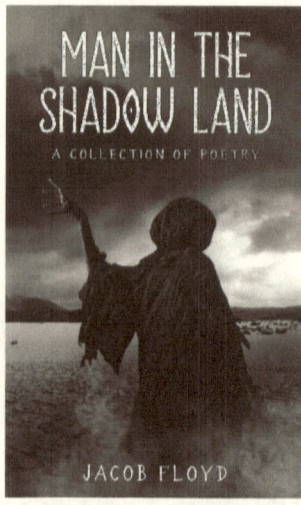

Welcome to the Shadow Land…

In this book, you will find poems about death, sorrow, madness, fear, and other aspects of life that haunt the Man in the Shadow Land. This collection spans ten years of the author's life, and contains some of his most authentic pieces. From his Poe-inspired poetry to those written from the darkest places of his heart, *Man in the Shadow Land* is a journey into a soul full of shadowy corners.

COMING SOON FROM ANUBIS PRESS:
Haunted Hotels of Virginia
Susan Schwartz

Kentucky's Strange and Unusual Haunts
The Frightening Floyds

Werewolves and Other Shapeshifters Stalking America
Pamela K. Kinney

COMING SOON FROM NIGHTMARE PRESS:
Retro Horror
An anthology

The Cursed Diary of a Brooklyn Dog Walker
Michael Reyes

The Untaken
Bekki Pate

Slice Girls
An anthology

All Roads Lead
Jennifer Winters

Viva La Muerte
Quinn Hernandez

Whoops! I Woke the Dead
Joseph Rubas

In Dormancy, They Sleep
D.G. Sutter

The Woodshed
Jacob Floyd

Slaughter at Seabridge
Cassidy Frost

Thank you for reading! If you like the book, please leave a review on Amazon and Goodreads. Reviews help authors and publishers spread the word!

To keep up with more Wild West Press news, join the Anubis Press Dynasty on Facebook.

www.ingramcontent.com/pod-product-compliance
Lightning Source LLC
Chambersburg PA
CBHW051955240626
47153CB00005B/1764